RAZORBILL

POPULAR

Gareth is superbly fabulous and something of a socialite himself.
Early twenties and not long out of Oxford University, he was
born in Belfast, but grew up in County Down. He wrote the
first chapter of *Popular* last summer and nearly all the book is
based upon events that have happened during his schooldays
– the more ridiculous they seem, the greater the chance that
they are close to real life. Gareth's accent is now best described
as polymorphous, shifting with the greatest of ease from
Northern Irish to English to American. And this pleases him
greatly. His first ever word was 'shoe'.

Books by Gareth Russell

Popular

POPULAR

Gareth Russell

FIC
T
Russe

razOr
bill
PENGUIN

RAZORBILL

Published by the Penguin Group
Penguin Books Ltd, 80 Strand, London WC2R ORL, England
Penguin Group (USA) Inc., 375 Hudson Street, New York, New York 10014, USA
Penguin Group (Canada), 90 Eglinton Avenue East, Suite 700, Toronto, Ontario, Canada M4P 2Y3
(a division of Pearson Penguin Canada Inc.)
Penguin Ireland, 25 St Stephen's Green, Dublin 2, Ireland (a division of Penguin Books Ltd)
Penguin Group (Australia), 250 Camberwell Road, Camberwell, Victoria 3124, Australia
(a division of Pearson Australia Group Pty Ltd)
Penguin Books India Pvt Ltd, 11 Community Centre, Panchsheel Park, New Delhi – 110 017, India
Penguin Group (NZ), 67 Apollo Drive, Rosedale, Auckland 0632, New Zealand
(a division of Pearson New Zealand Ltd)
Penguin Books (South Africa) (Pty) Ltd, 24 Sturdee Avenue, Rosebank, Johannesburg 2196, South Africa

Penguin Books Ltd, Registered Offices: 80 Strand, London WC2R ORL, England

penguin.com

First published in Razorbill, an imprint of Penguin Books Ltd, 2011
001 – 10 9 8 7 6 5 4 3 2 1

Text copyright © Gareth Russell, 2011
All rights reserved

The moral right of the author has been asserted

Set in Sabon MT 10.5/15.5 pt
Typeset by Palimpsest Book Production Limited, Falkirk, Stirlingshire
Printed in Great Britain by Clays Ltd, St Ives plc

British Library Cataloguing in Publication Data
A CIP catalogue record for this book is available from the British Library

ISBN: 978-0-141-33453-0

www.greenpenguin.co.uk

MIX
Paper from
responsible sources
FSC
www.fsc.org   FSC™ C018179

Penguin Books is committed to a sustainable
future for our business, our readers and our
planet. This book is made from paper certified
by the Forest Stewardship Council.

To
my parents,
Heather and Ian,
and
my uncle,
Richard Mahaffy

Contents

'It's better to be popular than right'
– Mark Twain

1

BUS PASSES AND BABY PINK

On the first Monday of September, Meredith Elisabeth Anne Harper stood staring at her own reflection in the huge mirror of her private closet on the first floor of her seven-bedroom, three-storey home in Malone Park, Belfast. The phrase most commonly used to describe Meredith Harper was 'the girl who has everything'. She was rich, popular, clever, elegant, manipulative, graceful and almost unnaturally beautiful. Thin and fashionable, she had long, perfectly coiffed brown hair, flawless pale skin and delicate facial features. At the age of sixteen, Meredith Harper was already a social legend.

Realizing that it would almost be time to go, she quickly checked her expertly manicured nails and not-too-shiny glossed lips. Her skirt was the perfect length – not too long (loser) and not too short (slut). She then picked up her black Birkin handbag that was now her schoolbag (backpacks were hideous things, used only by juniors and library-loving trolls) and swung it over her left shoulder while giving her reflection one more congratulatory smile. The only thing ruining how good she felt right now was the fact that her black school-uniform sweater was made of wool; Meredith was a devout and regular worshipper at the shrine of cashmere, and being forced to suffer wool five days a week was something she had never quite got over. She bent down and carefully adjusted her regulation knee-length socks and picked up her blazer, draping it over her right arm.

From downstairs came the sound of her father's voice reminding Meredith it was time to leave for school, so she exited her room and swept down the large staircase into the hall. She saw the cup of tea and plate of toast her housekeeper had left for her on the table but naturally walked straight past it and out to the waiting car.

The front door closed behind her and she stepped lightly into the back of the car as her father's driver took his place in the front seat and began the short journey to Meredith's school. The autumn leaves fluttered down from the majestic-looking trees that lined Malone Park and, all around her, Meredith could see the flurry of activity that marked the first day back to school. Yummy mummies were hustling their well-groomed offspring into waiting cars or were being eco-friendly and walking to a prestigious prep or grammar school nearby.

Meredith sat back against the cool grey leather of the car seat and checked her BlackBerry. She had a BBM from her best friend Imogen saying that she was walking to school that morning, at her father's insistence, because she had to accompany one of her younger brothers for his first day.

Five minutes later, the Harpers' car drew to a halt outside the main entrance of Mount Olivet Grammar School and Meredith alighted from the car, thanking the driver and turning her attention towards the impressive redbrick Victorian building that had been her educational home for the last eleven years. Of course, with just over twelve hundred students, the school had expanded a lot since a Protestant bishop had first laid the foundation stone one hundred and twenty years ago and there were now modern buildings sprawling out across the complex – including the Drama wing, the sports hall and the new Science block. The only eyesore, Meredith thought, was the truly hideous 1960s swimming pool, but thankfully it lay at the back of the school, so nobody but the sports freaks had to see it on a regular basis.

She was already aware of the many pairs of eyes watching her from the school courtyard as she walked towards the foyer doors. Clutching their new bus passes with maniacal zeal, a group of terrified-looking first-years gazed at her with a mixture of confusion and awe. By the end of the month, they would know who she was. Only the awe would remain. Meredith smiled a little at this reassuring thought and then widened the smile into a gracious thank-you as a third-year held the door open for her. Moving past the portrait of the Queen, which hung loyally in the lobby, Meredith was surprised to feel a leaflet being pressed into her hands by a fourth-year girl manning the Christian Union stand. 'Jesus loves you,' said the girl, smiling.

'Everybody does,' answered Meredith, handing back the leaflet.

Moving up a nearby stairway and past a group of nervous third-year girls, one of whom tried to squeak a 'Hello', Meredith arrived outside her house form room. Standing against the wall was Meredith's other best friend and neighbour, Cameron Matthews, who was almost six feet tall, thin and toned, with blue eyes and dark hair. He had his usual morning fix of Diet Coke in his hand and he was busy texting when he spotted Meredith and smiled.

'Hey!' he said, putting his phone back in his blazer pocket.

'Hello, lover. You are looking delightful this morning.'

'Thank you. You too. Of course. And how are we?'

'Better.'

'Than?'

'Everyone.'

At that moment, they heard the sound of a girl's shoes clacking along the corridor floor at immense speed as Kerry Davison hurtled into view, her pink handbag flailing along beside her and her perfectly styled blonde curls bouncing enthusiastically in rhythm to her running. She came to a skidding halt next to Cameron and Meredith, with a sort of demented gleam of happiness on her face.

'Oh my God,' she squealed. 'I've been bursting to tell someone all morning! OK. This is like *major* gossip.'

'This had better be good,' said Meredith. 'Not like the time you thought you'd seen Cheryl Cole in Nando's.'

'OK. So I was totally sworn to secrecy, so you can't tell *anyone* you heard it from me. Somebody told me at Titus Pitt's barbecue yesterday that Danielle Morrison apparently fooled around with Zach Stevens when she was still going out with Neil Pole. Isn't that *unbelievably scandalous*? What. A. Slut. But you didn't hear it from me. Seriously. I was *sworn* to secrecy.'

'I know,' replied Meredith icily. 'I told you that.'

Kerry's lip began to quiver and her voice became more whiny than usual at the prospect of a telling-off. 'Oh. Sorry. Well, still . . . it's not like we even like Danielle all that much. So it doesn't really matter, does it?'

Meredith considered for a moment before sighing. 'I suppose you're right. But just don't tell anyone you heard it from me.'

Mrs Vaughn lumbered into view, her arms weighed down with books as she desperately tried to find the room keys. Rather than offer to take the books, Cameron, Kerry and Meredith stepped lackadaisically out of her way, which Meredith counted as helping.

The class slowly filed in and Cameron headed over to the group's table at the back of the room. Within seconds of Kerry and Meredith sitting down next to him, their conversation was interrupted by the arrival of Catherine O'Rourke, hair swept up in a ponytail and sporting a bizarrely tiny blue backpack. Cameron and Meredith both inhaled in preparation for Catherine's several-decibels-louder-than-required greeting.

'Hey!' she bellowed. 'Happy first day back! Anyone want an Evian from the machine?'

It was then that Meredith spotted the backpack. 'What are you doing?'

'Just going to get Evian like I said,' Catherine chirped brightly.

'No. I mean, what are you doing with *that*?'

'Oh, my schoolbag? OK. Well, you know the way everyone says that wearing a bag on two shoulders is like a thing for losers?'

'Yes.'

'Well, I thought that it's been so loserish for so long that it might actually have become cool again,' explained Catherine, even as her smile began to falter. 'So *ta-da*!'

Meredith and Cameron shook their heads. 'No.'

'But I said *ta-da*.'

'There isn't a ta-da big enough in the whole world,' said Cameron.

'So you mean . . . I've walked through school looking like a loser?'

'I'm afraid so, but maybe –'

But before Cameron could finish his sentence, Catherine had hurled the bag off her back and on to the floor with a scream. 'Oh my God, oh my God, oh my God!'

'Catherine, calm down!'

'Calm down? Everyone will have seen me walking into school with a bag on *both shoulders*. Everyone will be looking at me tomorrow and they'll all be like, *Oh, look there's the two-strapper freak!*'

'I wouldn't worry,' said Meredith sweetly. 'It's not as if people know you well enough to start making fun of you. They probably didn't even notice you, Catherine.'

Catherine nodded, but she now wore the sort of shaky half-smile that Meredith's victims frequently sported when she delivered words of comfort wrapped in a barbed wire of bitchery. The moment the doors closed behind Catherine as she walked out to the vending machine, Meredith turned to the others.

'Can you believe that?'

Cameron nodded his head in agreement. 'I know. Why can't Catherine just take a look in the mirror before she leaves the house?'

'I mean, everybody else thinks the bag looks horrendous, right?' asked Meredith.

Kerry looked up from her hand-held mirror. 'What's happening?'

Meredith glanced at her with obvious irritation and left Cameron to answer. 'Catherine's bag. She was wearing two straps. She thought it looked cute. Instead, she looked like a weird extra from one of the *St Trinian's* movies.'

'Kerry, do you ever notice anything?' snapped Meredith.

Kerry's bottom lip began to quiver, threatening tears if the criticism wasn't immediately stopped.

'It's OK, Kerry! No one's mad at you – we're mad at Catherine. Don't cry, princess,' soothed Cameron. 'Meredith told her to get rid of the bag.'

Kerry brightened immediately and smiled at Meredith. 'For her own good, Mer?'

'What?'

Mrs Vaughn cleared her throat to begin taking the register, but naturally she had to clear it four more times before anyone paid the slightest bit of attention. The first name on the list was Coral Andrews. When Coral answered, Cameron turned round to glare viciously at her. 'Damn,' he hissed. 'She lived through the summer . . . Again.'

Coral Andrews was, in many ways (apart from the crucial elements of beauty and money), a sort of short, indie version of Meredith Harper. Coral was the unacknowledged queen bee of the 'anti-popular crowd'. Every school has one of these and they vary only in degrees of how annoying they are. They are the kids who make every effort to show that they don't care about popularity and that they definitely don't approve of cliques. The ironic thing is that they are infinitely more cliquey, judgemental and insular than the most shameless of plastics. They wear clothes that look as if they've been rejected by both Oxfam and the dry-cleaners. Their Bebo and Facebook profiles are littered with drawings of anorexic self-harmers or quotes from Kurt Cobain. They hate any form of music that is in the charts and their house parties generally consist of guitar-strumming, a large amount of marijuana and even larger amounts of self-pity. Shaking his head in disgust, Cameron turned back in his seat, muttering, 'Hippy bitch.'

Coral was sitting at a table on the opposite side of the room surrounded by her registration-class posse – the politically conscious bookworms Alice Fenchurch and Patsy Harris and the famously repulsive duo that was Hector Colliner (science-genius-smart) and Callum Quigley (science-experiment-ugly). These four had been Coral's devoted power-base for most of junior school, but by the beginning of fourth year she had outgrown them and moved on to the indie clique that spanned several form classes. She still took care to sit with her former followers in registration class, perhaps because she had no other friends there. She regularly and enthusiastically told them how much she loved them, how they were definitely going to be friends for life, how much they had changed her life for the better and gave them notes with song lyrics written on them. However, she never invited them to any of her house parties and didn't introduce them to any of her other friends. They, of course, failed to notice and worshipped her devotedly.

Mrs Vaughn continued with the register. 'Keith Bryce? Shaun Carson? Hector Colliner? Kerry Davison? Kerry Davison? Kerry Davison?'

'. . . which is why no one even knew about it until Danielle told Carolyn last week and she apparently told everyone the secret but left the names out, but she told it to Nicola Porter, who put the clues together and figured out that it must've been Danielle and Zach. So Nicola told Cristyn Evans, who she doesn't really like but that's not important, and Cristyn apparently told Meredith at Mass, which is when –'

'Kerry Davison. Kerry Davison! Can you hear me?'

Kerry turned round from her conversation and gave the world's surliest 'Yes, miss. Present, miss.'

Mrs Vaughn looked pleased with herself for securing this small disciplinary victory and she continued with the roll call with far more aplomb than usual. 'Alice Fenchurch? Billy Finster? Lisa Flaherty?'

At the mention of Lisa Flaherty, Kerry stopped dead in her conversational tracks and shot a look of pure venom at the peroxide-blonde object of her hatred. 'What the hell is that wab doing back here?' she hissed.

'She does go to this school, Kerry,' said Meredith, moving her Birkin to make room for Catherine as she returned to the table, Evian in hand.

'I can't believe she has the nerve to come back here after what she did to me! What a wab.'

Cameron rubbed Kerry's shoulder soothingly. 'Kerry, listen. What Lisa did was awful but –'

'That is not her name!' Kerry squealed. 'Her name is Dumbo-Eared McMotherfucker!'

'Yes . . .'

Kerry had gone to summer camp with Lisa Flaherty throughout childhood and they had maintained their friendship into high school, until there had been a falling out last summer, when Lisa had spread a rumour about Kerry and a boy she had kissed over the Easter holidays. Kerry responded with a not-necessarily-true story that Lisa's father was drug dealer for the IRA and that Lisa snorted printer fluid in her spare time. In retaliation, Lisa had

9

sunk to an unspeakable low by telling everyone that Kerry was a compulsive overeater and that her parents had to pay for regular liposuction because she was naturally a size 22. Needless to say, an enduring hatred had been born once that particular story became public knowledge.

Kerry's tirade was interrupted as the new homework diaries were passed around. In a transformation of delightfully bi-polar extremes, she beamed deliriously at the shiny new offerings. Catherine and Kerry plucked out their felt tips, glitter pens and stickers from their bags to begin the sacred annual decoration ritual.

Meanwhile, Meredith glanced at her new timetable and groaned. 'Oh my God, we have Mr Edgars for double Religion on a Friday afternoon. That is going to be hell! And the irony of that is not lost on me.'

'Quiet at the back, please,' said Mrs Vaughn in a trembling voice.

'Mutant,' muttered Meredith, before returning to her timetable.

In 1741, the teachings of the Italian scientist Galileo Galilei convinced the Catholic Church that the Earth was not the centre of the universe. However, even if Galileo had been alive today, he could never have convinced Imogen Dawson that she wasn't. With her lustrous blonde hair, perfect pale skin, luscious lips and plummy yet sexy English accent, Imogen was a bombshell and she knew it. At break-time, she sat in the school cafeteria with a bottle of Diet Coke in front of her, religiously checking Perez Hilton's blog from her BlackBerry. From Imogen's point of view, the world before Perez or her BlackBerry quite simply hadn't been one worth living in – they ranked alongside the Bible, high heels and Kimora Lee Simmons as the greatest products of civilization. Ever. At the centre of the table, she had left an enormous baby-pink folder, which contained the plans for Kerry's Sweet Sixteenth the following Saturday, including the guest list (with staggered arrival times based on how much Kerry liked each individual person).

Meredith and Cameron sauntered past the queue of terrified first-years. Cameron looked longingly at a white-chocolate-chip muffin, but just as his hand began twitching towards it he felt Meredith's icy stare on his back and he stopped. He picked up a Diet Coke and walked over to the table.

'I think this might be a record,' Imogen said as they sat down opposite her. 'It's eleven o'clock on the first day back and I'm already dealing with a full-blown emotional *emergencia*.'

'That's impressive,' congratulated Cameron.

Imogen bit her lip in exaggerated worry, timing her revelation perfectly as Kerry and Catherine approached. 'I'm an adulteress.'

Everyone around the table moved in closer at this shocking statement. Kerry all but swooned into the seat next to her, breathily asking, 'Are you cheating on Stewart?' in a voice that was trying very hard to be disapproving but still couldn't quite hide the wild excitement.

'Not physically,' said Imogen, 'but unfortunately I have fallen in love with Michael Laverty. You know – the six-foot-tall blond hotty with the abs of steel and eyes of passion? We met him at Zach Stevens's pool party in July. He's in sixth year at Immaculate Heart.'

'Oh my God! I know him!' gasped Catherine. 'His parents and mine go to the same golf club!'

'Good story, Catherine.' Meredith turned to Imogen. 'Imogen, I think you should ditch Stewart, immediately.'

'Oh, Mer, you're always so sweet, but it's not that simple. After all, I am technically in love with Stewart – we're even an official couple on Facebook – *and* his parents *worship* me. I mean, let's be honest, I am probably the best thing that's ever going to happen to him.'

'Well, what's happening with Michael, then?' asked Kerry. 'No kissing?'

'Nothing. Apart from the fact that we text each other, like, every day,' said Imogen.

Cameron, crippled by paranoia, was always the one to think ahead to possible espionage. 'What if Stewart goes through your messages and finds them?'

'It's OK,' answered Imogen quickly. 'I mean, I haven't quite been able to bring myself to delete them. Apart from the filthy ones – they *had* to go – but I have cunningly saved Michael's number as *Kerry New Mob*. So apart from the fact that Stewart thinks Kerry is a repressed lesbian, everything's fine.'

'But everything is not fine!' said Catherine sadly. 'This will break Stewart's heart if he ever finds out.'

'You're always trying to make her feel bad,' Meredith snapped irritably. 'Stewart clearly isn't providing Imogen with enough emotional support. If anything, *she's* the victim in all this.'

Kerry nodded in melodramatic and forlorn agreement, taking Imogen's hand in a gesture of solidarity.

'So we think it's OK to keep texting Michael?' Imogen asked. 'Just to see where it's going?'

'Absolutely,' said Meredith. 'I mean, it's not as if you're

planning on marrying Stewart anyway, is it? His family does have a history of gingers.'

'I know,' said Imogen, shuddering.

Just then, Mark Kingston sauntered over to the table and said, 'Hey, Cameron.'

At the sound of an outsider's voice, the change in the group was immediate. They all began doing an amazing job of pretending that they had been discussing nothing more interesting than the weather. Kerry valiantly tried to cover up by saying loudly, 'Yes, I love clouds!'

'Hey, Mark.'

'Sorry to interrupt. Cam, I just wanted to check if you're still up for watching the movies at Peter's on Saturday?'

'Yeah, definitely. It sounds like good banter.'

Mark stayed for a few more minutes to ask the girls what they thought of their new timetables, but neither he nor Meredith exchanged a single word. Meredith's face did not change one iota, but Cameron, sitting next to her, felt, rather than saw, her spine stiffen with the hatred she felt for Mark Kingston. Her eyes glazed over slightly as if she had deliberately drained them of all feeling and it was almost comical to compare Meredith's glacial reaction with Catherine's over-bubbly excitement. She was currently staring up at Mark with wide-eyed admiration, a star-struck grin plastered on her face and laughing far too loudly at every mildly humorous thing he said.

Ordinarily, Cameron would have found Catherine's desperate crush on Mark more than entertaining, but today he was too busy feeling uncomfortable in the face of Meredith's ice-cold disapproval. Mark Kingston had been Cameron's best friend since nursery school and the strong bond between them, coupled with a slight physical resemblance, meant that every now and then they were mistaken for brothers. Like Cameron, Mark had blue eyes and a tall, trim figure, although Mark was slightly better built and his hair a touch lighter than Cameron's. The main differences between them lay in the way the two boys carried themselves. Mark had more of a mannish swagger; his hands were usually in his pockets and his movements were forceful, deliberate and confident. Cameron, on the other hand, generally lounged back when people were talking to him, deigning to lean in only to exchange a secret with one of his best girl friends and it was often quite difficult to tell if he was actually listening to you or not, unless there was a sparkle of amusement in his eyes.

When Mark finished talking to the other girls, he nodded curtly to Meredith and walked off. She smiled icily then turned very briefly to Cameron and raised an eyebrow. In that single movement, she managed to convey that she definitely did not approve of whatever was happening on Saturday.

'Ladies, on Saturday, I think we should have a group day – a proper one to recover from the first week back at school: brunch, shopping, manicures, party-planning for Kerry's b-day, dinner at Deane's and then back to my house for a sleepover.'

Kerry's hand shot up in excitement. 'Oh, I have an idea! Let's watch *Marie Antoinette* and drink every time she wears a dress we like!'

'Sounds super-fun,' said Imogen.

Meredith smiled. 'Super. It'll be just the girls, since Cameron's got plans with Mark and the boys. Without us. Again.'

2

SARUMAN THE STUPID

Seven hours and eleven minutes into it, the boys were beginning to wonder if watching all three *Lord of the Rings* movies in one day had been a particularly good idea. In hindsight, picking the extended editions had probably been a mistake, given that they had only just finished *The Two Towers* and had yet to embark on the four hours and eleven minutes of *The Return of the King*. The long-term, brain-melting impact of their decision had been made obvious by their slowly developing signs of insanity. Cameron had steadily consumed five large bottles of Diet Coke and given the amount of sweets he and Mark had gone through it looked as if they were in a race to see who could give themselves diabetes first. The other two boys – Peter and Imogen's boyfriend, Stewart – were also beginning to show signs of Hobbit-induced Dementia, with Peter running around with his grandfather's skullcap on his head and Stewart having inexplicably removed his top somewhere between Helm's Deep and Osgiliath.

Adjusting the skullcap and looking deep in thought, Peter turned to Mark and asked in a serious tone, 'Mate, what is the deal with you and Meredith? How can you not like her? She's unbelievably hot. Like, I mean, unreal.'

'She's not just hot,' answered Mark. 'She's probably the

hottest girl I've ever seen who's not in the movies, but that doesn't change the fact that she's an evil bitch.'

Cameron giggled before remembering that in *this* group 'bitch' wasn't a compliment. 'Mark! Stop it. Meredith's one of my best friends . . . she never says anything bad about you.'

Stewart looked up from the DVD player, where he was inserting disc one of *The Return of the King*, and sighed. Meredith's name had always caused problems in the group and the sooner the topic was dropped, the better. 'Lads, forget about her. Cameron likes her, Mark doesn't. OK?'

The Return of the King began and the boys settled back on the sofa. For some time, Mark remained in a huffy silence, infuriated that Cameron had once again defended Meredith by telling him something which was clearly a lie. Did Cameron really think he was stupid enough to buy that kind of crap? Meredith Harper could have found something bad to say about a saint if she wanted to, so there was absolutely no way she had never said anything bad about him!

Had he been more analytical, Mark would probably have realized that he was angrier with himself than Cameron. For the last year or so, Mark had struggled to fight his strange fascination with Meredith. This fascination irritated him, for he believed quite firmly that had Meredith been ugly the only word used to describe her would have been 'bully'. But she was not. In fact, as he had just admitted to Peter, she was anything but. She was beautiful, she was clever, she was rich and she was glamorous. There was also no denying that she had a way with words and that helped her a lot as well. People found it harder to be angry with cruelty if it made them laugh and Meredith played upon that. She was also cleverer, by far, than most of the other people in school and there was quite simply no one who could read people or manipulate them like Meredith Harper.

Mark shifted uncomfortably in his seat and took a sip of his Diet Coke, annoyed at how frequently Meredith Harper appeared in his thoughts these days. Still, he, at least, was able to see her for what she really was; Cameron, on the other hand, seemed to delight in everything about her – especially the bad bits. Trying to break his best friend away from the popular set's busy socializing schedule was becoming especially difficult for Mark. Days like this – just hanging out with Cameron and the guys – were turning into things that needed several weeks' notice. Mark found it increasingly difficult to ignore what he knew were slightly petulant feelings at Cameron not being particularly upset about this. But, after all, if Imogen could make time to see Stewart on a regular basis, there was really no logical reason why Cameron couldn't do the same, unless, of course, Meredith was deliberately attempting to pull him away from his friendship with Mark – something that she seemed more than capable of doing.

'You know, Cameron, you want to try having some balls once in a while. And stop letting Meredith walk all over you,' Mark declared self-righteously.

Stewart sighed, picked up a Walnut Whip and threw it directly at Mark's face.

At precisely seven thirty, as the early Saturday morning sun lit up the day of Kerry's sixteenth birthday, an e-mail arrived in the in-boxes of Meredith Harper, Catherine O'Rourke and Imogen Dawson, announcing that a crisis had erupted in the middle of the night. Sometime on Friday evening, Kerry had gone into meltdown with the stress of the impending birthday. Apparently overwhelmed by her own fabulousness, she had very quietly excused herself from the dinner table and tottered upstairs to her bedroom, where she had crawled under the covers and proceeded to have a full nervous breakdown. Her mother, who had learned the hard way what to do in such situations, made a telephone call to Cameron and it was left to him to contact the others.

From: Cameron Matthews <manorexic@msn.ni>
To: Meredith Harper <sizezerois4heifers@msn.ni>, Imogen Dawson <eurovision_queen@msn.ni>, Catherine O'Rourke <sxcladyee@msn.ni>

Everyone,

As we all know, today is a v. important day. Kerry is sixteen but has unfortunately been in bed for the last twelve hours due to an FIB (Fabulous Induced Breakdown). So far, we have got things under control this end and her sister has managed to recurl her hair – we're hoping the 1 o'clock trip to the beauty parlour will force her to leave her room.

Now. This is very important: we have a list of things to do and I have numbered them so no one gets confused – Catherine.

1. Manicure, pedicure, wax (if Kerry cannot be persuaded to leave the house then Imogen will need to be here at 12.45)
2. Champagne (Kerry's Dad is picking this up on his way from the airport)
3. Costumes (EVERYONE had better have a good Marie

Antoinette or similar themed costume ready for this evening)

4. Snackages (please bring treats so that we line our stomachs in preparation for tonight)

5. No one – and I mean NO ONE – is to mention the following to Kerry over the next 24 hours
   a) Lisa Flaherty
   b) The Biology homework that was due in yesterday, which she has clearly completely forgotten about
   c) How her sister's lost weight (seriously – she looks AMAZING – you can hardly even notice that beak nose of hers)
   d) That Catherine's lost series 5 from her box set of S&TC
   e) How she really reminds all of us of Eddy from *Absolutely Fabulous*
   f) That they're definitely not making a sixth series of *Footballers' Wives*
   g) Or suggest that her curls are anything other than totally and utterly amazing

6. No one is to steal the limelight from Kerry in any way, shape or form. I know we would all like to, but while she cannot punch or bite like the rest of us, she does have the ability to cry and whinge about ANYTHING that goes wrong for years & years to come.

Love,
Cameron xxx

PS – Catherine, don't wear that weird Bo-Peep costume again.

Within an hour, every socialite who wasn't bedridden with stress was frantically getting ready to go over to Kerry's house. Cameron was pulling on a pair of Dolce & Gabbana jeans and furiously styling his hair, before hurtling into his father's car to be driven to Kerry's, receiving breathless phone calls from her every ten minutes. Meredith was strutting down her driveway in a pair of Manolos to get a lift with Cameron, Catherine had draped a rosary round her neck in the hope it would help with the crisis and Imogen was taking delivery of a package from London, which she had a sneaking suspicion might get her in trouble later since it definitely contravened point 6 of Cameron's e-mail.

By the time they had arrived at Kerry's house later that morning, it was clear the birthday princess wasn't going to be moved and it was time for emergency mani-pedi-waxing at the house. An expert with nails, Imogen began manicuring Kerry's cuticles, while Catherine carefully wiped away the tears that Kerry was periodically shedding. Cameron was downstairs in the kitchen, frantically calling the caterers to make sure all the cakes were the required pink and Meredith, never a team player, was drumming her nails on the marble-top counter.

'I mean an FIB is totally understandable,' she hissed, 'but she's been like this for fourteen hours.'

Cameron pulled the phone away from his ear and nodded. 'I've told you – if she's annoying you this much, hit her.'

'I can't hit her, Cameron. She bruises like a peach . . . selfish bitch.'

The doorbell rang and it was the waxing lady from the salon, who had agreed to make a house call in return for time and a half. Cameron dashed to the door and breathed a sigh of relief. 'Thank God you're here. It's a *total* emergency!'

'Where is she?'

'Upstairs – in the pink bedroom. I'll take you up in a minute. Can I get you a drink? Tea, lemonade, rosé?'

In the meantime, Meredith, Imogen and Catherine had gathered around Kerry, who had stripped down to her underwear in preparation. Having at last risen from her bed, she was now flouncing around her room trying to decide what type of wax to go for when she spotted Meredith's costume – a black velvet dress with gold and pearls around the neckline.

'What is this?' she asked dangerously.

'It's my costume,' said Meredith.

'It doesn't look very Marie Antoinettey.'

'That's because I'm going as Anne Boleyn. I love her. You know that.'

'Well, I love Strawberry Cheesecake Häagen-Dazs but I'm not going to a Marie Antoinette party dressed as it, am I?'

'They both got beheaded!'

'*That's not the theme!*' roared Kerry. 'It's Marie Antoinette's time and you're going as Anne Bo-freaking-leyn.'

'What's the problem?' Meredith snapped. 'It means one less woman wearing a similar style of dress to you. Less competition.'

'No!' screamed Kerry, her curls burling around her head. 'You're only doing this because Anne Boleyn dresses make you look really thin and because you want to stand out and steal the limelight from me!'

'*Everything* makes me look thin, Kerry. And do you know why? Because I *am* thin!'

At that point, the waxing lady entered and Kerry settled down for the wax. It was a couple of minutes into the 'what wax' discussion that Meredith finally deigned to speak again.

'You should get the Brazilian,' she said calmly. 'It's nowhere near as painful as people make out and you really should get it done at least once.'

'I thought it hurt like a mo-fo,' said Kerry, her lip trembling.

'Carrie Bradshaw got one, didn't she?' answered Meredith, playing the ace that could get Kerry Davison to do more or less anything.

'That's true,' she said thoughtfully. 'Series three – when they're in LA. All right! A Brazilian. You're sure it doesn't hurt that much, Meredith?'

With all the cool of a frequent liar, Meredith turned smilingly to her friend. 'Mine didn't.'

It was five minutes later, when everyone else was downstairs in the kitchen, that Kerry's scream echoed through the house and Meredith put down her fresh orange juice and smiled.

The shock of the Brazilian and the lingering fear of what a vengeful Meredith might trick her into next forced Kerry to get a hold of herself. By five o'clock, everything was prepared and Imogen had time to drive home to get changed. At half past six, an hour before the first guests arrived, Cameron was standing in full costume at the first-floor window, staring down Kerry's long driveway, when he saw Imogen get out of a car.

'O Holy Jesus,' he whispered.

Kerry laboured into view in a magnificent pink-and-white dress, with her blonde hair piled high atop her head with a little crown on it. 'What! What's wrong?'

Cameron turned to face her and began speaking in a voice full of mounting panic. 'Remember, Imogen's your best friend and you've always known that she is a ruthless, attention-seeking, self-centred she-beast, so don't freak out now.'

Kerry began to breathe heavily, panicking at what exactly Imogen had done that was so bad that Cameron was already swinging into damage limitation mode. Seconds later, she saw what it was and a waif-like Meredith was sweeping up the stairs in her Anne Boleyn dress, just in time to see Kerry hiss in rage and hurtle past her.

Imogen had somehow got her hands on one of the original costumes worn by Kirsten Dunst in *Marie Antoinette*. Having seen the film more times than Sofia Coppola had, Kerry recognized the dress immediately and was flying down the stairs like a diamanté-clad demon. She flung the door open to see Imogen, present in arms, smiling calmly as if nothing was wrong.

'*Quelle la fuck?*'

'Kerry, what's wrong?'

'Where did you get the black dress worn in the masquerade ball scene in the second third of the movie?'

'Oh, this? Daddy pulled some strings.'

'I'll be doing the same thing when I hang you!'

'What!'

'You have come as Marie Antoinette in an outfit from the movie to *my* birthday!'

'It's a Marie Antoinette theme. God, what's your problem?'

'No one else is actually supposed to *be* Marie Antoinette! I am the birthday girl. It's Kerry's day. *I'm the star!*'

'Kerry, calm down.'

'Take it off.'

'What?'

'Strip.'

'Bite me.'

'You know I will!'

'Kerry! What is your problem? I won't tell anyone else I actually *am* Marie Antoinette. It's just a dress.'

'Imogen, how could you do this to me on my birthday? What kind of friend are you? I mean look, look, at Meredith! She came as Anne Boleyn so that she wouldn't outshine me. That's *real* friendship!'

'You yelled at her about it earlier on!'

Kerry looked speechless with shock at having this totally accurate assessment of the facts thrown back in her face. 'I was in the middle of an FIB – a Fabulous Induced Breakdown. You know it can make people go *crazy*!'

'Don't explain an FIB to me. I'm not some retard like Catherine who can't remember the group lingo.'

Standing apart from this fracas, Meredith privately thought that in her svelte black velvet gown she had radiantly outshone Kerry, who, right now, looked like an over-frosted cupcake – a very angry, over-frosted cupcake. Everyone's attention was then mercifully distracted from the argument by Catherine's re-emergence, in the same Little Bo-Peep outfit she had been warned against earlier but which she had apparently decided to wear regardless, now that she had accessorized it with bangles, necklaces and a rather bizarre-looking wig that turned out to be a huge amount of toilet paper covered in a thick layer of talcum powder and stuffed into a bird cage.

The group went silent in shock and Meredith nodded authoritatively to Cameron. Cameron nodded back and looked at Bo-Peep. 'Catherine, can we talk to you for a minute, please?'

*

Four hours into the party, it was unfortunately clear that Catherine's outfit was not the worst offender when it came to authenticity. Most of the girls had opted for old 1980s-style bridesmaid dresses, which they had then covered with as much bling from Claire's or Accessorize as was humanly possible, while the boys had bought plastic swords and thrown-together outfits that generally made them look like a cross between a confused musketeer and a drunken pirate. This of course meant that Imogen's period-perfect and highly-flattering outfit was among only four that were getting complimented. Kerry had long ago made her peace with the fact that Cameron was getting noticed (male) and Meredith (wrong period), but every time someone said how nice/sexy/realistic/glamorous Imogen looked, Kerry looked like she had swallowed an insect. However, karma came in such an unexpectedly brutal form shortly before eleven o'clock that even the birthday banshee had to make her peace with Imogen immediately.

Cameron was in the kitchen talking to Mrs Davison, Kerry's mother, and doing what he imagined to be a very good job of acting sober – in fact, his wild hand gestures and overly enthusiastic answers made it perfectly clear to Mrs D that Cameron had long ago lost the battle with the birthday champagne, so she nodded politely in all the right places and moved the bottles of Bollinger as far away as she could. Just at the point when Cameron was about to explain that they would all be fine in their exams, Imogen hurtled into the room, her diamonds glinting in the light and giving her the appearance of a crazed, if beautiful, dragonfly.

'*Emergencia! Emergencia!*' The words, when they came, were more of a squeak and she had grabbed Cameron's arm in such a vice-like grip that he feared he was losing circulation.

'Imogen, dear, what's wrong?' asked Mrs Davison, worrying that Kerry had either burst into tears for some unknown reason or started a fight with one of the guests.

Imogen turned with a freakishly bright smile and answered in a pretending-to-be-fine-but-sounding-deranged voice, 'Oh, Mrs D! Hi. Hi! Hi! How are you? I'm great. Party is. GREAT. Everything is fine, A-OK, in fact. Cameron, can I talk to you over here for a minute? Would you excuse us for *one* second, please, Mrs D? Great, thanks.'

She pulled Cameron over to the drinks table and began breathing short, fast and furiously.

'Imogen, is everything all right?'

'Of course it's not all right! I just said "A-OK"! How could it possibly be all right? Michael is here!'

'Michael . . . Michael-Michael?'

'No, Saint Michael the Archangel . . . of course, Michael-Michael. I knew Kerry was pissed, but even I didn't think she would go this far! Oh my God, Michael is here. Here. And Stewart is out there . . .'

'Looking like Bluebeard.'

'Shut up, Cameron! If they run into each other, I'm going to be like a successful prostitute.'

'Well and truly screwed.' He nodded.

At that point, Meredith and Kerry entered the room, taking Imogen by an arm each and sweeping her into the nearby dining room, which had been made a No Party Zone by Mrs Davison's express orders. When Mrs D went to protest, Kerry held up her hands and shook her head. 'Emotional *emergencia*, Mother. We'll be out in fifteen minutes. If you try and stop us, Imogen will have absolutely no choice but to kill herself and you know we don't like to do anything on our own!'

Seconds after Kerry had locked the door behind them, Imogen lunged at her. 'I will kill you. Kill you. Or, better yet, I will call someone on the Ivory Coast and I will sell you into white slavery if Michael and Stewart run into each other, Kerry. I will sell you to Robert Mugabe!'

'I didn't invite Michael!' Kerry squeaked.

'You have to believe her, Imogen,' said Meredith, sitting on the window seat, bathed eerily in the moonlight. 'She would never have wanted her party to be upstaged by your break-up.'

Muttering under her breath, Imogen had to admit that this was right and took a seat next to Meredith. 'Don't turn on the lights. I don't want people to know we're in here until we've figured out a plan.'

'Say you're sick,' said Kerry. 'Go tell Stewart you're not feeling well and he should help take you home. That way you both leave and there's no way Stewart can run into Michael.'

'But my dress . . .'

'Apology accepted,' beamed Kerry.

'No, I mean, it's too pretty for me to leave early.'

For a moment, Kerry thought of how satisfying it would be to march back into the party, find Stewart and Michael, drag them to one side and say, 'Stewart, this is Michael; Michael, Stewart. Stewart is Imogen Dawson's boyfriend of one year; Michael is her newfound potential adulterous love-interest. Now, you two chat among yourselves!' But she realized that this would make her a bad person, so she remained where she was.

Cameron was too busy trying to stop swaying in the moonlight and feverishly plotting how he could get his hands on another bottle of champagne to be of any practical assistance, so it was Meredith who spoke again. 'I hate to say this, because it goes against almost everything I believe in, but the dress isn't the most important thing. Kerry's right. Imogen, stay in here and we'll send Cameron to go get Stewart.'

As Cameron shakily weaved his way through the party-goers to find Stewart, he was stopped by Mrs Davison, who asked in the voice of a woman who knew she should but probably didn't want the answer, 'What's going on in there?'

'I cannot say, Mrs D,' said Cameron, nodding with exaggerated seriousness, 'but it's sort of like a cross between *Dangerous Liaisons* and *Clueless*. So don't worry, it's very fabulous.'

'Oh, good . . . because that's what I was worried about.'

'Stewart! Excuse me, Mrs D, gotta go!'

Stewart was busy playing beer-pong with Peter and Mark when Cameron lurched into view. 'Stewart, Imogen's not feeling very well. She's got a massively bad headache and she's really sorry, but can you get in the taxi with her and take her home?'

'Shit, yeah, of course. Where is she?'

'She's in the dining room. She wants to go as quickly as possible, out the back door. She doesn't want to distract everyone from the party.'

For a moment, Cameron feared he had taken the lie too far. Surely, not even trusting Stewart could possibly believe that Imogen would ever pass up an opportunity for grabbing attention? Thankfully, Stewart just nodded his head and went to find Imogen, leaving Cameron to follow along after him. It was when he turned round to wave goodbye to the other two boys that he saw a suspicious look pass briefly over Mark's face.

Emerging from the dining room ten minutes later, with

Imogen and Stewart safely packed off in a taxi heading back to Malone, Kerry, Meredith and Cameron congratulated themselves on a job well done. Kerry all but glowed with self-satisfaction as she hit the dance floor, having managed the all-but-impossible twin tasks of elbowing her best friend out of the limelight while saving her from public humiliation – the moral high ground at no personal cost. As the three of them burled around to the music, in the sure knowledge that everyone was watching them and the firm belief that they were all admiring too, they caught sight of Michael smoking out on the terrace.

Wow, thought Cameron. *Imogen has seriously good taste.*

'I love my crown!' squealed an ecstatic Kerry, pointing to her tiara.

Double Biology on a Monday morning started at precisely half past nine, so it was perhaps no surprise to find Meredith, Cameron and Kerry standing next to the vending machine at twenty to ten. Meredith and Cameron were already clutching their morning Diet Cokes in their hands, waiting for Kerry to get her Rice Krispies Square before they slowly floated in the general direction of the Science block. However, today there was a delay and they were not happy.

It was one thing for them to be criminally late to class because of their own laziness and non-existent work ethic, but it was something else entirely when they were held up by somebody else. The current offender was a buffalo-sized second-year who had already bought four things from the machine and was currently hurling himself against it in an attempt to get his trapped chocolate.

'Excuse me,' said Kerry, 'but can I use it for one minute and you can go back to battering it then? It's just that I have to get to class and also –'

'Fuck off!' snapped the candy-bar maniac.

Cameron stepped in front of the offender and said in his silkiest, too-nice-to-be-genuine voice, 'Excuse me, Buddha Junior, but I think God is trying to tell you something by trapping that calorie log you call a snack. Maybe you could get out of our way and come back to it when you've got some manners – or a waist. Either/or.'

'Fuck off, faggot.'

'Look, Jabba the Hutt, I am not kidding around here. Beat it or we'll tell everyone that you were caught staring at the other boys in the showers after PE.'

'Yes,' said Meredith, 'and, unlike your haircut, this isn't a joke.'

The boy skulked off, leaving a grinning Kerry to begin purchasing her snack. Her joy, however, was short-lived. The Rice Krispies bar she wanted was selection 'F-10' but, as happened three times out of five, Kerry forgot that there was a separate button for '10' and instead typed 'F', then '1', then '0'. As 'F-1' (a Twix) hurtled into her hands, Kerry let out a gasp of shocked pain and her eyes filled with tears. Refusing to buy anything else from a machine that had clearly tricked her, she stormed down the corridor, bravely stifling a sob.

'I knew she was going to do that,' said Meredith.

'Why didn't you warn her, then?' asked Cameron.

'It entertains me.'

*

They passed the sign on the Biology room door and began drinking their Diet Cokes. Imogen was waiting for them at their usual table – the one nearest the door for a quick, easy and efficient exit. She had already stuffed a packet of McCoy's in her blazer pocket and was busy texting when Meredith, Cameron and Kerry trooped in, with Kerry hurling the Twix in the bin with a disgusted sigh.

'Oh my God,' Imogen hissed, pointing a perfectly manicured fingernail across the room. 'You will not *believe* the freak show that's going on over there.'

Meredith, Cameron and Kerry turned their attention to a table where Coral Andrews and her hippie sidekick Paula Flockley were busy drawing flowery tattoos on to their hands with felt-tip pens.

'What the hell is that on their feet?' asked Meredith, throwing her bag down on the table.

'Socks *and* tights,' answered Imogen. 'I know, it's so hideous.'

'Why are they doing it?'

'Well, it's just in case we didn't know that they're really independent and alternative,' sniped Cameron. 'Retards.'

'It looks stupid,' said Meredith, getting increasingly irate.

'Meredith, if you react to it, you'll only be doing what they want.'

'Just be thankful they haven't started "singing" again,' said Imogen comfortingly. 'Thank God, Jesus, Mary, Joseph and all the saints.'

But God, Jesus, Mary, Joseph and all the saints had apparently decided to play a well-timed joke, because at that precise moment Coral began to sing *Fields of Gold* and on cue Paula provided an annoying descant.

Meredith rolled her eyes. 'Why can't Coral just die?'

'Because women like her grow up to spend their gap year in Thailand trying to find themselves and then take lots of drugs and become Buddhists in Goa,' said Cameron.

'I hate her,' said Meredith.

'I hate her hair,' said Imogen, 'and, with that face of hers, it looks like someone stuck pubic hair on top of a potato.'

'What's happening?' asked Kerry, looking up from her nails.

'Coral. Socks. Tights. Singing. Pubis,' Cameron explained.

'Oh, her,' sighed Kerry, returning to her cuticles. 'She is *not* fun.'

Mr Roger Corbett stood at the front of the class and cleared his throat. Mr Corbett's most endearing quality was that Biology remained his passion, despite the total indifference of ninety-five per cent of his pupils, but maybe it had something to do with him only being out of teaching college for two years. Today he beamed down on his students and began to talk in his overly cheery voice. 'Now, this morning we're going to look at one of the most relevant parts of Biology, something which I think you'll find rather exciting. I certainly do, because it's all to do with *blah blah blah blah blah blah* . . .'

Frankly, Mr Corbett could have been speaking in Klingon by that stage for all Meredith cared. She had already turned back to her conversation with Kerry, Cameron and Imogen and they were busy doodling when they were rudely interrupted. 'Cameron, what's the answer?'

'Um . . . three?'

Mr Corbett's entire body flopped in a melodramatic gesture

of total disappointment. 'Ack, Cameron, no! Come on now! Were you listening?'

'Yes.'

'Were you?'

'No.'

Momentarily crushed by a combination of Cameron's total indifference and the smirking faces of his friends, Mr Corbett turned on the overhead projector and asked the class to take down the notes. Cameron, Meredith, Imogen and Kerry busied themselves with lining their paper in red ink, writing the subject title and date at the top of the page.

As Mr Corbett walked around the room, inspecting his pupils' progress, he was relieved to see that as he passed the group's table, all four of them had now turned over their pages and continued writing, proving that they were halfway down the projection slide and therefore making good progress. Had Mr Corbett ever stopped and turned the pages back over, he would have noticed that Cameron, Meredith, Imogen and Kerry had taken absolutely no notes from the first half and only turned their pages over when they sensed the teacher approaching. Had Mr Corbett then flicked back through their files at any point, he would have realized that this was a tactic they had been employing for over a year and that subsequently they did not have a full page of Biology notes between the four of them. In fact, for the last half an hour, Kerry had been absorbed in compiling a list of all the presents she had received on Saturday – and making a side note of which ones came with receipts, Imogen had been texting Michael under the table, and Meredith and Cameron had been passing notes on how rubbish it was that Coral Andrews was still alive.

As he passed the door, Mr Corbett glanced out of the glass

and spotted a pupil walking down the corridor outside. The boy was new to Mount Olivet Grammar, having just transferred from an American high school at the start of term. His name was Blake Hartman and he was in their year, but in another house – Chichester. Being monumentally self-absorbed and holding fast to the view that Chichester was for freaks, none of the four socialites sitting at the table nearest to the door had even noticed yet that a new boy had enrolled. As Mr Corbett turned back towards the door to ask Blake for the homework due in last Friday, they had no idea that this was about to be their collision course with destiny and Blake Hartman. It was also about to be a collision course between Mr Corbett's head and the door.

In his over-eagerness to reach Blake before he disappeared out of sight, Mr Corbett almost hurtled over his own feet. As he opened the door, Mr Corbett tripped and his forehead wedged on to its corner. For one breath-holding second, the door and Mr Corbett's head were as one – there was a squelching noise as the door first gashed open part of his eyebrow and then separated again from his flesh. The teacher reeled backwards, holding his eyebrow, defiantly refusing to admit that he had been wounded and, with his spare hand, he gestured to Blake to come into the room. Blake edged in, apparently terrified that he would be blamed for this near lobotomy.

'Just, eh, wait there for a moment, Blake, please,' said Mr Corbett pleasantly, before raising his blood-spattered hand in a defiant, Nelson Mandela-like pose. 'It's OK, everyone, I can still teach. The lesson will carry on.'

But as Mr Corbett held his handkerchief to his head and began talking about stamens again, the lesson did not continue for Cameron Matthews, Meredith Harper, Imogen Dawson and Kerry Davison. The four of them had seemingly frozen in the poses they had adopted in the second after the accident – their hands had reached out slowly and taken the person's next to them, so that all four of them were now linked together in total, stunned silence. What had just happened was quite simply too funny for any of them to even begin to know how to react.

'Oh my . . .' said Meredith quietly. 'Did that just happen?'

'No,' said Imogen, 'it didn't. It couldn't. No.'

A giggle popped out of Kerry's mouth and, before they knew it, all four of them were convulsed with laughter. While Mr Corbett tried to turn his handkerchief into a makeshift eye-patch, Meredith flopped forward on to the table, sobbing with laughter and Imogen and Kerry collapsed into each other, with Imogen carefully tracing a finger under one eyelid to check if her mascara was running.

It was Cameron who halted long before the others, when he was directly addressed in Blake's soft American accent. 'Em, has he forgotten about me?' he whispered, with a smile, still standing between the doorway and Cameron's desk. 'Do you think I could go? I seriously haven't done that homework.'

Cameron smiled back and nodded. 'Oh God, yeah. Cut and run!'

'Cool. Thanks. I'm Blake Hartman, by the way.'

'Cameron Matthews. Hi.'

'Yeah, I know who you are. Don't tell him I've gone!'

With that, Blake left the room, leaving Cameron feeling curiously nervous about what exactly Blake had heard about him and worried in case he had looked stupid when laughing so hard. Staring over at Mr Corbett, though, he assured himself that the laughter had been worth it.

3

THE IRRESISTIBLE RISE OF SO BEAU

Monday and Friday afternoons were a special piece of Purgatory for Cameron Matthews, not just because he was afflicted by double Religion last thing, but also because on each occasion he had to walk to those classes alone in the company of Catherine. Trying to find a topic of conversation that she would be able to follow and Cameron would be able to stomach was always a particular challenge and today, after enduring five minutes of hearing about her nail-beds, he was done with being polite and swooped in with an interruption.

'Catherine, did you know there was a new kid in our year? Blake Hartman? He's American.'

Catherine spun to look at Cameron, her face alight with breathless excitement. 'The hotty who looks like Zac Efron?'

'Yeah, he does kind of look like him, doesn't he?' Cameron agreed.

'Kind of? They're, like, unbelievably beautiful twins. Well, before Zac got like old and stuff. It really shows that when God puts His mind to it, He can turn out some amazing work. He's in my English class, you know?'

'That's really interesting,' said Cameron, in a toneless voice he had perfected for dealing with one of Catherine's many tedious digressions.

'So how do *you* know him, then?'

'I don't. He was in Biology class earlier today.'

'When Mr Corbett smacked open his own head? Oh my God – funniest thing, *ever*.'

'You weren't there, Catherine.'

'I know! But Imogen does the best impressions.'

Yeah, you should see the one she does of you, Cameron thought. He tried one last time to find out about the new boy. Slowly – for Catherine's benefit. 'So, what's he like?'

'Who?'

'Blake.'

'Oh,' said Catherine. 'Well! He's apparently really nice. He's from America, but not the OC, and his father's some sort of minister or priest or something and he's working at some Baptist church outside Belfast for, like, the next two or three years or whatever, so Blake and his brother have come over with him to finish school here and stuff.'

'He has a brother?'

'Yeah. He's in first year. So, can Protestant priests have, like, kids and stuff?'

'Yes.'

'Weird.'

'Does Blake have a girlfriend?'

'No, I don't think so. Loads of girls fancy him. But he's sort of quiet and doesn't really go out to any parties. Apparently, he's like really good friends with the other boys in his school house, Chichester.'

'Why?'

'Someone has to be, I suppose. Does my hair today make me look like I've got meningitis?'

'Not really. Why?'

'Meredith sort of said it kind of did.'

'She probably meant it in a good way.'

'Yeah, probs.'

From: Kerry Davison <pinkmanolosprincess@msn.ni>
To: Imogen Dawson <eurovision_queen@msn.ni>

Imogen,

I just got your text but I was basking in my own radiance so couldn't reply right away. OK, DON'T panic. You are a sick little princess, which means you deserve sympathy. Some people don't understand this – I do. I am very spiritual. The reason why you can't get Michael out of your head is because you have MENTAL INFLUENZA ('the flu') – which is when you get so obsessed about someone that you get the fever for them and your whole life becomes about the illness. Like when you have the real flu, only worse. The real flu doesn't make you text someone 20 times in one day. So, in conclusion, you have the flu for Michael (who, by the way, we're going to need a code name for! I'm thinking Ernesto ... or something fabulous like that?).

Anyway, here's the plan. You can't stop thinking about him because he's the perfect imagined man. See? You haven't actually spent enough time with him to get a real picture in your head of what he's like, so you imagine him to be gorgeous and perfect. Sort of like what I think about Jamie Dornan, or what Lisa

Flaherty thinks about whoever's working behind the counter at Krispy Kreme. Text him and ask him to meet up in town for a coffee. (This is a VERY feminist thing to do!) Go and have a coffee with him. If you want, we'll go sit in a coffee shop nearby for emotional support and any emergency interventions. Meredith needs to get her hair done this Saturday anyway. Sound good? Call me in the next 20 mins and we'll run through possible texts to send him and make sure we get the right air of casualness. K?

Love you lots m'a-fucka'a,
Kerry xXx

Cameron, Catherine and Kerry were perched in the Starbucks on Cornmarket at half past twelve that Saturday when Meredith swept in with her newly feathered hair and a macchiato in her hand.

'Oh my God, Meredith, it looks amazing!' said Kerry, in her genuinely-serious voice, which she liked to practise in front of the mirror and which she modelled on Reese Witherspoon's final speech in *Legally Blonde*.

'Thanks. I got there at nine and Fabio did a great job in such a short time. Any word from Imogen? Cute shoes, Catherine.'

Catherine looked like she had seen the Risen Christ at receiving such an unexpected compliment from Meredith. 'THANKS! Your boots are just beyond.'

'I know,' sighed Meredith. 'They're *killing* me, but it's worth it.'

'No word from Imogen,' said Cameron. 'It's either going really well and she and Michael have run off to sunny Mexico together or Stewart caught them, in which case she's thrown herself in front of a bus.'

'This frappolatte is delicious,' said Catherine. 'Really yummy.'

Meredith's head snapped up at this remark, flicking her new hairstyle back with professional flair. 'What?'

'My frappolatte,' answered Catherine. 'It's yum. Should I get another one?'

Kerry began to speak. 'It's not called –'

'Yes,' said Meredith. 'Yes, you should.'

As Catherine skipped off downstairs, Cameron buried his face in his hands to hide the laughter. 'How does she get dressed in the morning without injuring herself?' he asked.

'I think that was mean,' said Kerry piously. 'I mean, she may be stupid, but, still, she's our friend.'

Refusing to engage in a conversation that had absolutely nothing to do with defending Catherine and everything to do with Kerry's determination to be seen as the 'nice' member of the group, Cameron turned to Meredith. 'Meredith, do you know anything about that new American kid that started in our year?'

Meredith nodded. 'Blake Hartman? Of course. I know everything. But he's not that popular or interesting. Why?'

'I just can't believe there's someone in the year I don't recognize.'

'Oh,' said Kerry, 'there's about sixty I don't even know exist until I see their sweaty faces next to me in the cafeteria queue.'

'True.'

Cameron lapsed into a sort of thoughtful silence, while Kerry sat next to him humming the tune to 'I'm Just the Girl Next Door' and Meredith looked over at Cameron, watching him closely. A thought flashed through her mind as she said, 'I mean, Blake is very good-looking . . . I suppose that's why a lot of people have noticed him.'

Cameron looked momentarily startled, but he answered in an even voice. 'Yeah, I suppose, he is quite good-looking. Catherine thinks he looks like Zac Efron.'

'Yeah,' said Meredith, running her finger slowly round the rim of her coffee cup.

'They laughed at me!' squeaked Catherine, as she threw herself back into her chair. 'Apparently, there's no such thing as a frappolatte!'

'Really?' said Cameron. 'What bitches.'

'Oh! There's my phone. Texty times,' smiled Kerry. 'I wonder who loves me?'

Go back to my house ASAP. I am on my way there now. I am in love. Imogen xxxxxx PS – Get me a millionaire cake.

'It was perfect,' sighed Imogen dreamily, lying on her bed. 'He's just so mature and so clever and so funny and so great. And he has amazing arms. Where's my cake?'

Meredith flicked her hand. 'Catherine, where's the cake?'

'What about Stewart?' said Kerry, with heavy hesitation.

'I know!' moaned Imogen, rolling on to her side. 'Stewart. Stewart. He has great arms too! But should I end it with him?'

'Only if you're certain that Michael will start properly going out with you,' Meredith said, sitting down next to her. 'What if he doesn't and you're left alone? And what will you tell Stewart when he asks why you're breaking up with him?'

'He might be too busy crying,' Imogen pondered aloud. 'At

least there'd be no questions that way, but I'd definitely feel like a bitch.'

'Stewart cries?' asked Kerry.

'Yes,' agreed Cameron. 'Surprising, I know. And once he starts there's literally no stopping him. I've only seen it happen twice – once when his grandfather died and once during *Billy Elliott*.'

'We all cried during that,' Meredith muttered.

'Yes, but he cried because of the story, not because it was so crap that it would have been more fun forking out his own eyes.'

'What am I going to do?' snapped Imogen, furious at being upstaged by a fictional ballet-dancing miner. 'I can't let the love of my life get away. Stewart's lovely, but he's my Aidan; Michael is *clearly* my Mr Big.'

'Do you ever think we might pay too much attention to *Sex and the City*?' Catherine asked quietly from the foot of the bed.

The other four turned to look at her as if she had just suggested that they voluntarily gain thirty pounds or join the Young Farmers' Club.

'Well, if that's true,' Meredith said slowly, 'then maybe you should take a series-three approach to the whole problem?'

'You mean . . .'

'Well, as long as no one finds out and it only goes on until you've reached a decision about whether you prefer Stewart or Michael – why not? As long as you're clever about the whole thing, and make sure neither of them have any friends in common, I say you have three weeks to test the waters.'

Imogen lay very still on the bed and there was a long silence; no one wanted to second the plan for cheating in case she decided not to do it, in which case they would be the immoral bitch who advocated sabotaging a relationship, but equally no one wanted to be the prude who objected to Imogen pursuing a love affair with a man she had spent the last two weeks referring to as 'Delicious McHotty'.

After two minutes, in which the only sound had been Catherine having an attack of her famous nervous hiccups, Imogen spoke. 'I'm not coming to the Beach Club tonight. I have other plans. Cameron, is Stewart going to be there?'

'Yes.'

'Definitely?'

'Absolutely.'

As they got ready at Meredith's for their night out, Kerry stepped into the enormous closet carrying her fuchsia-pink silk-satin Jimmy Choo sandals in her hand. Meredith was standing in front of the accessories drawer in her dressing gown, picking up a Chanel belt and clearly debating in her head whether or not she should wear it. Kerry sat on the seat in front of the make-up mirror and took a deep breath before speaking.

'Meredith?'

'Yes?'

'You know that there is absolutely no way that Imogen will be able to keep this thing with Michael down to just three weeks?'

'She might. Do you think the Chanel with the lilac?'

'No.'

'Me neither.' And she began running her fingers through the rest of her chains and belts.

'Mer, if she picks Michael, it's bound to eventually get back to Stewart that they started up when she was still dating him.'

'No, not at all. Who'd tell him? Stewart's too nice for anyone to want to hurt him, especially after he would already have gone through a traumatic break-up with Imogen. And he isn't close friends with any people who are major gossips, apart from Cameron, who *can't* tell him. So, no, if – or when – she chooses Michael, there's no reason Stewart would find out that they had been going out beforehand. The only one in that group who will probably know anything about it is Mark.'

'Mark?'

'Of course. He's friends with everyone in the year. More or less. Someone he knows is bound to know someone in Immaculate Heart and one way or another the rumours about Michael and Imogen will get back to him, eventually.'

Kerry didn't like the sort of icy, matter-of-fact way Meredith was speaking. It was this tone of voice that gave Kerry the firm belief that Meredith could kill someone without feeling even a twinge of remorse; what made it worse was that she knew without a shadow of doubt that Imogen and Cameron would help her hide the body.

'But if Mark finds out, he'll go ballistic.'

'Yes,' said Meredith, taking her dress off the hanger, 'but, again, he wouldn't want to hurt Stewart once the break-up had already happened. So Mark will go ballistic in his stupid, self-righteous way, and he'll blame me, because he hates me; Imogen, because she's the one who did it; and Cameron, because he must have known about it but never told Stewart. Oh, cute belt!'

As Meredith was slipping into a lilac Versace party dress and putting a golden chain round her waist, Kerry began to suspect the horrible direction this plan was going in. 'And Mark will yell at Cameron . . .'

'Yes. And he'll be so angry he's very likely to say something unforgivable and Cameron holds a grudge more than any of the rest of us, so it's pretty safe to say that one way or another that irritating little friendship between the two of them will be over for good and I will finally have Mark Kingston out of my life.'

'Meredith, encouraging people to commit adultery, which will destroy a relationship and a friendship, just so we can be temporarily amused and trim down our guest lists, is the kind of thing that makes us bad people.'

'No, Kerry! Punching orphans makes people "bad". We're being cruel to be kind. Cameron totally deserves friends who don't morally judge him for the occasional act of Fabulous Induced Viciousness – like us. And Imogen deserves someone special and glamorous, not safe and boring, like Stewart. Stewart is a nice guy, he's very handsome, he's on the rugby team, but he's just not good enough for someone in our group in the long term. Neither is Mark. This plan is even more perfect than I thought and everyone is going to be much happier in the end. You'll see. If you want to make an omelette, you've got to break a few eggs.'

'I hate my diet,' sighed Kerry. 'I'd sell my own mother for an omelette right now.'

Their worryingly good fake IDs having passed inspection, Meredith, Kerry and Cameron entered the Beach Club, jumping ahead of the others who were queuing throughout the arena. The moment they entered, Cameron quickly clocked Stewart over by the bar and he breathed a sigh of relief that there was now no chance of him interrupting Imogen's date with Michael the

Immaculate Heart Hotty. At over six feet in height and extremely toned due to his constant exercise as outside centre for the school's First XVs, Stewart wasn't exactly hard to spot when you were looking for him. Spying him from the entrance, Cameron reasoned that by anyone else's standards but Imogen's, apparently, Stewart Lawrence seemed like the world's most perfect boyfriend. With his light brown hair freshly showered, he was leaning confidently against the bar in a red Jack Wills rugby top with a popped collar and Abercrombie & Fitch jeans, talking to Peter and Mark, both of whom stood several inches shorter than him.

Remembering his instructions, Cameron began texting Imogen to let her know that her dinner with Michael was safe and there was no chance of Stewart being near the restaurant that evening. Kerry meanwhile had completely forgotten that she was supposed to be watching Stewart as well and had instead handed over money to the nice barman in return for a Hawaiian flower necklace. Seeing that keeping Imogen informed was going to be completely up to him, Cameron began waving his arm around, trying to get a signal.

'Hey, Cameron. Have you seen Imogen?' asked Stewart, who had walked over to him during Cameron's frantic signal search. 'I thought she was supposed to be coming tonight?'

'Yeah, she was,' said Cameron, taking the Budweiser Stewart had bought for him, 'but her dad's making her go to this family thing.'

'What family thing? They all live in England, don't they?'

'I didn't say "family",' said Cameron, acting confused, 'I said "church".'

'You said "family", mate,' laughed Stewart.

'God, sorry – I meant "church". With her mum. There's some

46

fundraiser on for the Our Lady of Lourdes thing at Saint Brigid's tonight and they're both on the committee.'

'Oh, right,' said Stewart, smiling. 'Gotta love that Catholic banter. I wonder how late it'll go on . . .'

'Probably not that late, but she'll have to hang around afterwards. She was really upset that she couldn't come.'

'Pity.'

'Yeah, I know. Would you hold this for me for a minute, please? I need to go send a text.'

'Sure thing, mate,' smiled Stewart, taking back the Budweiser.

Cameron moved quickly out of the club to try to message Imogen, but no luck was to be had anywhere in the arena, so eventually he had to step outside into the night air, where he was finally rewarded with three bars.

Stu is here. Asked where u were. Told him ur at a CHURCH thing. R Lady of Lourdes. Fundraiser. Ur dad made u go. V last minute. U hav 2 hang around after which is y u can't come out 2nite xxx

Within minutes, he had received a message back from Imogen.

Perfect! Thanx babes. U r a sexcellent biatch. Michael is amazing. Even more delicious than the strudel we're sharing for dessert, which is absolutely yummylicious btw. Let me no immediately if there is any other gossip xxx

Smiling, Cameron turned round to head back inside and bumped straight into a very angry-looking Mark, who had been standing right behind him.

'What's wrong?'

'Were you going to say hello to us tonight?'

'I didn't see you and I've only just arrived,' Cameron said. 'The only person I saw was Stewart. I said hi.'

'That's crap. I saw you see all of us, when you came in with *her*.'

Cameron sighed. 'That's what this is really about, isn't it? Meredith. As usual! Why do you hate her so much?'

'Are you kidding? Why do I hate her? Are you kidding? Because she's the devil, Cameron! That's why. And what's worse is the moment you're around her, you become this horrible little lick-ass, who I don't even know!'

'Calm down, Mark. You're too drunk for this conversation.'

'Yeah, maybe I am, but I mean it. It's like there are two Camerons – there's the one who I've known since we were kids and then there's the one who's Meredith Harper's favourite toy.'

'I'm not going to stand around drinking beer at the bar with you all night while you drunkenly bitch about Meredith when I could be dancing with my real friends!'

Mark looked, for a moment, like he had been punched. 'That's fair enough, Cameron,' he snapped. 'I'll see you later.'

'Mark, wait!'

But Mark turned round and moved, slightly unsteadily, back into the arena. Cameron was left standing outside, furious at himself for being so tactless, and equally angry at Mark for creating a fight out of nothing. At least Meredith kept her hatred for Mark down to little more than a few nasty one-line remarks, some of which were actually quite funny; Mark went on about *her* all the time. He was like the inverse of an obsessed boyfriend and it was beginning to get really, really annoying.

Irritated and confused, Cameron sat down on the wall behind him to calm down.

'Cameron?'

Cameron turned to look, prepared to cut down whoever had interrupted his mental strop, when he saw Blake Hartman standing next to him. 'Blake, hi.'

'Hey. Thank goodness you remembered my name. Otherwise that could've been awkward! I didn't think you would . . . remember.'

'Well, it was a pretty memorable occasion when we first met. It's not every day you see a grown man impale his own head with a door.'

Blake laughed. 'Poor Mr Corbett! Is everything all right?'

'With Mr Corbett?'

'With you.'

'Kind of. I just had a fight with my friend.'

'Yeah, I saw. Sorry to hear that. Is anyone else here with you?'

'Not right now, no. I'm a loner.'

'Yeah, so says the most popular guy in school.'

Cameron felt that sort of pleasurable rush that Imogen achieved when she saw a hot guy or Meredith when she slipped on a pair of new shoes. 'Well, that's not true,' he answered with false modesty.

'Oh, come on, Cameron. On my first day at Mount Olivet, you and your friends were actually pointed out to me in the cafeteria, like mini-celebrities: Imogen is the hot one, Kerry's got Daddy's credit card and Meredith's the one who'll kill you as you sleep.'

Cameron giggled. 'Yeah, but she'd do it with style. Who told you all this?'

'Everyone,' said Blake, avoiding Cameron's stare as he sat down next to him.

Cameron nudged his shoulder. 'Well, that's clearly a lie. You just don't want to give away any names.'

'Kevin Law,' answered Blake, defiantly. 'He was the first one to say it.'

'Is he the one with really short dark hair and smells like rope?' said Cameron, looking at Blake and feeling momentarily unnerved as he realized just how close Blake was to him. He really was as good-looking as everyone said. It was no wonder Catherine looked as if her lungs were constricting every time someone mentioned him.

Blake looked up and smiled. 'Yeah, I suppose he kind of does kind of.'

'God, I didn't even know he could talk.'

'I mean, don't get me wrong. It's really cool that everyone knows who you are. I think it's amazing.'

'Everyone thinks we're amazing, Blake,' said Cameron, only half-jokingly.

'No, but seriously, I mean, how often is it that you find a high school where a gay guy can be one of the popular kids?'

Cameron turned to look at Blake in shock. 'I'm not gay.'

'What?'

'I'm not . . . I'm not gay.'

'Oh.'

'Who told you I was?'

'No one.'

'Kevin?'

'No! No one. I just assumed.'

'Well, don't!' said Cameron, standing up, feeling suddenly panicked. 'Don't.'

'OK, God, I'm so sorry, Cameron. Please, don't leave. I don't have any ID. I can't get in and anyway I'm not exactly in a position to throw away friends. Please. I'm so sorry.'

Now embarrassed at how worked up he had been, Cameron hesitated before slowly sitting back down. It was a few moments before either of them spoke again and it was Blake who broke the silence. 'For the record, I don't think of it as an insult.'

Imogen burst into Meredith's kitchen at half past eleven the next morning, just as Meredith and Kerry were sipping their first coffee of the day. They could tell that her date with Michael had gone spectacularly because she was sporting a happy expression on her face, one which was unique to Imogen – it managed to combine utter joy with a scary level of determination. It meant that some sort of plot would be needed in order to secure her happiness permanently and God help the besty who didn't help as required.

'I've met the man I'm going to marry! My flu has a *raging* fever!' she proclaimed, while pouring coffee into a mug for herself. 'I am going to be Mrs Imogen Dawson-Laverty. Where's the milk?'

Kerry sat biting her lip nervously, silently waiting for what Imogen was about to suggest next. It was absolutely certain that whatever scheme she had come up with would involve contributions from her friends and being caught up in one of Imogen Dawson's intrigues was something Kerry Davison had learned to fear more than surprise tests in Spanish class. She had still not quite forgotten the time when Imogen had taken it into her head that her ex-boyfriend, Alistair, had blocked her number and had forced Kerry to call him thirty-seven times from a withheld number in the space of twelve minutes, only to make her pretend to be a market researcher when he did pick up on call thirty-eight.

'The milk's on the table,' answered Meredith. 'Where's Cameron?'

'He went to get coffee with Mark this morning,' Kerry answered first. 'They had a massive fight last night and he's trying to patch it up.'

'Patch it up? He should let it go. When is he going to get over that friendship? I'm so done having to listen to Cameron bitch about how moody and grumpy Mark Kingston is, but then he runs off first thing in the morning to patch things up with him. God! Am I the only one capable of having an opinion and sticking to it?'

'Yes, you are,' said Kerry. 'I am so flaky that I disgust myself.'

'Anyway,' said Imogen, sitting down, bored already by the conversation that wasn't about her, 'obviously, adultery is now the name of the game and this will require several things if it is going to work. Firstly, I am going to confession right before Christmas. This means that by that time I have to have made a decision about which man to stick with and be pretty sure I'm not going to cheat again. God is a big enough factor to keep on schedule for, right?'

Meredith nodded. 'Sure.'

'Perfect. Secondly, I'm going to tell Michael that I've broken up with Stewart, obviously. The story I'm going with is that Stewart and I just went through a very stressful break-up, which we're keeping quiet because he's had a tough time at home recently and doesn't want people at school to be all over him with fake sympathy. Which is why I have to keep the me-and-Michael thing on the down-low until Stewart's fine again.'

'That's an OK plan,' said Meredith, 'but doesn't it sort of make you look like the sociopath who's dumped a guy when he's having a tough time at home?'

'Damn.'

'How about you tell him that Stewart cheated on you and you're just so frightened about getting back into a relationship that you need to take things slowly and don't want to go "public" with it yet?' said Kerry, who was warming to the scandal now that she realized she wasn't going to be personally inconvenienced by it in any way.

Imogen clapped her hands together excitedly. 'Sexcellent.'

'Also,' said Kerry, delighting in her own genius, 'it means Michael will have to be extra nice to you and work really hard to win you over. Guys like that kind of thing and it never hurts to get them to make more of an effort.'

'God, Kerry, that's a really good idea,' smiled Imogen. 'I don't care what the teachers said at parents' evening: you *are* competent.'

'Does anyone want more coffee?' asked Meredith.

'Me, please,' said Kerry, looking slightly wounded at the unnecessary reminder of parents' evening.

Mark and Cameron had been sitting in a fairly uncomfortable silence in Mark's bedroom for the last five minutes, when Mark finally spoke, still irritable and accusatory. 'Look, is there a reason you're here or did you just come to make me feel awkward?'

'Rude, much? I came to apologize for last night.'

'Which bit?'

'What I said about Meredith – the "real friends" bit.'

'Oh.'

'That wasn't fair.'

'Yeah, but you meant it,' sighed Mark, getting up from his bed and walking across his room to lean against the far wall, 'didn't you? And it probably *is* fair. You're bound to have more fun with her than you've been having with me lately.'

Cameron fidgeted, discomfited by Mark's change of mood. 'Mark, no. Different types of fun, maybe, but not better.'

'I'm sorry too, Cam, honestly. It's just hard, being replaced and seeing you change . . . I sound like a gay.'

'I'm not replacing you! I'd never do that, Mark. C'mon. It is true that Meredith is spectacular levels of fun, but it wasn't Meredith who I met on the first day at prep or Meredith who comforted me the day I cried for six solid hours because I had to get braces, or Meredith who rubbed my back when I was thirteen and started vomiting after drinking an entire bottle of Buck's Fizz . . . Is that a smile I see?'

Mark walked over and punched Cameron lightly on the shoulder with a shy smile. 'OK. You win. Arse.'

Sadly, even Imogen's flamboyant descriptions of her first date with Michael and discussions on what the possible theme of their wedding might be (Tuscan?) had not lifted Meredith's irritation at how bored she had been by her weekend. Thinking it over on Sunday evening, she realized that the only person who was responsible for her own entertainment was herself and so she decided to do something that had not been done in the group for almost a year: she was going to make up a new word and launch it the very next day.

She entered Biology class fifteen minutes late and sat next to Imogen. Mr Corbett, now sporting seven stitches in his head, looked up disapprovingly. 'Meredith, what time do you call this?'

'Quarter to ten, sir,' she said breezily, as she set her practically useless folder on the table.

'Right, well, don't be so late again,' mumbled Mr Corbett lamely. 'Class, today we're going to be discussing the way in which insects and pollination work together and . . . *blah blah blah blah.*'

'Eugh,' sighed Kerry. 'I'm *so* tired.'

'I know, totally,' agreed Cameron.

'Totally.' Imogen nodded.

'What do you think of this top?' asked Kerry, holding up a catalogue for approval.

It was then that Meredith, gazing disinterestedly into her hand mirror, made Mount Olivet history. 'I love it –' slight pause – 'it's *so* beau.'

For a split second, the other three didn't move – Kerry still held the magazine in her hand, Imogen had stopped twirling her hair on her pencil and Cameron's fingers were held slightly above the table where they had stopped, mid-drum. It was Imogen who broke the silence with a faint 'What?'

'Oh!' said Meredith, with a tiny silly-me-I-forgot-you-wouldn't-know laugh. 'It's just my new word. *Bee-yah*. It means "beautiful". Only it's shorter, different and better. *Bee-yah-tiful.*'

'*Bee-yah*,' enunciated Imogen. 'So, like, I'm *beau*. You're *beau.*'

'Coral Andrews is *not* beau,' nodded Meredith, waiting for one of them to use it in a sentence, which was the clear sign she had succeeded.

'That is *such* a beau word,' said Kerry. 'I love it. So beau.'

By Friday, *beau* (pronounced *bee-yah*) had swept Mount Olivet quicker than the bubonic plague had Medieval Europe. With her usual cunning, Meredith had picked a shortening of the word that technically didn't sound anything like the way it was written, meaning that there were delightful opportunities to punish people who pronounced it 'bow' or, worse, 'be-oh'. Catherine was so traumatized by the fear of pronouncing it wrong and earning a retribution nip from Imogen that she had stuck six Post-its with *bee-yah* round her bathroom mirror and checked over them religiously before leaving the house every morning. The sure sign of *beau*'s power had come on Wednesday, when the semi-popular kids started using it, and by Friday afternoon, two first-years waiting at the bus stop were heard to say it about Kerry's hair as she strode past them. By the weekend, someone had started up a Facebook group: 'Mount Olivet girls – they're so beau!'

Cameron was walking home alone that Friday afternoon, reflecting on how *beau* had even outdone the popularity of *snarf*, the word they had come up with in third year (to be used in the context of, *Oh my snarf* and, eventually, *Snarfalicious!*). His thoughts were interrupted when he was tapped on the shoulder by Blake, who had unexpectedly appeared behind him and looked slightly out of breath.

'Hey, Cameron!'

'Hey . . .'

'Hey.'

'Yeah.'

'Are you walking to Malone?'

'Well, I live there. So, yes.'

'Cool,' smiled Blake, holding his side slightly. 'Do you mind if I walk with you?'

Still not quite ready to let go of how awkward he had made him feel last Saturday, Cameron's tone was non-committal. 'No. Not at all. But why are you going this way? You're not from Malone.'

'My little brother's made friends with Imogen Dawson's brother, Chris. They hang out together after school, so my dad's picking me up there at five. I saw you up ahead of me and I knew you lived in this direction, so I sort of ran to catch up. No point walking alone, is there?'

'Not usually.'

'Did you and your friend patch things up after Saturday?'

'Kind of . . .'

'Cool . . . It's really nice out today.'

'Yeah, it's so beau.'

Cameron thought he caught Blake smile momentarily and it was a few seconds or so before the other boy spoke again. 'Hey, listen . . . um . . . do you wanna hang out sometime? The boys in my class are cool, but they're a bit . . . well . . .'

Irritated by anyone attempting to be nice simply for the sake of it, Cameron helpfully interrupted. 'They belong in a circus.'

Blake smiled again. 'That's not nice.'

'That's why it's true.'

As they walked along together, Cameron decided that while he was shocked that someone outside his group had dared to ask him to hang out, he did actually like Blake despite his inappropriate gay comment last Saturday.

'What about Sunday?' he said, after a few minutes.

'Sure!' smiled Blake. 'Do you wanna come over to my house?'

'Can't. My sister has Pilates that evening, so I won't be able to get a lift. You can come to mine,' Cameron answered, with a slightly aren't-I-gracious tone on the last sentence.

'Cool! Half seven?'

'Why not?'

'So . . . Cameron?'

'Yes?'

'*Beau* . . . what is that all about?'

4

Pray for Us Sinners

'Imogen's being weird,' said Stewart as he pulled on the trousers of his dinner suit.

'How d'you mean?' asked Peter.

'I don't know. She's just been very distant or something. I don't know. I can't put my finger on it, but things haven't been going great between us recently.'

'Mate, maybe she was just stressed about tonight. You know how girls get about these kinds of things. And it's a pretty big fucking deal.'

Stewart put on a smile. 'Yeah, you're probably right. Tonight's the biggest night of her year.'

'Why don't you ask Cameron?' suggested Mark, polishing his shoes. 'He's bound to know if it's anything else. But I'm sure it's nothing, big lad. Do you have any spare hair gel?'

The Our Lady of Lourdes Annual Fundraising Ball was the social event of the autumn season. Five hundred guests bought obscenely expensive tickets in return for a five-course gourmet meal and a spectacular ball, with the proceeds going to local hospitals and to help with the pilgrimage of the sick to the shrine at Lourdes. The guests generally consisted of the great and the good of Northern Irish high society and it was bound to get at least a ten-page spread in *Ulster Tatler*. Imogen and her mother, Clarissa, had been on the Events Committee for the last two balls and Imogen had made sure that every single one of Mount Olivet's glamazons would turn up to the palatial building where the party was being held. For the last six months, she had been obsessed with every detail of the Lourdes ball, and balancing that along with her mounting relationship troubles proved that if she had ever bothered to turn her willpower to her studies, she could have been on her way to Yale in no time. As it was, Imogen had last been seen flouncing across the foyer in an Oscar de la Renta ball gown, demanding to know who had authorized white freesias instead of lilies for the entrance display.

Meredith made an entrance into the main dining hall on the arm of her father, half an hour after the doors opened. As they descended the marble staircase, many admiring heads turned to look at them – the wealthiest and most eligible man in Northern Ireland with his beautiful teenage daughter. With a keen eye for the theme of the party, Meredith had dressed in a Vera Wang gown and the only jewels she wore were her diamonds and a Breguet ring. Everything on her was either diamond-pure, white or blue – the colours of Our Lady of Lourdes.

Anthony Harper, who had been divorced for the last six years, was a millionaire many, many times over, but the centre of his world remained Meredith, his only child. He all but glowed with pride looking at her and his warm, welcoming smile took in her friends as they reached the bottom of the staircase – Kerry, in a silk-organza Ermanno Scervino dress, and Catherine, in a strong orange number by Marchesa. He escorted all of them over to their table, smiling and nodding to acquaintances as he went. Meredith's diamonds sparkled in the light glowing from the silver candelabras dotted across the room as she weaved her way elegantly through the guests. After he had pulled out seats for all three of the girls, Anthony Harper went to mingle and Meredith quickly took in the room.

She saw that there were many faces that she recognized and that Mount Olivet's socialites had turned out in force. All of the senior school queen bees were there: Cecilia Molyneux, the lusciously blonde head of the pashmina brigade in upper sixth, was at Table Nine; Cameron's sister Charlotte, the fourteen-year-old leader of the Malone princesses, was at Table Seven with her two best friends, Jenny Thompson and Melissa Russell; and, to Meredith's delight, Anastasia Montmorency could now be seen entering the room in an exquisite floor-length Valentino number.

Anastasia Montmorency was the queen bee of sixth year and her group included four other girls – Mariella, Natasha, Lavinia and Tangela – all of whom were known as 'the Heiresses', thanks to their incredibly wealthy parents. In many ways, Anastasia and Meredith were highly similar – both were popular, very attractive and fabulously wealthy, both of their mothers were born outside Northern Ireland and both of the girls had slight accents to prove it (Meredith's mother was American, Anastasia's was English). By general agreement in the school, Anastasia was the wealthiest girl at Mount Olivet and the second most beautiful; Meredith was the most beautiful and the second wealthiest. They should have been enemies, but since they both controlled separate year groups they got on very well and as Anastasia sailed over to her table on the arm of a good-looking, olive-skinned gentleman, Meredith rose to hug her.

'Meredith, I love your dress.'

'Thank you,' smiled Meredith. 'You look amazing.'

'That's so sweet of you. Meredith, I want you to meet a friend of my family's. Francesco Modonesi, allow me to introduce a very dear friend of mine from school, Meredith Harper. Meredith, this is Francesco; he's at boarding school with my brother and he's spending some of his half-term visiting us before going back to see his family in Italy. Francesco, these are Meredith's friends – Kerry Davison and Catherine O'Rourke.'

The only way to describe Francesco Modonesi was beautiful – stunningly, stunningly beautiful. He was tall, tanned, elegant and devastatingly charming. Faced with a man who they felt belonged in a Christian Dior campaign, Kerry and Catherine had fallen into a stupefied silence, punctuated by a gasp from Catherine when Francesco nodded politely in her direction. At this, she kicked Kerry so hard under the table that she left a slight bruise. Thankfully, Kerry was still too stunned at the lusciousness in front of her to notice. Meredith, on the other hand, simply smiled radiantly and extended her hand to Francesco as he took it to kiss.

'It is very nice to meet you, Miss Harper,' he said in flawless English.

'*Sono lieta di conoscerla, signor Modonesi*,' she answered. '*Quanto si trattiene ancora in Irlanda del Nord?*'

Clearly impressed and delighted, Francesco slowly let go of her hand, but held eye contact. '*Lei parla Italiano?*'

'*Un poco, si*,' answered Meredith, gesturing to the chair next to her.

'There!' smiled Anastasia. 'I knew you two would get along. Oh, excuse me one moment, Lavinia's just arrived. Francesco, I'll be right back! Meredith, I think the *Tatler* photographer wants to get a snap of the two of us together at some point.'

As Anastasia greeted her best friend/sidekick, Lavinia, dressed in a blood-red Galliano dress, Meredith turned her attention back to Francesco, who was staring at her avidly.

'I go back to Genoa on Tuesday,' he said, answering her earlier question. 'But in the meantime, would it be all right if I fetched you a drink?'

'Yes, thank you.' Meredith nodded. 'That would be lovely.'

'What would you like?'

'*Sorprendimi*,' she smiled.

As Francesco walked over to the bar the power of speech was finally restored to the other two girls. 'If he was in a room with Blake Hartman,' sighed Catherine, 'I would explode. It would just be too much sexiness and stuff.'

Just then, Imogen sat down at the table with an exhausted sigh. 'Who was the Adonis?'

'A friend of Sasha Montmorency's. They're at Winchester together,' explained Meredith. 'His name's Francesco Modonesi; he's over visiting from Italy.'

'Well, he was hardly from Finaghy, was he?'

'Where's Stewart?' asked Kerry.

'Don't know . . . Not here yet.'

'Aren't you worried about Michael showing up?'

'No!' giggled Imogen. 'He couldn't afford the ticket – one of the benefits of dating the poor.'

'His father's a dentist,' said Kerry.

'Exactly. One of the help.'

'Imogen! That is *very* politically incorrect!' roared Kerry, who liked to take a stand on politically correct vocabulary as if it might compensate for how much evil bitchiness she tolerated in all other aspects of her life.

Imogen sighed. 'Blah, blah, blah. I hope Stewart hurries up. Him, Cameron and Peter are sitting at our table and I don't want there to be three empty seats when Father Jerome makes his opening speech. Wait! Where's Orla?'

For a moment, Catherine pretended not to hear her, but when Imogen repeated the question, she knew it was time to 'fess up. 'She's not coming,' said Catherine, 'but I managed to give her ticket away, so there won't be an empty place at our table.'

'Who to?'

'Well . . . Orla only came down with stomach flu this morning, so it was *very* last minute and I called a couple of people and eventually Stewart said he had a friend who wanted to come but couldn't get a ticket.'

Meredith's head snapped in Catherine's direction. 'Who'd he give it to?'

'Well . . . em . . .'

'Catherine, who did you sell your sister's ticket to?'

Just then, Stewart could be seen walking down the staircase accompanied by the tuxedoed Peter, Cameron – and Mark. As they watched their descent, Meredith turned to Catherine and said, through clenched teeth, 'I am going to kill you as you sleep.'

'Hey, beautiful,' said Stewart, leaning in to kiss Imogen as he arrived at the table. 'Ladies, you look lovely.'

'Thanks,' simpered Kerry. 'It's Ermanno Scervino.'

'Means nothing to me,' answered Stewart good-naturedly.

As Cameron lowered himself into his seat at the table, Meredith got up. 'Cameron, can I talk to you for a minute, please?'

'Sure!' he exclaimed.

'Over here,' she gestured, moving towards the bar. 'Imogen. You too, Kerry. Catherine, you can stay here.'

Kerry, Imogen and Cameron dutifully rose from their seats and followed after Meredith. Mark couldn't hide his annoyance and was heard to mutter, 'For fuck's sake,' under his breath. Desperate to gloss over the awkwardness, Catherine decided to strike up a conversation on the charity. 'Soooo,' she said, trying to force brightness into her tone, 'Lourdes and stuff?'

'What the hell is he doing here?'

'Meredith, I didn't know he was coming until he was in the car when they picked me up! And, anyway, it's not as if spending time with you is Mark's idea of the perfect night out either, is it? It's not like he planned this,' said Cameron. 'Apparently, Orla got stomach flu yesterday but didn't realize how bad it was until today and Catherine needed to sell the ticket.'

'Wasn't there someone more fun that she could've sold it to?' asked Meredith. 'A crack addict? A mass murderer? A farmer? I don't know!'

Plucking a cosmopolitan from a passing waiter, Imogen shook her head in disgust. 'Well, I think she's really crossed a line. It's one thing to sell the ticket to Mark, but to sell him a ticket at *our* table when she knows what you think of him is *so* not OK.'

'It's ridiculous,' snapped Meredith. 'He's going to ruin my night. I don't want to have to sit opposite *that* all evening. His judgemental face is going to ruin my starter.'

'What are we having?' asked Kerry.

'Pressed cantaloupe ice cubes with melon-seed milk,' answered Imogen.

'Ooo, delicious!'

Meredith looked as if she would dearly like to plunge her stiletto in Kerry's neck. Luckily, just then, the lights dimmed and Father Jerome took to the podium to make his speech. Everyone took their places at their appointed tables and applauded the priest before he began.

As Father Jerome spoke of the importance of the Our Lady of Lourdes Society and its work with the sick and the wider community, Mark's eyes kept travelling over to Meredith, who was serenely watching the speaker. Sitting in the dim light and bathed in the glow of the candles, Mark had to admit that she was almost painfully beautiful. When the priest mentioned the organizational work done by all the ladies of the committee, he singled out Imogen and her mother especially and, at that, Meredith put her arm on Imogen's in a gesture of silent congratulation. Imogen turned to look at Meredith and smiled. Mark felt a twinge of unease, as most people do when someone they've turned into a two-dimensional object of hatred displays any sign of human warmth. Deep down, he began to wonder if he was entirely right about Meredith, but, just as he was thinking that, she reached to pick up her glass of champagne and her eyes momentarily caught his. She held his stare for a second and the coldness Mark saw in her immediately re-affirmed all his worst prejudices. By the time she had turned her attention back to the podium, Mark Kingston's brush with uncertainty was over.

When the priest concluded his speech, polite applause filled the room and after it died down some people got up to mingle before the meal was served. A well-dressed, middle-aged couple began to approach their table and Catherine, who could see them coming, squeaked and gestured as subtly as she could to Imogen, who turned all too late to see who it was.

'Oh my God, oh my God, oh my God!' whispered Catherine under her breath. 'This is a disaster!'

'Why? What is it?' asked Kerry, leaning in with evident delight at potential scandal.

'Michael's parents.'

Imogen had stood up in a pre-emptive gesture to try to steer them away from her table, but they were already standing next to Meredith's chair and the best she could now hope for was damage limitation. 'Hello, Imogen,' said Michael's father with a cheery smile. 'We spotted you from across the room. We're sitting just over there.'

'How lovely,' she answered, her fingers digging into the back of her chair. 'Dr Laverty, Mrs Laverty, these are my friends – Meredith, Stewart, Cameron, Peter, Mark, Kerry and Catherine.'

'Nice to meet you,' said Mrs Laverty. 'Isn't it a lovely party, Imogen? We didn't know you would be here or we would have got a ticket for Michael as well. When we heard Father Jerome mention your name, we said to ourselves, *We've got to find her and stay hello and congratulations*, didn't we, Paddy? And then we saw you were sitting over here with Catherine O'Rourke and we thought, *Well, now we have to go over!* Didn't we, Paddy?'

Dr Laverty nodded in agreement with his wife. Cameron, Kerry, Meredith and Catherine had almost stopped breathing, clearly hoping that if they stayed as still as possible, the impending car crash in front of them would not happen. Finally recovering her wits, Meredith pulled her phone out of her clutch and immediately texted Anastasia from under the table.

'Yes!' smiled Imogen. 'I'm on the committee . . .'

'Michael will be so disappointed that he couldn't make it. He's got ever so fond of you,' beamed his mother. 'You two are pretty much inseparable nowadays. I suppose you'll be over again tomorrow and . . .'

Anastasia had materialized, as if from nowhere. 'Hello, I'm so sorry to interrupt. Imogen, Meredith, the *Tatler* photograph needs us as soon as possible.'

'Oh, well, we'll let you go!' smiled Mrs Laverty, 'Lovely to see you again, dear. And well done. See you soon, no doubt. Nice to have met you all, as well. Have a lovely night. And, Catherine, tell your mummy I was asking about her.'

As the Lavertys moved away from the table in one direction and Meredith, Imogen and Anastasia moved away in the other, the tension could have been cut with a knife.

'She introduced me as her friend,' said Stewart quietly. 'And who the fuck is Michael?'

'He's her dance partner,' said Cameron, with hardly a second's pause. 'She's taken up samba. It's the latest work-out thing. She's obsessed.'

'Really?'

'Yes. But I don't think she really likes Michael that much. He's a good dancer, though.'

'Most gay men are,' put in Kerry helpfully.

Scuttling into an abandoned ladies' bathroom on the second floor, Imogen, Meredith and Anastasia stood in front of the mirrors. Meredith and Anastasia began reapplying their make-up, while Imogen stood next to the basin, breathing deeply.

'What was that all about?' asked Anastasia.

'Man trouble,' explained Imogen, still clearly shaken. 'Oh my God. That was close. Way too close. Do you think Stewart suspected anything?'

'Oh, gosh,' whispered Anastasia, understanding at last. 'Another guy's parents?'

Imogen threw her clutch down on the marble countertop. 'Fuck! Fuck! Fuck! Meredith, what am I going to do?'

'You're going to have to end it with one of them,' she said. 'Seriously, Imogen, it's been way longer than three weeks. It's time to dump Stewart.'

'But I'm not sure it's him that I want to dump!'

'If there's someone else then that's usually a pretty good indication,' advised Anastasia.

'Maybe . . . maybe. I'm not sure . . . Mark knows. I know he knows! I saw his face. He's been really suspicious around me for ages. I thought it was just because he didn't like you, but it's because of this!'

'What's he doing at your table anyway?' asked Anastasia. 'I thought you hated him.'

'I do,' said Meredith, 'but Catherine gave him her sister's ticket.'

'Stupid bitch,' hissed Imogen.

'You know what's so strange to me? Mark Kingston is so incredibly B-list,' said Anastasia, who could be counted upon to politely share the prejudices of anyone she was currently talking to. 'But half the school seems to think he's like a really good-looking saint.'

'Which makes them blasphemous, as well as blind!' Meredith

snapped. 'Anyway, enough about him. I better go back and check if Michael's parents have left the table yet. I'll come and get you when they have.'

'Thanks, babes,' smiled Imogen, leaning against the basin as Meredith swept out of the bathroom.

'You know,' said Anastasia as she lightly touched up her mascara, 'Catherine's little mistake isn't going to do Meredith any favours.'

'I know. It's completely ruining her evening.'

'No, not like that. I mean with the rumours.'

Like a hound that had scented blood, Imogen turned to focus fully on what Anastasia was saying. 'Pardon?'

'You know: about her and Mark Kingston.'

'That she hates him?'

'No, silly. *Quite* the opposite. Olivia-Grace and Sarah-Jane told Lavinia that they heard some of the girls in your year saying that everyone thinks the reason Meredith and Mark carry on the way they do is because they secretly have a thing for each other.'

'I hope you told them not to be so fucking stupid?'

'I couldn't do that,' said Anastasia, as she sprayed her wrists with perfume, 'Olivia-Grace has amazing hair.'

Imogen nodded thoughtfully. It was impossible to be rude to someone who'd had a haircut as spectacular as Olivia-Grace's most recent one. 'They said everyone thinks she fancies him?'

Anastasia nodded. 'That's what they told Lavinia, who told me and asked me not to tell anyone. So if you do tell people, don't tell anyone I told you.'

'OK . . .'

'I didn't say I agreed with them.' Anastasia shrugged. 'But

it is a bit weird that she seems to care so much about him being around her, you know? And people are going to wonder why he was at her table tonight if she really hates him as much as she says she does. Oh, well. What did you think of the cantaloupe ice cubes?'

One of the traditions of the Our Lady of Lourdes Ball was that one of the Mount Olivet girls would have a post-ball house party and that year the duty had fallen to Anastasia Montmorency, who had a huge country house out at Helen's Bay.

As the drinking began in earnest, Meredith, Imogen and Kerry went upstairs to Anastasia's room to get changed out of their ball gowns into something a bit more comfortable that wouldn't cost thousands of pounds if it was spilled on – Ralph Lauren, Karen Millen and French Connection, respectively. Standing alone on the stairs before she went up with the other girls, Meredith was checking her BlackBerry when Stewart walked over to speak to her, his bowtie and his top buttons undone. 'Hi, Meredith.'

'Hello, Stewart.'

'We didn't really get a chance to talk at the ball,' he said, leaning against the bottom of the banister.

'No. You look very nice in your suit, by the way.'

'Thanks,' he smiled. 'You look lovely too, Meredith.'

'Thank you.'

'Listen,' said Stewart, clearing his throat slightly, 'I couldn't help notice the tension between you and Mark at dinner.'

Meredith regarded him coldly, but her tone remained polite. 'That's hardly unusual, is it? Mark and I don't particularly get on.'

'No, I know that, but it's just that tonight was an important night for Imogen and I thought maybe the two of you would have been mature enough to bury the hatchet for her sake.'

In a sign that her close friends would have realized as a warning, Meredith arched one eyebrow at what Stewart had just said. 'Pardon?'

'Well, it's a bit childish, the way you and Mark carry on, don't you think? He's a cracking lad and you're a great girl . . .'

'I see. Well, Stewart, if I seemed cold with Mark, the answer to the problem is not to tell me that I'm immature, but to make sure that Mark doesn't turn up to any more events where he doesn't belong.'

'He doesn't *belong*?'

'Clearly someone like Mark doesn't belong at the Our Lady ball, Stewart. Be realistic.'

'I'm pretty much the same type of person as Mark, Meredith. Do you think I didn't belong there tonight?'

Meredith paused momentarily before answering. 'You're Imogen's boyfriend.'

'And Mark is Cameron's friend.'

A mocking smile played on Meredith's lips as she replied, 'As fabulous as Cameron is, I don't think the criteria for admission to an A-list event like tonight's is being one of the people he mistakenly made friends with in prep school. And, even if it was, Cameron wasn't the one who invited him, was he? And doesn't that tell you something? Even though he won't admit it, Cameron is more than aware of Mark's . . . limitations. That's why he wasn't the one who brought him tonight; you did.'

'And Catherine,' reasoned Stewart. 'She gave him the ticket. She clearly likes him.'

'Well, I would hardly use Catherine's judgement as your defence in any argument, Stewart.'

Stewart shook his head in bewildered disbelief. 'Wow. Harsh.'

'Sorry. That's just how it is.'

Stewart ran his tongue along the inside of his mouth, just below his bottom lip and nodded his head slowly but decisively. 'Well, as you said, I am Imogen's boyfriend and for that reason, although apparently no other, I'm welcome in your little circle for the time being. So I should make it clear that as much as I like you, Meredith, and respect you, and I really do, Mark Kingston is one of my best mates and he is an excellent, excellent guy. So, as long as I'm part of this group, he's going to be as well. Hope you enjoy the rest of the party.'

Stewart walked off into the crowd of party-goers, with Meredith's eyes following him as he went. She smiled a cold, determined smile and then turned, lifted the hem of her dress and walked up the stairs to Anastasia's rooms, where Imogen and Kerry had been joined by Anastasia and three of her posse – Lavinia, Mariella and Natasha. Gossip immediately turned to Imogen's close shave with Michael's parents, once Anastasia and her group were up to speed. Of course with a bottle of champagne in her and the shared sisterhood of getting changed together, it seemed a wonderful idea to Imogen for her to tell them every last detail of her romantic shenanigans.

'Oh my God!' said Lavinia, with a long sigh on the end of the word which basically got rid of the *d*. 'That's *so* horrible and stuff.'

'I know!' exclaimed Imogen, hurling herself on to the bed. 'What's going to happen to me?'

'Well, maybe you should, like, you know, like, pick one and stuff,' suggested Mariella. 'Who's cuter?'

'Michael,' answered Meredith, as Natasha helped her out of her dress.

'I don't know!' wailed Imogen. 'Can we get Facebook up and I'll show you their pics?'

It took twenty minutes of Facebook stalking before the group had cast their votes: Meredith, Anastasia and Lavinia for Michael, Mariella and Natasha for Stewart, with Kerry unhelpfully voting for both. By then, the music from downstairs had got much louder, so the sensible thing to do was to go and see what was going on. If truth be told, all seven of the girls were distinctly irked at the idea that there *could* be a party without them.

As they entered the living room, it was clear just how much alcohol had been consumed in their absence. The twenty-five guests were dancing, laughing and there was a game of Never Have I Ever going on in the corner, which had already descended into the sordid, shaming version that usually occurs about four questions in. Meredith's attention was temporarily distracted by the sight of the regal Francesco standing next to the sound system with Anastasia's brother, Sasha. However, within two seconds her eyes had already taken in the most shocking sight of the evening – there, on the couch, was Catherine, still in her Marchesa ball gown, making out with Mark Kingston.

'Oh no . . .' whispered Kerry.

Anastasia and her clique hastily made for the other side of the room, passing Cameron as he walked over to join Meredith, Kerry and Imogen.

'What is she doing?' asked Kerry.

'It's called "making out", Kerry,' said Imogen. 'I know it's been a while since you've done it . . .'

'Shut up!'

'Ick, Catherine's technique is *awful*,' tutted Imogen. 'This is *the* most cringe thing I've ever seen and I'm including last year's teachers' Christmas pantomime when I say that.'

Just then, Kerry saw a sight that made her squeal in disgust. 'Tongue on face! Tongue on face! Tongue on face!'

Meredith had turned her back on the pashing and was pouring herself a drink, torn between her desire to pluck out Catherine's tongue and her refusal to make a scene at a party. For a moment she felt a sudden surge of fury at the thought that Catherine and Mark might actually start dating after this, and the idea displeased her immensely. It wasn't just the fact that Meredith's daily exposure to him would be doubled, as he would now be both Cameron's best friend and Catherine's boyfriend, but also because it would be disgustingly inappropriate for someone as bouncing, dim-witted and shallow as Catherine to become the other half of someone as serious and frustratingly self-righteous as Mark Kingston.

They would look ridiculous together and the idea of seeing them draped over each other, performing the same kind of lip-locking acrobatics on a daily basis, made her feel physically sick. Meredith quickly suppressed her feelings of nausea, rage and panic and thought rationally: firstly, it was silly to start caring too much what B-listers like Mark Kingston did with their spare time and, secondly, even if she did care, which she didn't, her social instincts told her that relationships do not start with drunken kisses. In fact, if anything, they make the likelihood of future dating almost non-existent. She had nothing to worry about. She took a sip of her drink, steadied her nerves and turned back to look at the kissing with haughty disapproval.

'This must be why she gave him the ticket!' exclaimed Kerry, interrupting Meredith's thoughts. 'She's a secret planner!'

'Let's hit her!'

'Easy, Imogen,' soothed Cameron. 'Why don't we just . . . Mother of God, when are they going to come up for air?'

Catherine and Mark were now involved in a kiss so energetic it was more like a game of Olympic tongue-wrestling than anything else and the sight was so disturbingly awful that none of them could look away, like with a car accident or really bad highlights. They were so mesmerized, in fact, that they didn't even notice when Stewart, who Imogen had been doing her best to avoid since the ball, came up to stand directly behind them.

'Hey, babe.' He placed his arm round Imogen's waist and pulled her gently in towards him.

Meredith, who had been tilting her head in morbid fascination at Catherine's antics, rolled her eyes at the sound of his voice.

'Can I talk to you for a minute?'

'Sure, honey . . .' Imogen replied carefully. 'But Kerry just asked me to have a chat with her. It's kind of urgent, but I'll come get you when we're done!'

'No. It's OK, Imogen,' said Kerry, who was still smarting from the 'making out' jibe earlier. 'It's all sorted now. You can go with Stewart.'

'But . . .'

'No, seriously, it's fine,' she smiled. 'You can go!'

'OK . . .' said Imogen, shooting a poisoned glance at Kerry. 'Well . . . Super . . .'

'Let's go outside,' Stewart suggested, as he steered her towards the patio. 'It's too noisy in here.'

'Great.'

It was freezing outside, so Stewart gave Imogen his tuxedo jacket and stood shivering in the cold. There was an awkward silence for about a minute, before Stewart finally spoke. 'I don't know why I'm so nervous.'

'Are you?'

'Yeah . . . really. I wasn't even this nervous when I first asked you out.'

'Well, don't be. It's only me,' she said with a light laugh.

'Is it, though?'

'What do you mean?'

'Something's not right, Imogen,' he said, rubbing his arms to keep warm. 'With us, with you. You've been so distant over the last few weeks and I thought it might just be organizing the ball, but tonight when those people came over to our table, you introduced me as your friend and then they said you'd been spending so much time with their son, I thought . . . well, I thought for a minute you were seeing someone else.'

'Oh.'

'But then Cameron and Kerry said he's just some gay guy you've been taking dance lessons with, but, I don't know. Something's . . . something's still not right.'

'Stewart . . .'

'I mean, look at us, Imogen – look! I can't even put my arms round you right now.'

'Well, why don't you?' she asked softly.

'Because I'm afraid you don't want me to.'

'Stewart . . .'

'Something's changed, Imogen. Something's not right.' He paused, as if the next sentence was stuck in his throat. 'Do you want to break up with me?'

Imogen answered quickly. 'No.'

'Is there someone else?'

'No.'

'Really?'

'Really,' she said, swallowing away her guilt. 'Stewart, there's no one else but you.'

5

MISTLETOE AND WINE

Sitting inside Deane's the following morning, as the late November rain poured down over Belfast, Meredith, Cameron, Imogen and Kerry were ordering brunch and reflecting on the events of the previous evening.

'Did you see Natasha by the end of the party?' asked Kerry. 'She was *so* rabidashed.'

'I know.' Cameron nodded, sipping a Diet Coke. 'But then that number of tequila slammers would rabidash anyone.'

'Those members of the group who unexpectedly ended up kissing Peter Sullivan,' Imogen began, pointedly looking at Kerry whom she still hadn't quite forgiven for leaving her at the mercy of Stewart's freakishly accurate suspicions, 'are in no position to throw stones.'

'Shut up, Imogen. I only kissed him for like six seconds and/ or minutes,' snapped Kerry.

'Oh good,' Meredith said sarcastically, 'because what we really need right now is for another one of us to be romantically involved with one of those boys.'

'Don't bitch at me just because you're annoyed at Catherine the Happy Hooker,' huffed Kerry. 'Peter has always been really nice to us and we didn't turn our kiss into a circus show, like Catherine and Mark.'

'Dirty bitch,' muttered Cameron.

'What are the odds she becomes obsessed with him?' asked Kerry.

'High,' declared Imogen. 'Catherine has always been that way. I'll bet you a new pair of shoes she's in her dance class right now imagining what Mrs Catherine O'Rourke-Kingston sounds like.'

'She wouldn't hyphenate,' said Meredith icily. 'Too many letters for her to remember.'

'Is she coming here after?' asked Cameron.

'Yes, she is,' replied Meredith, 'because *someone* couldn't not reply to her text messages.'

'Sorry,' whined Kerry, filling her eyes with tears just in case she was yelled at. 'It's not my fault that I'm nicer than the rest of you.'

'Once again, you're confusing "nice" with "weak",' said Meredith.

'I like Catherine,' Kerry said stoutly, brilliantly ignoring that only a minute earlier she had referred to her as 'Catherine the Happy Hooker'.

'You know the series-five discs of *Sex and the City* that you lent to her over summer?' smirked a triumphant Meredith. 'She says she just keeps "forgetting" to return them to you, but she actually lost them and just hasn't told you yet.'

Kerry gasped. '*What?* She's ruined my box set!'

'Well, don't look now,' whispered Cameron, who could see Catherine entering the restaurant, 'but she's about to ruin your brunch as well.'

As she took her seat between Imogen and Kerry, Catherine

was still too elated from her kiss with Mark the night before to notice the chill emanating from her four companions. 'Oh my God! Dance class was *so* good today. Like, I mean, *so* good and stuff. I'm so hungry . . . what'll I have?'

'I know what we'll have,' said Imogen. 'An explanation.'

'About what?'

'Third World debt.'

'Oh my God! You mean, last night?' she giggled. 'I know! I'm *so* embarrassed. But Mark was, like, all over me and stuff.'

'Yeah,' muttered Cameron sarcastically. 'It really looked like you were trying to fend him off.'

'He's *such* a good kisser, though. Like, *so* good. And he's really, like, into me. He texted me this morning and . . .'

'How did he get your number?' asked Meredith.

'He, like, *made* me give it to him last night and stuff. And, anyway, when he texted me today, he was, like – *Just wanted to check you got home OK? Last night was really fun. See you in school, Mark x.* X! X! Cameron, does Mark usually give an X?'

'Not really, but then I don't usually count.'

'Nobody does,' snapped Meredith, looking at Catherine as if she was deranged. 'Xs mean pretty much nothing, especially to boys.'

'But from him it probably meant something,' persisted Catherine, determined not to let go of her plans to one day marry Mark Kingston.

'All it means is that you're a twelve-year-old for noticing things like that, you crazy, crazy stalker!' said Meredith.

'He's *so* into me, Meredith, I'm so sure!' beamed Catherine, the barbed insults bouncing off her new Mark-obsessed bubble. 'I'm, like, in love.'

'You know, Catherine,' sighed Meredith as she picked up her menu, 'sometimes conversations with you are like a really brutal form of self-harm.'

When the doorbell went that evening, Cameron was expecting it to be one of the neighbours or a friend of his sister, Charlotte. He was not expecting to see a stressed-looking Mark standing on his doorstep.

'Where are you going?' asked Mark, taking in Cameron's immaculate appearance and new sweater.

'Out,' Cameron answered. 'Soon. Sorry.'

'Well, it can wait,' muttered Mark, walking past him. 'I need your help.'

'Is this about Catherine?' asked Cameron, glancing surreptitiously at his watch.

'She keeps texting me,' Mark groaned. 'She won't leave me alone. She thinks we're going to be a couple or something, but it was just a drunken kiss! Cameron, what am I going to do? You have to help me.'

'Mark, I don't know what I can do; Catherine's boyfriend-obsessed – I mean, you literally couldn't have picked a worse person to make out with. She was counting the number of Xs you put at the end of your text message to her today at brunch.'

'But that doesn't mean anything!'

'I know that, but she doesn't. And until you have a proper talk with her, she's not going to stop.'

'No, no. No way,' said Mark, shaking his head emphatically. 'I don't do the whole *let's talk* thing. No. No.'

'Well, then, just be prepared for the fact that by the end of the week, she'll have picked out your wedding china.'

'Are you serious?!'

'Yes! Of course, I'm serious. She's insane,' said Cameron. 'I mean, for her, this is practically playing it cool. Look, Mark, I *really* have to go. I'm already late, but I promise I'll come over and see you after dinner, OK?'

'Yeah, that's cool,' agreed Mark. 'Thanks. Where are you going, anyway?'

'Ehm . . .'

'Meredith's?'

Cameron nodded his head quickly.

'Whatever. Just call me when you get in,' said Mark, opening the front door again. 'And don't tell anyone else about this Catherine thing, will you?'

'I won't. I promise.'

'OK. Have fun with Meredith, then. Make sure you take a bucket of live mice to feed her.'

'You're so funny,' muttered Cameron, nudging him through the door. 'Get out.'

Cameron weaved his way through the crowds at the Victoria Square shopping centre, shuddering as he swept haughtily past four emos, loitering disaffectedly on the second floor. He pulled his grey cashmere sweater down for the hundredth time, before re-arranging it slightly to make sure it was sitting with just the right air of nonchalance over his Hermès Etrivière belt. A similarly fraught process had gone into ensuring his hair had seemed tousled without appearing either too messy or too contrived.

As he scooted absent-mindedly around a middle-aged couple, who were moving with frustrating slowness, and stepped on to the second set of escalators, Cameron trailed his fingers over the points on his wrist where he had earlier dabbed his Tom Ford cologne, and hoped he hadn't put on too much. Stepping off the escalator with his BlackBerry clutched religiously in his right hand, he moved over to the Gourmet Burger Kitchen where Blake Hartman, in jeans, trainers, T-shirt and a navy-blue zip-up, stood waiting for him. He beamed a wide, friendly smile as he saw Cameron approaching and wrapped him in a hug, which rather took Cameron by surprise, especially when he realized that he had temporarily forgotten to breathe during it.

'Hey. You came!'

Cameron smiled. 'Well, I wasn't going to stand you up. I'm a man of my word.'

'That you are. Are burgers OK?' asked Blake. 'I didn't know what kind of food you were into, but who doesn't like burgers, y'know?'

'Right,' agreed Cameron, as the name 'Meredith' blared in his head.

Blake stood back and held open the door to the restaurant with slightly theatrical politeness to allow Cameron to walk through before him. The waitress seated them at a table for four, along a side wall, and took their orders for drinks – a Diet Coke for Cameron and a regular Coke for Blake.

'What?'

'What?'

'You looked really surprised for some reason,' said Blake, as he unzipped his jacket and hung it over the empty seat next to him.

'Oh, it's nothing.'

'No, go on, tell me.'

'It's just that I'm not used to people ordering fat Coke,' said

Cameron, remembering how Kerry had once taken to her bed, face down in the starfish position, for three hours after imbibing a full cup of it when she mistakenly ordered it as her mixer on a night out. 'You're very brave, Blake Hartman.'

Blake laughed. 'I'll take my chances – to be fair, I think luck's already on my side.'

'Luck?' asked Cameron, leaning back in his seat and mentally preparing for the sparring banter that he sensed instinctively was coming his way.

'Having dinner with the one of the most popular people in school,' Blake teased. 'How many people would kill to be in this position?'

'One hundred and thirty-seven,' answered Cameron quickly. 'Or thereabouts.'

'This school is insane, Cameron. You do know that, don't you? The way people are split up into cliques here is unreal. I've never seen anything like it.'

'You didn't have this in America?'

'Not in my school, no, but then we don't start high school until we're fourteen. Before that it's middle school, from like ten to thirteen, and a lot of the kids who're really popular or plastic or whatever in middle school tend not to be once everyone transfers to high school. But here it's obviously different, because you guys have had five years to build your empire.'

'OK, well, actually a lot of people did get kicked out of the group around third year *and* not everyone who's in my group now has been there from the beginning,' said Cameron huffily.

Before Cameron could launch into an impassioned defence of the Divine Right of Queen Bees, the waitress came and took their order, along with another Diet Coke for Cameron, who had learned to drink it and drink quickly, else lose it to Imogen and her frantic desire to suppress her appetite with enormous amounts of caffeine.

Blake too leant back on his chair, biting his bottom lip and regarding Cameron with amused curiosity. 'So, people got kicked out of the popular group?'

'Yes.'

'Out of the Garden of Eden?'

'Yes,' smiled Cameron. 'And you should think of Imogen as the angel with the fiery sword stopping them getting back in.'

'Did you help kick them out?'

Cameron looked up quickly and stared at Blake, checking for any sign of judgement or condemnation, such as he was now used to receiving from a perpetually disapproving Mark. Finding none, he shook his head. 'No. No. I wasn't in our group until I was fourteen.'

Blake looked up from taking a drink through his straw in evident surprise. 'You weren't?'

'No.'

'That's very surprising, Cameron.'

Cameron nodded his head slowly and then looked around the restaurant for a moment, hoping that Blake would change the topic of conversation. The years before he was allowed to sit at Meredith's table were ones Cameron didn't like to think about, any more than Mark liked to think about the years that came after it.

'This is the part where you tell me what happened,' teased Blake. 'That's how conversation generally works. One person shows an interest in the other person's life and the other person volunteers the information. See? Now, tell me how you clawed your way into Meredith Harper's magical bubble.'

'I didn't claw my way in,' Cameron snapped. 'I was invited.'

Blake leant across the table and said firmly: 'Cameron, I'm not getting at you or making fun of you. I'm genuinely interested, OK?'

Cameron sighed, recognizing defeat. 'I was quite fat, from the age of about eleven to thirteen,' he began.

'Yeah, but that was just puppy fat, obviously.'

'It was disgusting,' Cameron retorted quickly, before continuing with his story. 'I had been really good friends with Mark Kingston – you know who he is, right? – since prep school, but he wasn't in my house once we started at Mount Olivet. He's in Antrim; I'm in Stormont. And for the first three years, you kind of have all of your classes with your house – apart from Science.'

'OK.'

'And because I was quite shy and overweight, people didn't really talk to me in my house class. Like, I had too much of a Malone accent for people who weren't from there to like me and I was too ugly for people who were from Malone to want to be friends with me. So, I ate my lunch with Mark and his friends – Stewart and Peter and some of the other boys – but I didn't really have any friends in class.'

Blake looked at him sympathetically, which both touched and irritated Cameron in equal measure. 'Then what happened?'

'I got thin,' Cameron said simply. 'Over the summer between second and third year, I stopped eating and had a growth spurt and on the first day back Meredith came over to my table and told me that I could eat lunch with them that day. So, I did and from then on I got to sit with them in class too. I was thin and

I came from the same part of Belfast as them, so there was no reason not to speak to me any more. And that's how it happened.'

'Wow. And you're happier now?'

Cameron answered without even a second's hesitation. 'Yes. I hated my life before I was friends with them. I was miserable and I never want to be that way again. Ever. The only downside is that sometimes I'd still really, really like a white-chocolate-chip muffin at break-time and Meredith won't let me have one. I've never told anyone this before, by the way, either the misery or the muffin-longing.'

'It'll be our secret,' Blake whispered, with a half-smile. 'What did the guys make of your new lunch buddies?'

'Peter and Stewart don't really care. Mark hates it and he hates Meredith. Like, I mean, it's actually quite weird how much he talks about her and how much he complains about every little thing she does. He really *hates* her, Blake. Sometimes it feels like he hates me a little too because I'm friends with her. But, what can you do?'

Their food arrived and as Blake doused his burger in ketchup he asked: 'So by the time you had arrived Meredith and Imogen Dawson had kicked out all the others?'

'Oh no,' replied Cameron. 'Imogen only joined the group about a year before I did. I mean, she helped with kicking out one of the girls and that was pretty savage – you *don't* want to get on the wrong side of Imogen – but the original two are Meredith and Kerry.'

'Are you serious?'

'Yes. They made friends on the first day of school and it was those two who picked who got in, who stayed in and who got kicked out.'

'And was it always obvious Meredith was in charge?'

'To everyone except Kerry,' Cameron said wryly. 'Every now and then she can get a little bitchy about it and likes to remind people that she's been in the group just as long as Meredith has. But don't tell anyone I said that.'

'OK, I won't. So, who were the others?'

'In the group? Originally, they were all girls in our house – Lisa Flaherty, Carolyn Jeffreys, Aisleagh McGorian, Melanie Stevens and, obviously, Catherine O'Rourke. And, somehow, Catherine's the only one left.'

'And how did that happen?'

'I don't really know how. I think it's either because she's too stupid to realize how much we bully her or because she would actually kill herself if she didn't get to sit with us. But, I mean, it's not like we have to spend massive amounts of time with Catherine outside of school. So it's bearable. See, in the middle of second year, Meredith made friends with Imogen and Imogen kind of took Catherine's place as, like, a major part of the group.'

'How'd they meet?'

'The only class we had that wasn't with our house was Science and one day Catherine fell off her seat, just as Imogen was walking past, and so Imogen kicked her and Meredith thought this was like the single funniest thing she'd *ever* seen, so they started hanging out together. Imogen had been in our school since Day One, but because she had just moved from England and there were no, like, fun people in her house, a lot of people didn't really speak to her until she became friends with Meredith.'

'A bit like you, then?' asked Blake.

Cameron, who was coating his chips in vinegar, luckily didn't take offence. 'Kind of. Except that it never really bothered Imogen. She doesn't need people to like her. She knows she's better than everyone.'

Cameron looked up and shrugged, waiting for Blake to say something. Blake nodded and set his burger down on its plate, weighing up what to say next. 'OK, two things. The first is that you could never, ever be ugly and the second is that you should take a leaf out of Imogen's book.'

'Kick people when they're on the floor?'

'No! Stop feeling like you would be nothing if you weren't friends with who you're friends with. Honestly, you don't need to think like this. I'm just really glad that *we're* friends.'

Cameron swallowed a little harder than he had intended and nodded awkwardly. 'OK.'

'OK?' laughed Blake. 'Is that it?'

'I don't know what to say,' said Cameron, wriggling slightly in his seat, but smiling.

'Learn to take a compliment!' smiled Blake, patting him lightly on the hand.

'I can! It's just that usually I'm expected to give one back.'

'OK. Well, go for it.'

'What?'

'Give me a compliment, Cameron. If it'll make you feel better.'

'You're such a douche, Blake!' said Cameron as he rubbed his face, trying to think of something to say. Ordinarily, he would have made a funny, unemotional riposte, but Blake was one of the few people who made him feel like that was both unnecessary and, temporarily, inappropriate. 'OK . . . em . . . I'm really glad we're friends too.'

Blake flashed that perfect Colgate smile of his. 'See? That

wasn't so hard, was it? Now, will you eat more, please? I'm starting to feel like the fat girl at the popular table.'

Meredith was sitting in front of the fireplace in her bedroom, curled up on the sofa with an old copy of *La Reine Margot* open in front of her. She wore a long Brunello Cucinelli grey cardigan, a plain white top underneath and a pair of Chloé jeans. Her BlackBerry sat on the sofa next to her tucked-in feet and a cup of hot chocolate sat on the coffee table in front of her. Outside, the early evening's drizzle had turned into a nighttime downpour, making Meredith slightly glad that there had been no plans for socializing that evening.

Just as she was returning to her book, there was a knock on her bedroom door and Pauline, the family's middle-aged housekeeper, popped her head round the door. 'Imogen's here to see you, Meredith.'

'Oh, yay,' smiled Meredith, closing her book and standing to hug a slightly bedraggled-looking Imogen.

'Can you believe this fucking weather?'

'I know.' Meredith nodded. 'It's hideous.'

'Imogen, can I fetch you a cup of hot chocolate to warm yourself up?' asked Pauline.

'Oh, yes, please, Pauline, thank you!'

Pauline smiled. 'Meredith, do you need a top-up?'

'I'm fine at the moment. Thanks, Pauline.' Meredith smiled as the housekeeper left. 'She makes the best hot chocolate.'

'I know. Super-scrummy,' said Imogen, hurling herself down into the sofa. 'I just had the most exhausting cinema date with Stewart. I nearly called him "Michael", at one point. And then right before the movie I swear I thought I saw some of Michael's friends from Immaculate Heart across the lobby, so I had to hurry Stewart into the theatre without buying anything. I hate going to the movies without popcorn. It's literally pointless.'

'Poor you.'

'I know!' exclaimed Imogen, arching her head melodramatically backwards on to the arm of the sofa. 'Oh, and you'll never guess who we ran into afterwards?'

'Who?'

Pauline re-entered with the hot chocolate and a plate of biscuits, eliciting thanks from the two girls, before exiting downstairs to the kitchen once more. Imogen took a sip of her drink and purred appreciatively. 'Mark Kingston's mother. She stopped to talk to Stewart for, like, fifteen minutes.'

'Excessive, much?'

'I know. Clearly, she needed to keep me standing there in the chill for fifteen minutes on a Saturday night while she talked about how amazingly boring her life is. No wonder she's divorced. She's really piled on the pounds since the last time I saw her. Heifer!'

'Well, if you'd produced Mark Kingston, wouldn't you start comfort-eating?'

Imogen sighed. 'If I tell you something, will you promise that when you get mad, you'll punish anybody but me?'

'OK.'

'Somebody told me that some of the girls in our year and the two years above us think you have a crush on him.'

'On Mark?' snapped Meredith. 'Who?'

'I was sworn to secrecy but it was Anastasia. Lavinia told her and she apparently heard it from Olivia-Grace Wallace and Sarah-Jane Rogan. But, seriously, I can't tell you anything else.'

'I hope you told them they were retarded?'

'Well, you do hate him an awful lot and there's a definite atmosphere any time he's around you, so . . .'

Meredith regarded Imogen coldly. 'Do you agree with them?'

'I don't know,' she admitted nonchalantly. 'Sometimes we do fancy the ones who annoy us the most.'

'Have you forgotten what happened?'

'No . . . but technically it wasn't him who did it, was it?'

'No. That doesn't make it any better, though, and I don't see why I'm not allowed to take a tiny amount of pleasure in hating him without some idiot with amazing hair starting the rumour that I fancy him!'

'Oh, sweetie, don't be silly,' cooed Imogen. 'I didn't mean that *at all*. By all means, take pleasure in hating him. All I was saying was that if you *do* hate-love him then that's totally cool as well. I won't judge you for it. And, to be fair, Olivia-Grace didn't start the rumour – she just heard it from somebody else.'

'I don't think you get it,' said Meredith. 'It's not that I can't tell the difference between hating someone and being in love with them – I don't like him as a person, Imogen! He's so prudish and dull and so irritatingly self-consciously *nice*. And he's one of those people I really hate – the ones who judge anyone like us, but then refuse to admit that they're judgemental. At least we know we're judgemental!'

'Well, I've never really noticed any of that about him,' said Imogen, stretching out lackadaisically. 'I just find him quite boring. But that's not his fault, I suppose. It's God's.'

'Oh, of course he's boring!' laughed Meredith mirthlessly. 'Maybe "moody" is a better word. It's as if he's trying to cultivate "Mr Darcy chic", but doesn't have the money or class to pull it off. I can't believe people think I fancy him. As if people like me end up with people like Mark!'

'I'm not saying that you *do* fancy him,' reasoned Imogen. 'It's just that I can see why people would think that.'

'I hate him, Imogen,' Meredith repeated.

'Well, then, carry on, sweetie,' shrugged Imogen.

Meredith nodded and tossed her hair behind her, thinking that it would all be a lot easier once Imogen got on with it and ditched Stewart. 'So,' she smiled, 'tell me about the date with Stewart. Give me all the details.'

Non-uniform days at Mount Olivet were just as stressful as Paris Fashion Week and slightly more divisive than the Berlin Wall. The students got a non-uniform day at the end of each term and on Saint Patrick's Day. Every time it rolled around, Meredith predictably looked amazing, in some flawlessly elegant day-wear number, Chanel or Ralph Lauren being her favourites, with the obligatory pair of Louboutins or Manolos and an accompanying large handbag. It was Meredith's firm policy to always choose beauty over edginess and because of this she always looked effortlessly glamorous. In contrast, Imogen usually turned up in something cutting-edge chic, complimented by her beloved oversized jewellery, Kerry embraced pretty, pink, preppy and princess and Catherine, who worshipped Karen Millen and Jack Wills, went for a cute top and skirt combo. For his part, Cameron was generally a monument to Euro-American metro-chic, always basing the outfit around a perfect pair of jeans. This winter, he was also heavily into scarves and he had spent a very pleasant Wednesday afternoon buying six of them with Meredith.

But non-uniform day was a source of both amusement and alarm to the group as they observed the inexplicably hideous fashion mistakes of their peers. Meredith had been nothing short of disgusted to see that some of the girls in the year below were wearing 'fuggs' (fake Uggs), with ripped jeans/tights and no make-up, in some sort of mistaken ultra-boho gesture, while Kerry screamed in fright at finding herself standing next to a girl with black lipstick in the girls' bathroom and a knee-length top with the words 'I hate myself and want to die' on it. When a small army of surly boys in skinny jeans had swarmed into Chemistry class, Imogen was heard to coo in a voice dripping with cruel sarcasm: 'Oh, look at them: they're wearing skinny jeans. They must be really in touch with their feelings. I bet they're in a really cool band after school.'

Along with the fashion freak show, that Friday also proved how Cameron's prediction about Catherine had come satisfyingly true. On Tuesday, she changed her Facebook relationship status to 'It's complicated'. On Wednesday, she ran into the girls' bathroom in floods of tears because she saw Mark flirting with one of the girls in his Business Studies class and by the end of the week genuine obsession levels had been reached.

'What's Mark's favourite movie?' she asked during form class, as Mrs Vaughn pottered ineffectually around the room.

'*Gladiator*,' answered Cameron.

'Oh, beau! What's it about?'

Cameron gave her a withering stare. 'A gladiator.'

'Right . . . And what's Mark's favourite food?'

'Mexican.'

'Like chapalinos and stuff?'

'Jalapeños, retard,' said Meredith, from behind her magazine.

'OK, class, well, em, now is, em, time to go to assembly,' mumbled their form teacher. 'And have a happy Christmas! See you next year.'

'God, I hope that "next year" comment wasn't supposed to be amusing,' sighed Meredith as she swept towards the door.

'I thought it was quite cute and funny,' said a defiant Coral Andrews, with a studded dog collar, mauve flowing shirt that came down to her knees and enormous baggy jeans.

'Well, judging by your outfit you have far more of a sense of humour than I do. I especially like the dog collar. Hilariously appropriate.'

'Are *you* trying to call *me* a bitch?'

'No, Coral,' said Meredith with a smile, as someone opened the door for her. 'I'm trying to call you a mutt. Keep up.'

Cameron was walking alone from the boys' cloakroom to the cafeteria after depositing his Latin books in his locker when Blake walked past with some of his housemates. He smiled and waved as he passed, which Cameron briefly returned, knowing that other Mount Oliveteans would be shocked to see him bestow acceptance on anyone else other than the girls.

'Hey, Cameron!'

Cameron looked back at the sound of Blake's voice, to see that he'd spun round a couple of metres away. Blake reached into his schoolbag with a mischievous grin and tossed something to Cameron, who caught it in both hands. The American winked at him and turned to catch up with his friends.

Looking down into his hands, Cameron started to laugh at the white-chocolate-chip muffin he saw there. He put it into his schoolbag and felt himself starting to grin, just at the point Kerry appeared at his side from the girls' cloakroom.

'What did that Australian boy throw at you?' she snapped. 'Was it a hate crime?'

'What? No! It was just something I lent him in English class – and he's American.'

'Fine. Listen, when we get into the cafeteria, back me up about where we go tonight. I want to go to Rain. And if I don't . . . well, it'll be Kerry-the-She-Beast time.'

'OK,' said Cameron.

'Do you ever wonder what it would be like to have Tourette's?'

Sitting at their table in the cafeteria, looking disapprovingly at the tacky Christmas decorations and laughing at the indie kids as they walked by, Meredith contemptuously tossed an uneaten festive mince pie into a nearby bin and turned her attention back to which club they would grace with their superior presence.

'It has to be Rain,' said Kerry authoritatively. 'Everyone's going. It's a Thursday.'

'I think Box would be super-fun,' opined Catherine. 'And I heard that's where Mark's going, so it'd be so perfect and stuff.'

Imogen rolled her eyes. 'It would not be perfect, Catherine. Try not to be retarded.'

'Speaking of not being perfect,' asked Cameron, 'how's the hideously dangerous adultery coming along?'

'It's a disaster,' sighed Imogen. 'I just can't seem to stop it and Christmas confession time is getting pretty damn close!'

'What do you mean, you can't stop it?'

Imogen gathered her thoughts. 'Adultery is sort of like a Roberto Cavalli outfit: you never think it's going to suit you until you try it on and then you're surprised at how delightful it is.'

'I hate Roberto Cavalli,' snapped Kerry huffily.

Imogen opened her mouth in shock. 'You have three of his outfits!'

'I know,' smiled Kerry, 'and it really is surprising how delicious they are once they're on.'

'That's the point I just made!'

'Yes, but you'd been leaving me out of the conversation for too long.'

'At least there's no danger of getting caught tonight, Imogen,' said Meredith.

'I know!' Imogen replied. 'Thank God Michael's going to that concert.'

'I have four Roberto Cavalli outfits, *actually*,' said Kerry.

That night, the clubs were packed as all of the Belfast grammar schools finished for the Christmas holidays. In the end, both Rain and Box were packed out by university students and the only place left for them to go was the Beach Club once again, much to Meredith's fury as she had spotted several people in checked shirts and desert boots in the queue, meaning that farmers were likely to be inside. Kerry loyally pretended to be angry as well for about three minutes before delightedly capering to the reception to buy three Hawaiian flower necklaces for herself and squealing with pleasure as they were placed round her neck.

Try as she might, Catherine could not keep from twitching her head around in various directions to see where Mark might be, or if he had even arrived yet. She texted him four times, each time pretending to her friends that she was texting someone else. Finally, just after eleven o'clock, she saw him – kissing Heather Blount, a pretty girl who was in his house at school, who Imogen had despised for a year and a half ever since she had allegedly stolen her haircut.

'Marky!'

At the sound of Catherine's greeting and her slap on his shoulder, Mark stopped kissing Heather and turned round. 'Catherine . . .'

'How could you?'

'Oh my God,' said Heather, pulling away from Mark. 'Are you two . . . Is something going on? Oh my God, I'm so sorry, Catherine – I had no idea.'

'Don't even, Heather,' shouted Catherine, who was so distraught that she had lost her usual compulsion to be nice to everyone. 'First you steal Imogen's hair and then you steal my boyfriend!'

Heather spun round and stormed off into the crowd and Mark quickly pulled Catherine to the outside smoking area. 'Look, Catherine, I'm sorry if I've given you the idea that I want a relationship, but I'm really not your boyfriend and I don't want to be.'

'But we had a magical kiss,' she said, looking miserable and fairly drunk.

'Yeah . . . I'm sorry about that. I just don't see you that way. You're a nice girl, but, yeah, no, sorry. I don't want to go out with you.'

For an agonizing moment, Catherine looked too stunned to move then she finally spoke. 'Right, well, that's actually really good and stuff, because I'm not looking to get into a relationship right now either, actually. I have to concentrate on my dance sport.'

'But you just said . . .'

'That's because I didn't want to upset you! You see, I actually care about people's feelings, Mark!'

And with that she flounced off into the crowd.

Imogen, Meredith, Cameron and Kerry were standing upstairs next to the balcony, cradling their drinks from the bar. Leaning against the balcony rail, staring down disinterestedly on to the dancing masses beneath her, Meredith suddenly did a double-take, smirked slightly and then tapped Cameron, pointing to the scene below.

'I love the end of term,' sighed Meredith contentedly. 'It's always so busy.'

There was Catherine, locking lips with Peter, and a piercing scream echoed in their ears as Kerry, standing next to them, looked down and saw what was going on.

'Now, Kerry,' said Cameron, spinning her round and going into full damage control, 'Catherine is drunk and she's probably trying to get over Mark and you did say you weren't interested in Peter in any way, shape or form!'

'He only kissed me a couple of weeks ago!' she screamed, tears beginning to fall down her cheeks. 'He's supposed to be in love with me! That's what happens. That's what happens to me! People fall in love, people chase, people get obsessed.'

'Let's go down and slap her,' suggested Imogen, beginning to make for the stairs.

'Imogen, enough!' said Meredith. 'Physical violence in public is always a no-no.'

While Imogen was busy arguing for vengeance, Kerry had

suffered an entire nervous breakdown and she was now sobbing blindly on Cameron's shoulder. Totally confused by the conflicting advice her friends were offering her, Kerry began to display bizarrely schizoid social behaviour. She decided to carry on dancing, because that was what little princesses did, but she couldn't quite get over the humiliation of Peter not being in love with her and every two or three minutes she would burst into tears, throwing herself on to Cameron's chest. Deciding that this was not an efficient use of her time, she started dancing and crying simultaneously – burling around in her pink skirt and waving her arms in rhythm to the music, but still stomping her feet and wiping tears away as the night progressed.

By the time Catherine rejoined the group, Kerry had calmed down but not enough to stop her yelling, 'What the hell was that? Do you not remember last Saturday, Catherine?'

Quite unexpectedly, Catherine was suddenly crying as well. 'I'm sorry! I just wanted to make Mark like me again, but it didn't work.'

'Oh, Catherine, that's because he never really liked you in the first place,' said Meredith.

'I know that!' she sobbed. 'And I've just made a complete idiot of myself and everyone's going to think that I'm some sort of massive slut! Oh my God, what was I thinking? I really don't feel well.'

'Do you feel sick?' asked Imogen.

'I need the bathroom,' she responded, dashing to the ladies'.

Cameron was standing in the queue for the cloakroom, knowing that within fifteen minutes Meredith would be insisting they drag a possibly comatose Catherine home to avoid any further group humiliation when he saw Blake talking to an indifferent-looking bouncer.

'Blake, is everything OK?' asked Cameron, walking over to the two men.

'Cameron! Hi! No. My wallet *and* my phone have been stolen out of my jacket.'

'I've told him there's nothing we can do about it, mate,' shrugged the bouncer. 'Sorry.'

'But . . .'

'Blake, there's really nothing they can do about it. They can't shut down the club and search everyone,' said Cameron, steering him away from the bouncer. 'Thank you.'

'What are you thanking him for?' snapped Blake as they walked away. 'He didn't do anything!'

'That's because he couldn't,' reasoned Cameron, holding out his BlackBerry. 'Do you need to call your dad and cancel your cards?'

'Pardon?'

'Do you need to cancel your credit cards?' Cameron repeated.

'I didn't have any credit cards in my wallet!' replied Blake incredulously.

'Oh.'

'My dad doesn't even know I'm out here tonight,' Blake groaned, running his hands through his hair. 'I'm supposed to be staying at Eóin's house, but I can't find him and I've got no money to call a cab!'

'Well, you can stay at my house,' offered Cameron.

'Really?'

'Of course, it's absolutely no problem,' he smiled. 'My

parents are away for the weekend and with you there it means that Samara won't crawl out of the television and get me.'

'What?'

'Nothing.'

'Do you have Eóin's number on your phone? I feel like I should call him,' Blake asked worriedly.

'Eóin is indie,' said Cameron. 'I definitely do not have his number in my beautiful BlackBerry.'

Blake laughed. 'OK. Thank you for this, Cameron. I really appreciate it.'

'You don't need to thank me. Honestly.'

'Catherine, don't aim for the lid!' roared Imogen. 'Aim for the bowl.'

'I want to die,' sobbed Catherine. 'I'm so embarrassed.'

'For the vomiting or the kissing?' asked Kerry.

'You're not helping,' hissed Meredith, as she pragmatically held Catherine's hair back for her. 'Catherine, don't talk. You'll be fine as long as you don't hit me or choke. Imogen, call a taxi for us. She can stay at my house.' As Imogen went to call the cab, Meredith patted Catherine's back. 'Oh, that's a lot of fake tan,' she said, trying to wipe her hands clean on the toilet paper and hide the revulsion in her voice.

'I'm so sorry,' Catherine said, her make-up running down her face. 'Look at me! I'm disgusting.'

'Mmmmm,' said Meredith, still trying to scrub the fake tan and back sweat off her hand on the toilet roll next to her.

'The taxi's on its way,' said Imogen, appearing in the doorway of the cubicle.

Meredith briskly helped Catherine up from the floor.

'Thanks, Imogen. Catherine, we're going to get Kerry to redo a bit of your make-up for the walk out? The taxi's here.'

'Thank you,' she mumbled. 'I'm really sorry.'

'Kerry, could you fix her, please?' asked Meredith, as she texted Cameron to meet them outside.

'There!' said Kerry, with a triumphant hiccup a few minutes later. 'Your make-up's as good as new!'

'Look at how much make-up Kerry has slapped on her,' whispered Imogen to Meredith. 'She's made Catherine look like a drunken geisha.'

'Shut up,' said Meredith. 'Let's just get her out of here.'

Cameron was waiting at the exit of the arena outside the club with Blake at his side. 'Blake's wallet has been stolen and so has his phone, so I told him he could crash at mine tonight,' he said as the four girls approached.

'That's very clever,' Kerry whispered to Cameron. 'Samara Fear, remember?'

Cameron nodded and the two exchanged dark looks – ever since they had watched *The Ring* together late one evening, their lives had never quite been the same again. The main result being that when either of them was left alone in the house for more than two hours at a time they artfully invented excuses for people to come over, thus preventing the evil sewer-baby Samara crawling from the television set and eating them or whatever it did to people. It had been hard to follow the story over the sound of Kerry screaming to Jesus to save her.

'The taxi's on its way,' sighed Meredith, trying to support Catherine and completely ignoring Blake's arrival.

'Oh my goodness,' said a stunned Blake, looking at Catherine. 'Is she all right?'

'No,' snapped Imogen, lighting a cigarette. 'The only thing Catherine handles worse than men is her drink. And she's –'

Blake edged towards Imogen. 'Imogen, I'd move away from there before they –'

'Give me a minute! I need to light this –' Unfortunately, within that minute the fountains outside the arena were turned on for the midnight show and Imogen was standing directly on the grate. Once her screams had died down, she hobbled to dry land where Blake gave her his coat.

And that is how the most glamorous group at Mount Olivet scuttled away from their end-of-term party – with Kerry's eyes still puffy from her crying, a blanched Catherine being supported between Meredith and Cameron, and Imogen, wearing a boy's coat, soaked from head to toe, missing a shoe and with a sodden, broken, unlit cigarette still dangling from her lips.

'So?' said Blake with a slight laugh. 'How was your night?'

The fifteen-minute taxi ride back to Malone Park was a further orgy of embarrassment, with Catherine having to stop the cab four times to be sick on the roadside. 'She's a recovering bulimic,' explained Kerry, assuming in her drunken mind that this was a masterfully clever lie.

'She's as pissed as a fart,' said the taxi driver.

'That's such an unattractive word,' whispered Meredith.

'Catherine's being sick out the door and *that*'s what you find unattractive?' answered Cameron.

Imogen was still shivering in the corner of the cab, huffing at her humiliation and shooting venomous glances at Catherine, as if the whole thing had somehow been her fault. She all but kicked open the door of the taxi when they arrived at Meredith's house, followed by Catherine stumbling out after her and Kerry who had started singing ABBA songs. Meredith had taken a £50 note from her bag. 'Just keep the change,' she said to the driver, before getting out on to the street. 'Now, listen, Catherine, you can't be sick any more. This is Malone.'

'Do you need any help getting her into bed?' asked Cameron, secretly hoping the answer would be a 'no'.

'No, it's fine,' answered Meredith helpfully. 'You two can go. I'll put her in one of the guest rooms and leave a bucket by her bed, just in case.' In her current mood, Meredith had absolutely no intention of indulging Cameron's penchant for B-listers. Good-looking or not, Blake Hartman was not 'in' and as a result he was definitely not coming into Meredith's house.

'Worst. Night. Ever,' seethed Imogen, who was limping up Meredith's driveway in her one remaining heel.

'Poor Catherine,' said Blake, as he and Cameron started walking away from the girls.

'Yeah, I do feel sorry for her. She's so desperate for a boyfriend, Blake, that it's embarrassingly pathetic. It used to be annoying, but after tonight I think everyone just finds it quite sad.'

'But going from one boy to the next isn't going to make any guy want to go out with her.'

'I know that; you know that; Mark knows that; Peter knows that; Meredith, Imogen and Kerry know that; every agony aunt and chat-show host in the world knows that, but Catherine doesn't or, at least, didn't. Seriously, if a half-decent guy paid her any amount of attention, she'd go out with him in a flash. It's sort of worrying.'

'Wow. Well, at least you helped her tonight. That was nice.'

'To be fair to Meredith, when you're actually in a massive amount of trouble, she is great at taking over. I hope the guest room is OK, by the way. It's been a while since anyone's stayed there, but I'm sure it'll be fine. The housekeeper cleans it all the time.'

'I'm sure it'll be great. Has she ever had to help you out like that?' Blake asked.

'Meredith? No. She's never had to,' said Cameron. 'I think that's why she likes me so much.'

'Well, if you ever need someone to help you, with anything . . . you know I would.'

Cameron nodded, as he fished the keys out of his pocket. 'I know.'

Three days after the drunken antics of the Beach Club night, Imogen's father sat staring down at her with a suspicious gleam in his eyes. 'You're staying with Kerry all week, aren't you?'

'Yes, Daddy.'

'Good, because if you come back here, while your mother and I are away, to throw parties, you're going to be in big trouble, young lady. Especially after last year.'

'Daddy, that wasn't my fault. I told them not to let the petting zoo into the house!'

Imogen's mother burst into the room. 'Edgar, stop limiting her! And hurry up! We've got the three boys out in the car. All right, sweetie darling,' she said as she leant in to kiss her daughter. 'Much love. We'll be back in four days and if anything goes wrong you have the number of the ski lodge, don't you?'

'Yes, Mummy.'

'Good. Come on, Edgar!'

Edgar Dawson continued to regard his daughter suspiciously as he followed his wife and three sons to the car. Clarissa ran back quickly to whisper in her daughter's ear. 'Just make sure everything's left back in its proper place and make sure you throw Cameron an absolutely kick-arse birthday bash, sweetie!'

Edgar meanwhile was calling from the car. 'Imogen, be good!'

'I will, Daddy!'

Ten seconds after their car had disappeared from sight, Imogen hit the '2' button on her mobile. 'Meredith? They're gone. Bring the party plans over ASAP!'

Meredith and Kerry promptly appeared with the guest list, a digital camera and a notepad. They followed Imogen around the house, photographing the exact location of everything and Kerry dutifully took notes as Imogen fired out important details. 'Door to lounge left open at forty-five-degree angle . . . Dining room double doors – one on right, locked, left still open . . .'

Meredith was reading aloud from the guest list. 'The table's booked at AM:PM for half past seven. Everyone's RSVPed as a yes, except for Catherine . . .'

'Why? Where's she?' asked Kerry, for whom the idea of missing a besty's birthday was utter anathema comparable to punching a pensioner in the face or wearing dungarees.

'She's in Prague,' Meredith answered smoothly. 'Orla was going for the week and after Catherine's shameful drunken display at the Beach Club, she asked to go with her. I persuaded her it was the right thing to do. Although it has messed up the seating plan. I was going to sit her down at the other end of the table with Freddie Carrowdale and Victoria Stephenson, but now I'll have to move them up closer to Titus Pitt and

Peter. Can't put them too near Anastasia, because she hates Victoria.'

Imogen was still moving around the house like a detective. '. . . three bottles of Evian, one of fat Coke, a tub of mayonnaise – half full – and new bottle of ketchup in fridge. Nothing else.'

'Cameron will get his gifts there and the dinner should be over by about half ten. The other guests have been told to arrive here at eleven, just to be on the safe side. Stewart's bringing over the alcohol and mixers at three o'clock, which means everything needs to be ready here before he arrives, to give us enough time to get dressed afterwards.'

'. . . all appliances disconnected . . .'

'Cameron's going to arrive at AM:PM at quarter to eight and he's coming with his sister, Charlotte, and two of her besties, who're also on the list, but they're not coming here afterwards.'

'One high chair still at counter . . . two more at approximately fifteen centimetres from countertop. Photo, Kerry, please.'

'And I think that's everything,' concluded Meredith. 'Apart from the cake, which I've sent the driver to collect from the bakery now.'

'What did we go for?' asked Kerry sharply. 'You know Cameron's a picky little he-beast when it comes to cake. It can't be chocolate.'

'I know that, Kerry, I've known him longer than you have. The cake *I* organized has vanilla buttercream icing. Imogen, sweetie, we've done enough preparation. We're not going to make a mistake this time.'

'Everyone makes mistakes – even God – e.g. World War One.'

'You need to calm down,' Meredith advised. 'It's only ten

o'clock now. We have time for a massage. Three hours at the spa will do us all the world of good.'

'You're so right, Meredith,' said Imogen, gathering her coat. 'Party planning is so stressful. I feel like a war veteran or something.'

Cameron's birthday dinner at AM:PM, one of the most fashionable restaurants in Belfast, was delightful and pleasantly drama-free. Twenty of the birthday boy's closest friends, including his beautiful blonde sister, Charlotte, were gathered around the table, laughing, joking and taking photos for the obligatory Facebook album to come later. Blake was scanning through the menu worriedly when Peter leant in and whispered to him, 'Don't worry about it. Cameron's dad has already paid for everything. Seriously, mate, if you order something small the girls will think you're trying to lose weight and ask what your secret is.'

'Really?' said Blake. 'Well, in that case I'll have the steak.'

Later, Blake got a less pleasant surprise at the presents his new friend received. Meredith had bought Cameron a surprise weekend in Dublin at one of her father's hotels, leaving tomorrow and with tickets for her, Imogen and Kerry as well. Imogen gave him an Armani jacket, Kerry got him a new BlackBerry, Charlotte produced a Louis Vuitton man-bag, and Anastasia Montmorency, whose family had known Cameron's since childhood, bought him a beautiful new pair of cashmere gloves.

'All I got him was a book,' he whispered under his breath.

'Don't stress, Blake,' said Mark. 'The guys don't usually get him anything. I didn't. I'll be back in a minute.'

Mark went to use the bathroom and when he was emerging

he bumped into Meredith who was just about to walk into the ladies'. 'Tonight must be quite a challenge for you since Catherine's away. Who'll carry your things for you? Who'll fetch your drinks?'

'We don't ask Catherine to fetch the drinks,' said Meredith. 'She has a tendency to spill.'

'What I meant was –'

'I know what you meant, Mark. Your point was about as subtle as that jumper you're wearing. Nice birthday present for Cameron, by the way.'

'I don't feel the need to buy his friendship.'

'Oh my God, please don't say you're delusional enough to try getting by on your personality?'

'I can understand why you feel the need to buy him ridiculously expensive presents.'

'Because I'm ridiculously rich?'

'No. It rhymes with rich, though.'

'Hilarious. You should do stand-up. I buy Cameron these presents because I come from the same world that he does and because he's my best friend. I like to have a good time with him – you remember fun, don't you, Mark? It's the thing you usually set out to kill? Anyway, I completely understand why you don't get him gifts because – as with so many other things – you just can't keep up with me.'

'I can keep up with you, Meredith. I haven't walked away from being mates with Cameron and I'm not going to. You keep trying to elbow me out, with the presents, the holidays, the parties – whatever. I don't need to do any of that, because I'm Cameron's best friend, I'm the one who looks out for him and I always have been. And no matter what you do I'm not going anywhere.'

'Could you not stand so close when you're talking to me, please? With your breath, it's like having a walrus breathe its lunch all over me.'

Meredith walked into the ladies' bathroom and calmly removed her BlackBerry from her clutch. While her face and body language remained completely unemotional, inside Meredith had just felt a sudden surge of anger at Mark Kingston stronger than anything she had experienced in over two years. Mark had now become so comfortable in her world that he felt entitled to speak to her in that way! Who did he think he was? God only knows how disrespectfully smug he would become if he heard the ridiculous rumour that she had a crush on him! It would be beyond humiliating if he ever thought that, especially given the history between them.

Meredith started at her reflection in the mirror, fighting a rising sense of frustration. This had gone on long enough. She had been patient, she had been reasonable and she had tried to shimmy Mark Kingston out of her life without making too much of a fuss about it, but no one was helping her. Well, they had had their chance and now time was up. She would just have to sort it out all by herself.

And if getting her revenge meant throwing Stewart under a metaphorical bus, then so be it.

She hit SEND and dropped the phone back into her purse.

After the meal was finished, taxis took everyone back to Imogen's house, where the twenty lesser-friends had already begun to turn up. Inside, the girls had arranged bottles of champagne, whiskey, vodka, martini, mixers, frosted glasses, finger food, a chocolate-caramel fountain and dozens of photographs of Cameron, from babyhood onwards. As the party got into full swing, a fierce wind was blowing outside and by the time the spectacular cake was brought out to a chorus of *Happy birthday!* the weather had reached gale force.

The cake had already caused some tension, because Meredith had paid for a photograph of Cameron, along with Catherine, Imogen, Kerry and herself to be crafted on to it and Mark was distinctly unimpressed, but he joined in the singing as Cameron leant in to blow out his candles.

'Make a wish, buddy!' called an unidentified male voice, which came from a handsome seventeen-year-old who had just arrived at the party and immediately bent down to give Imogen a kiss on the lips.

'What the hell!' shouted Stewart, storming over to the newcomer and pushing him back against the wall. 'What the fuck do you think you're doing?'

'I'm kissing my girlfriend,' said Michael, pushing Stewart back. 'Who the hell are you?'

'I'm Stewart. Who're you?'

'You're Stewart? Well, sorry you had to find out this way, mate. I'm Michael. I'm Imogen's new boyfriend.'

A horrified silence had descended upon the room and the hearts of half the guests had stopped, waiting to see what would happen next. Stewart clenched his fist and punched Michael in the face, then he turned round and walked away. Kerry looked like she was going to faint at such a level of drama in one room and was doing an excited yet terrified little dance in the corner of the room. Imogen nodded decisively in Meredith's direction, who swept over to take care of Michael, while she ran off after Stewart.

'Michael, maybe we should take you upstairs?' said Meredith, smoothly steering him towards the stairs, before depositing him into the care of Anastasia, who had followed to help, dragging her sidekick Lavinia along behind her. Cameron turned back to his guests, trying to smile and carry on with things, but he saw Mark staring daggers at him from across the room and lost his nerve. 'Would you all excuse me for one minute?' he asked. 'I'm just going to check if Imogen's OK.'

Imogen re-entered the house, looking windswept and ashen. 'He's gone,' she said softly. 'He didn't want to talk to me.'

Meredith and Cameron clustered around her, with Meredith smoothing her hair, when Mark stormed out of the kitchen in a high fury. 'You've been dating another guy behind Stew's back?'

'Cameron, take Imogen upstairs to the music room. Anastasia and Lavinia are up there right now,' ordered Meredith. 'I'll deal with this.'

Cameron looked like he was going to protest. 'But . . .'

'Just go.'

Mark stood looking directly at Meredith. 'I'm going up there.'

'No, you're not, Mark. This isn't your house or your business.'

'What? Are you fucking joking?'

'Does anything about my tone suggest merriment?'

'I'm going up there to sort out that guy – Michael or whatever the fuck his name is! I know he's up there! How could Imogen do this to Stew?'

Mark pushed past Meredith and began running up the stairs, when he heard her say in a cold, clear voice, 'Because sometimes people stop loving each other, Mark. Kind of like your parents.'

Mark stopped abruptly on the stairwell and turned to look at her. 'What did you say?'

'I think you heard me.'

'What?'

'No wonder you're so angry at Imogen; you'll get to yell at her the way you never got to yell at your father.'

'Excuse me? What the hell has this got to do with my father?'

'Oh, Mark,' she smiled. 'The cheating, of course. The way Imogen did on Stewart and your father did on your mother. Oh, didn't you know? Oh, dear. Well, anyway, now you can keep your sanctimonious opinions on Imogen to yourself. People in glass houses, et cetera. Maybe you should make yourself useful and go and find Stewart? I'm sure he needs some comforting after tonight's upset – not someone looking to make it ten times worse or more public. Anyway, there's no need for you to stay and ruin Cameron's party, or life, any more than it already has been.'

Meredith turned and walked back to the kitchen, leaving Mark trembling on the stairs with anger and shock.

Yes, his parents were divorced but his father hadn't had an affair. She was making it up. She was messing with his head. She was just trying to distract him from the despicable thing one of her plastic princesses had just done to his friend.

He couldn't believe she'd stooped to this level, though. He shook his head at that thought. Of course he could.

Mark turned back and continued up the stairs, breathing slowly and deeply to try to calm himself. At the top, he saw Cameron looking down at him, shocked.

'You knew,' said Mark. His voice was low, but dangerous, and Cameron jumped slightly when he spoke. 'You knew, didn't you? About Imogen and that guy.'

Cameron stalled for less than a second. 'Mark, I don't really think we should get involved in this. It's not our business. It's between Imogen and Stew.'

'You lied for them, Cameron! I know you did. You sat there, God knows how many times, and you heard Stewart worry about Imogen and talk about how much he loved her and you never said anything to him!'

'I couldn't tell Stewart about Michael without screwing Imogen over. She swore me to secrecy.'

'So you chose them over us?'

'Oh, that's what this is really about, isn't it? It's not about Stewart – it's about you once again not liking that I'm even friends with the girls in the first place!'

'Well, look what you've become!'

'Popular! I've become popular, Mark. And I'm sorry if that annoys you or makes you feel jealous, but I need those girls. Have you any idea what life without them would be like for someone like me? Do you? It's all right for you – you're one of the lads and you're safe and you're likable. What the hell would I be without Meredith? I would be the kid that everyone thinks is gay and when people think that about you they think it gives them the right to say anything they like to you. Anything. You know, before I became friends with Meredith, there wasn't a day – not one, single day – when someone in school didn't make some comment or joke about me when I walked past. I still get a tightness in my chest when I have to walk down the corridor alone and there are people there, Mark. I still feel nervous when there are guys around that I don't know, because I think they're going to start making fun of me! You have no idea what that's like and maybe Meredith and Imogen aren't always good, but they are great, Mark. Great friends. You didn't have to make the choice between being popular or always nice, but I did! And if you're going to keep getting in my way, then I can't be friends with you any more. I'm not going back to being average, not for anything or anyone!'

Now he had somewhere to channel his anger, Mark couldn't seem to stop himself. 'Well, maybe if you stopped acting so gay, people wouldn't think you were!'

'Get away from me,' said Cameron, angrily trying to push Mark away. But Mark was stronger than he was and stayed standing in front of him. Cameron's eyes flashed with anger and his voice caught in his throat. 'Get away from me. I didn't deserve that.'

They were standing very close to one another now and the lights above them flickered, momentarily distracting Cameron. The tension was broken and Mark leant up against the wall next to Cameron. 'What's happened to you, Cameron?'

'What needed to happen,' he said simply, looking back into Mark's face just as the power cut kicked in and the lights went out entirely.

'God, Cameron. We used to be so close. I don't know . . .' Mark's voice sounded strange, somehow different in the darkness. 'I don't know you any more.'

Blake found Cameron standing alone against the wall, head in hands. 'Cameron?'

'Blake, hi. God, I'm so sorry. Tonight's just . . . a disaster. Michael wasn't supposed . . .'

'You don't have to explain any of that to me, dude, you really don't,' said Blake, putting his arm around Cameron.

'Mark and I had a huge fight. He was really aggressive. I've never seen him like that. And then . . . I don't know how it happened . . .'

'I'm really sorry.'

'He makes me feel like an awful person every time I'm around him. I don't know, Blake, maybe I am. Maybe that's what I've become.'

Blake turned Cameron towards him. 'Cameron, don't think that about yourself. It was just a fight between friends that got out of hand. Mark wouldn't want you to hate yourself. You're a good friend.'

'Blake, that's really nice of you, but . . .'

'You're funny, you're smart, you're good-looking, you're popular, you've got so much personality and . . . I really admire you.'

'Really?'

'Yes,' said Blake. 'Cameron, I think you're amazing.'

When the lights failed downstairs, Meredith grabbed Kerry's hand and steered her out of the back door, to where the moonlight provided some light. 'Damn,' said Meredith. 'This is just what we need. Kerry, go upstairs and find Imogen. She's in the music room. I'll find some candles and we'll gather everyone in here until the power comes back on.'

'Why do I have to go upstairs in the dark?' whined Kerry.

'Because my heels are higher than yours,' answered Meredith.

Cursing her low heels and taking quite some time to overcome her fear of the dark and wander towards the staircase, Kerry finally arrived there only to see, through the darkness, a rather curious sight. People were kissing at the top of the stairs, both of them tall and unrecognizable. It took her about a minute to figure out that they must both be men or one freakishly tall and masculine-looking woman. When this realization hit, Kerry put her hand over her own mouth to stifle a gasp and hurled herself through the open bathroom door. There she waited to see if she had been right and hopefully see who the two boys were. This was Grade-A scandal! She was so excited that she even did another silent little dance, only this time it was one of joy. Two minutes later, she heard the sounds of footsteps descending the stairs and she stepped out of the bathroom to see who it was.

'Cameron!' she squeaked before she could stop herself.

'Kerry,' he said, turning round in evident shock. 'What are you doing here?'

'I was sent to find Imogen, but that was ages ago and I got scared so I waited in here. Where were you?'

'I was going to get Imogen as well, but then the lights cut out, so . . .'

'Where is she?'

'The music room, I think . . .'

'Did you go alone?'

'Yes,' he answered quickly. 'Where's everyone else?'

'Meredith's got them all into the kitchen. Shall I go up and get Imogen, then?'

'No,' said Cameron. 'It's fine. I'll go back up. I completely forgot about it when the power went out. You stay here and I'll pick you up on the way back.'

'Thanks,' she said, watching him move up the stairs again. 'I'll be waiting.'

6

THE HANGOVER FROM HELL, THE SWEATER FROM HEAVEN

The storm was still raging outside the next morning, something it had in common with Imogen's hangover. She was lying on her bed in physical and emotional agony, with an icepack placed against her temples by a solicitous Kerry. The only task Imogen seemed capable of managing was flicking through Perez Hilton to see what the news of the day was, but after a while even that became too much for her when the light from the laptop screen started to make her feel nauseous. Meredith sat nearby at Imogen's make-up table, brushing her long brown hair and occasionally glancing over at her prostrate friend.

'How are you feeling now?' asked Kerry.

'Fine,' Imogen lied.

'Just how drunk did you get by the end of last night?'

'I woke up with a jello shot-glass suctioned on to my right nipple and a crushed Smirnoff lid stuck to my foot.'

'Classy.'

'Well, what do you expect?' Imogen moaned. 'I cheated on Stewart. I got caught. I got dumped.'

'God, you're so brave,' said Kerry. 'I would have needed a Valium to even utter that last sentence.'

'At least I still have Michael. Although I have all these weird feelings of regret or sickness, or something.'

'It's guilt,' explained Meredith, rising from her seat. 'You'll get over it. Well, I should go and check if Cameron's ready. I'll see you at the station.'

Kerry shifted uncomfortably, remembering that three months ago, as Kerry had been clutching her delightful fuchsia-pink silk-satin Jimmy Choo sandals, Meredith had more or less predicted the entire outcome of the previous evening. 'I'll be back in a minute,' she said to Imogen, following Meredith out on to the landing and closing the door behind her. 'Meredith?'

'Yes?'

'You didn't have anything to do with Michael turning up here last night, did you?'

'Kerry! Of course not.'

'But he wasn't invited. He didn't even know about the party.'

'And?'

'And . . . well . . . Stewart's now out of the picture and so is Mark. Isn't that what you wanted?'

'Yes, but I also wanted there to be more than one season of *Glee*, but that doesn't mean I had anything to do with it. I have no idea how Michael knew about Cameron's party. Maybe someone else texted him . . . I mean, there were, like, forty people there. I don't know.' She smiled and leant in to kiss Kerry on the cheek, before bouncing down the stairs and out through the front door.

Kerry stood in silence for a minute or so, debating in her head how far Meredith would go to get exactly what she wanted. Something didn't quite make sense about last night's events and, even if Meredith hadn't told Michael about the party, she must know who did. After all, by her own frequent admission, she knew everything. *Well*, thought Kerry, who had been friends with Meredith far too long not to be able to sense a scheme brewing, *if she's not going to tell me stuff about Imogen, then I'm not going to tell her stuff about Cameron. We'll see how much she likes being excluded!* Then, she turned round and went back into Imogen's bedroom.

'What was all that about?' said Imogen suspiciously, rising from the bed. 'Did something else happen last night?'

'Yes,' Kerry answered. 'Lots.'

'Big enough to take my mind off Stewart?'

'Yep.'

Cameron was sitting on the floor of his bedroom, staring off into space, looking pale and exhausted, with an untouched cup of tea at his feet and his weekend bag packed on his bed nearby. From downstairs, he could hear his mother talking to someone, who then began climbing the stairway. Looking up, he saw a slightly windswept Meredith standing in his doorway with a large shopping bag from her favourite boutique, Cruise, on her arm.

'You went shopping in this weather?' he asked.

'Oh, yes,' she replied. 'You can't let a gale stand in the way of your destiny, can you? Can I come in?'

'Why couldn't you?'

'I really hope you're not going to be super passive aggressive about the whole Mark thing,' she sighed. 'I'm sure he's not spending any time worrying about how you're feeling.'

'Why did you tell him that about his father?'

'Because he was being inappropriate and needed to be put in his place. Why do you care?'

'Because he's one of my best friends!'

'Oh, Cameron, your tense is all wrong. *Was* – he *was* a best friend,' she said with a careless smile as she crossed the room and opened the doors to Cameron's balcony to let in some fresh air.

'I can't believe you made fun of his parents getting divorced. I didn't know you hated him that much.'

'Well, now you do. Cameron, can't you see how much better off your life is going to be without him? He never understood you, or us, or any of *this*. He was never really happy about how fabulous you've become and his jealousy of your popularity was a really, really unattractive quality in him. He's the High Priest of Average and you know how I feel about that. And, even if he wasn't so bland, what does it say about your friendship when he automatically assumed the worst about you last night?'

Cameron sighed and adjusted the heavy navy woollen cardigan he was wearing. 'Maybe. But Meredith . . .'

'Ugh! Can we please stop talking about this? You need to get changed so we can catch the train. And look, I bought you a present for the journey.'

'You didn't have to get me an apology present,' he said.

'Actually, I didn't, because I have nothing to apologize for. It's a feel-better present. It was going to be part of your Christmas present, but I thought you may as well get it a few days early in time for Dublin.'

Cameron pulled the box from the bag she set at his feet and opened it. Inside was a white Gucci sweater that he'd commented on a few weeks ago. 'Oh my God, Meredith!'

'I know.'

'This is so nice of you and you really didn't have to get me anything else after the birthday present.'

'Don't be silly.'

The two stood up and hugged. Inwardly, Meredith breathed a small sigh of relief. Last night had been a very risky gamble, because there was every possibility that Cameron could have been more annoyed at Meredith for taunting Mark, than with Mark for yelling about it. However, despite everything, she had been fairly confident that the outcome all depended on who got to Cameron first the next morning and she counted on the fact that Mark was too proud, or too guileless, to make the first move. Now she could rest easy in the knowledge that the long battle for Cameron's friendship, as well as two years of waiting for revenge, was finally over. She never had to worry about Mark Kingston – or what people thought of the two of them – ever again.

'I'll get changed and then I'm ready to go!' Cameron smiled, moving into his closet.

'God, that's sexy!' said Imogen, a cigarette clamped between her fingers as she struggled to find her phone charger for the weekend.

'I know,' said Kerry.

'Don't tell anyone else,' advised Imogen.

'I haven't!' she replied self-righteously. 'Even Meredith doesn't know. She'd just take over the whole thing if we told her. And, anyway, it's not like she tells us all of her secrets. Do you think I need to get my roots done again?'

'Yes. And you have no idea who the other guy is?'

'None. It was just after the power cut. I mean, it could have been a really mannish, tall girl, but whoever it was they were pretty much the same height as Cameron. So . . .'

'God. Scandal-o-rama. Still, I have to say, it's not a massive surprise about Cameron, is it?'

'No,' said Kerry, flicking her curls behind her head and thinking how much she looked like a young Shakira. 'I've always thought he was probably gay. In fact, I've always known. Before any of the rest of us did. Yeah. I knew.'

Imogen opened her bedroom window and blew the smoke out. 'God, you really are stupid, aren't you, Kerry? Cameron's not gay. Neither is this mystery guy. They're bisexual.'

'What?'

'They're bisexual,' said Imogen, warming to her theme. 'It's the Age of the Bisexual. Heterosexuality is o-v-e-r. Well, not for women, but it is for men. Over.'

'Everyone's bisexual?'

'Apart from women. Yes.'

'Most women?'

'Probably,' said Imogen, beginning to falter. 'Although I haven't really watched enough of *The L Word* to be sure about that.'

'Are you?'

'No. But don't think I haven't tried!' she snapped. 'God, I'd love to be bisexual. So glamorous.'

'What do you think Meredith will do to us if she finds out we knew before her and didn't tell?'

'I'd prepare for anger,' Imogen said, nodding sagely. 'In fact, I don't think we'll have seen her so angry since Melrose didn't win cycle seven of *America's Next Top Model*.'

Kerry shuddered. 'Those were dark times.'

*

Mark, Stewart and Peter were going for a walk along the roads that surrounded Saintfield, the village outside Belfast where Stewart lived. Wrapped up against the cold winter wind, the three lads kept silent until Stewart finally spoke. 'How long was it going on for?'

'I don't know,' Mark admitted. 'None of us did. Apart from Cameron – and it's not like he was sharing the information in a hurry.'

'It can't have been that long,' Peter said, pulling his woollen hat further down over his short black hair.

'I can't believe Cam knew about it,' said Stewart, shaking his head.

'I know, Stew, but he's Imogen's friend as well,' Peter reasoned. 'It's not like he wasn't put in a difficult position about the whole thing.'

'Why are you defending him?' snapped Mark. 'When I spoke to him, he didn't seem to feel guilty about it at all!'

Peter's usual calm was ruffled at this and he answered aggressively. 'Stew's already lost his girlfriend, Mark – do you want him to lose one of his best mates as well?'

'That was Cameron's decision, not mine!'

'No, Pete's right,' Stewart said. 'Obviously, I wish Cameron had told me, but not half as much as I wish Imogen hadn't done it in the first place. I feel like a fucking idiot! She lied right to my face about it, y'know? I asked her at Anastasia's if there was anybody else and she looked straight into my eyes and said no, there wasn't.'

'Maybe there wasn't at that point?' suggested Peter.

'Maybe, but either way it's not really Cameron's fault. I

honestly don't see how he could've told me without ratting her out. Imogen is as close to him as I am, probably closer, actually, so I don't think he could've . . . It's such a mess.'

'But he –'

'I'd still like to be his friend after all this has calmed down,' Stewart said decisively. 'And that's that.'

'Me too,' said Peter, trying to make a joke out of the whole thing. 'Bros before hos.'

'Well, I can't,' muttered Mark. 'I won't. Sorry.'

'Shut up, Mark. You're best mates. You and Cam argue like this all the time. It's always all right eventually.'

'Not this time. No way. He crossed a line. We both did.'

'What line?'

'Just a line! OK? I don't know! Seriously, the way we ended things, we're never going to be friends again. Meredith must be doing a dance of joy right now.'

Snug in the First Plus carriage of the express train from Belfast to Dublin, Kerry was watching Meredith closely as the train passed through Drogheda and the conversation about last night's events continued.

'He was running up the stairs to yell at you.'

'Are you serious?' Imogen said indignantly. 'He was coming to yell at me?'

'That's what he told me,' Meredith replied. 'And, believe me, he was unsettlingly angry. It was actually quite frightening.'

'I had no idea that's what he was planning to do,' said Cameron. 'I thought he was coming up to yell at me.'

'Not initially. It was Imogen he wanted to scream at.'

'But she's a girl. You can't yell at girls like that.'

'Not everyone's been brought up as well as we have, Cameron,' said Meredith, sipping her tea.

'I can't believe that! God, I wish I could just cigarette-burn his eyes!' hissed Imogen, who considered the idea of being personally reprimanded by anyone the equivalent of being water-boarded at Guantánamo Bay. 'What an over-opinionated wanker. I wish he was dead.'

'I know.'

'I mean, I'm not a snob,' said Imogen, 'but I think that kind of behaviour is really lower-class.'

'Isn't it?'

'Imogen, I'm so, so sorry,' apologized Cameron. 'I had no idea he was going to try and shout at you.'

'It's all right, sweetie. The troll is banished back under the bridge now, isn't he?'

'Yes,' interjected Meredith. 'He is. The next step is deleting his number from your phone.'

'Yes,' Cameron nodded slowly. 'Yeah, I suppose so. I can't believe he was running upstairs to yell at a girl.'

'What an oik!' snapped Imogen, tossing her blonde hair behind her back with aplomb. 'He should be gelded. Delete his number, Cameron. I'm glad his parents are getting divorced. I hope he's really, really miserable and gets a spot on his face the size of Catherine's shame and dies a virgin.'

Meredith laughed, but out of the corner of her eye she could feel Kerry watching her closely and she had the same knowing look on her face as she had when she figured out that it was Meredith who leaked the rumours to the entire school about Melanie's sluttiness back in third year, just so they would have an excuse to kick her out of the group. Kerry had known then that somehow Meredith had been responsible and Meredith had an uneasy feeling that Kerry's instincts were once again serving her well.

Two days after Cameron's disastrous birthday party, cold winds and a torrential downpour were lashing the streets of Belfast as Blake Hartman ran towards the Victoria Square shopping centre. Taking shelter in the Queen's Arcade, he saw Catherine O'Rourke standing next to him with a broken umbrella. 'Catherine?'

'Yes?' she asked, only then turning to see that it was Blake Hartman next to her, at which her voice rose several octaves. 'HI!'

'I thought you'd be in Dublin?'

'Why?'

'Isn't that what Meredith got Cameron for his birthday?'

'Oh, yeah,' she said quickly, not meeting his eyes. 'I think it was last minute or something and I'm usually away over the holidays and stuff. Like, I was in Prague until yesterday with my sister and they'd already left by the time I got back, but yeah, no, it's fine. I just wasn't around for it. And I'm leaving again tomorrow to go to Scotland to spend Christmas with my mum's family and stuff. So, yeah.'

'That sounds cool.'

'Yeah, it is. Really cool.'

'We should meet up for coffee or something when you get back,' he said, hoping to put her at her ease. 'Before school starts again.'

It did not put her at her ease. 'Oh my God!' she squeaked.

'Em, well, yes, like, totally, and stuff. Yeah. Coffee's such a good drink . . . and stuff.'

'Yeah, it's pretty great,' laughed Blake. 'Well, I better go. I'm late for dinner with the guys and the rain's finally stopped a bit, but will you be OK getting home?'

'That's so sweet! Yeah, I will. Thanks. My sister's coming any second now to pick me up. Thanks . . . you. Thank you, not thanks you.'

'Great. I'll see you next week and happy Christmas!' he said as he walked off.

'Happy Christmas!' she screamed after him, immediately regretting her volume and burying her head in her hands.

Sitting in Pizza Hut with a mountain of food between them, Mark, Stewart, Peter and Blake were laughing about one of their teachers in school. Blake leant forward, eager to be included in the conversation. He had been surprised, and a little touched, by Mark's unexpected invitation that he should join the lads for a meal.

'Yeah, she's pretty obvious about it too,' said Stewart. 'Miss Adams would let the Malone kids get away with anything because deep down she wants to be one of them. Story of their lives.'

'She's pretty fit, though,' said Peter. 'I would.'

Mark burst out laughing again. 'What the hell?'

'I've eating way too much cheese,' said Stewart, putting down his tenth slice of pizza, 'but if they're going to put pepperoni inside the cheesy bites, then I'm going to have to rise to that challenge.'

'Are you trying to tell me that you don't fancy any of the teachers in our school?' Peter asked.

'Not really,' answered Mark. 'Maybe Miss Donahue. Blake?'

'None,' he said. 'They all kind of scare me. Teachers are generally pretty weird.'

'Better sticking to someone our own age, I think,' said Mark.

'Yeah, like Catherine O'Rourke,' Stewart teased.

'I'll second that,' joked Peter. 'Oh, no, wait, I already have.'

'Catherine's nice,' said Blake. 'A bit . . . hyper.'

'She's crazy,' said Mark. 'Like a mad bag of cats.'

'Who's the hottest girl in the year, then?' asked Peter. 'Mark?'

'The hottest girl in the year is . . . hmmm, I don't know, actually.'

'The most beautiful girl in the year is clearly Meredith Harper, right?' opined Blake, earning him a momentarily dark look from Mark.

'She is unbelievable,' said Peter, 'but that's the problem.'

'She's also Satan's bitch,' added Mark, 'which doesn't really help.'

Stewart sighed slightly at Mark's return to his favourite theme, as Peter moved in to keep the conversation going: 'I think the hottest is Kerry Davison.'

'She's a head-melter, though,' said Stewart. 'She's so dramatic about the tiniest things.'

'Yeah . . . still, though.'

'I think Catherine O'Rourke's pretty hot,' Blake said, 'but Nicola Porter's really sexy too.'

'Yeah,' Peter agreed, with a grin on his face. 'She's dirty.'

'Definitely part of the attraction,' Blake added.

'You know,' mused Peter, 'Meredith's a great example that

there's a difference between being beautiful and being hot. She is beautiful, but the sexiest, hottest girl in the year is . . .'

'Imogen,' finished Stewart.

'The hotel is so nice,' said Cameron, as he and Meredith walked down Grafton Street, while Imogen and Kerry frolicked in nearby Brown Thomas. 'Thank you so much for this present. I really needed it.'

'Don't thank me. It's been so much fun,' smiled Meredith.

Sipping his caramel macchiato and strolling along in a grey sweater, Abercrombie & Fitch jeans, Brora cashmere gloves and a black Burberry overcoat, Cameron cut an elegant figure that afternoon in Dublin and standing next to him in heels, an emerald-green coat and cute leather cloves, Meredith looked like his equally well-groomed girlfriend. To passing observers, they looked like the perfect teenage couple.

'I'm really not looking forward to going back to school after Christmas,' sighed Cameron. 'It's going to be awful.'

Meredith nodded thoughtfully as she dropped her empty coffee cup in a nearby bin. 'There's bound to be a lot of rumours about Imogen and Stewart,' she said, 'but nothing we can't cope with.'

'I'm more worried about having to run into the guys.'

'Stewart will be fine with it, eventually. He's not interesting enough to hold a grudge.'

'And what about Mark?'

Meredith shrugged indifferently and linked her arm through Cameron's. 'I don't know. Maybe there's a bright future for him as an aid to bulimic girls.'

'What?'

'Well, I want to throw up every time I look at him.'

'I can't believe some of the things he said to me that night. What a dick. The whole thing was just . . . awful.'

Picking up on the tone of Cameron's voice, Meredith looked at him intently. 'Did anything else happen that I should know about?' she asked.

Cameron stopped walking and turned towards her, deliberating about how much he should tell. Seeing genuine interest in her face, he inhaled slightly before starting, 'Well, it's kind of a long story . . .'

7

PS I Love You

It was a freezing day in January when Mount Olivet reconvened for spring term. Sitting in the back of the Harpers' Mercedes, Meredith, Imogen and Cameron wore heavy winter gloves, coats and scarves over their uniforms to guard against the cold. Cameron had spent twenty-five minutes agonizing over his thirty-piece scarf collection that morning, before opting for one in light-grey cashmere. Next to him, Imogen smelt like a tobacco factory, having smoked herself to a tumour due to her nervousness at seeing Stewart for the first time since Cameron's party.

'Do you think everybody will know?' she asked.

Cameron and Meredith exchanged looks. 'Well,' said Cameron, 'there *were*, like, forty people at that party.'

'Thirty-nine,' corrected Meredith, with her encyclopaedic social memory.

'Bollocks!' cursed Imogen.

'Why are you worrying?' Meredith asked serenely. 'You've got us on your side and a lifetime's knowledge on how gossip works. What's Stewart got? Mark, Peter, a familial history of gingers and a grudge.'

'I hope you're right.'

'I'm always right.'

The car pulled to a halt outside the school gates, unfortunately stopping right next to where Mark was standing in conversation with Blake, a sight which Cameron had certainly not been expecting. 'What the hell?'

'Don't make a scene,' ordered Meredith as she stepped elegantly out of the car. 'Hello, Blake.'

Clearly surprised that she had stopped to speak to him, Blake smiled awkwardly, while Mark stayed silent. 'Hi, Meredith. How was your Christmas?'

'Fabulous,' she beamed. 'How was yours?'

'It was really nice, thanks. I spent most of my time with Mark and the guys, just hanging out.'

'Oh, well, never mind,' she smiled. 'Better luck next year! Bye.'

Mark looked as if he would quite like to reach out and punch her, but all he could do was watch as Meredith, Cameron and Imogen began walking across the courtyard to the main entrance.

'What a frigid little fuckface,' said Imogen indignantly. 'Did you see the way he looked at me? Like I was Chlamydiana, Queen of the Sluts!'

'I know,' agreed Cameron. 'And since when did him and Blake become such besties?'

'That *is* a little unexpected,' said Meredith. 'I thought better of Blake.'

'You thought well of someone?' asked an astounded Imogen.

'I said *better* not *well*, Imogen; he's not Yves Saint-Laurent.'

Imogen crossed herself mournfully, before moving on. 'So, we hate Blake now?'

'No . . . not exactly,' said Meredith. 'We're just disappointed.

Sort of how we feel about Catherine every minute of every day.'

'Nauseated?'

'No, Imogen: disappointed. Like I just said.'

'I never really liked Blake anyway,' Imogen said thoughtfully. 'Too much of a Nate Archibald for my tastes and I'm a Chuck Bass kind of girl.'

'Thank God for *Gossip Girl*,' said Cameron. 'We haven't had anything to morally affirm us since *Sex and the City*.'

Ten minutes later, Meredith, Kerry, Cameron and Catherine were sitting in form class, watching as a nervous Mrs Vaughn took the register. 'I feel as if there's something we've forgotten,' said Cameron, 'but I can't think what it is.'

'It's probably not important, then,' replied Meredith absent-mindedly.

'Now,' said Mrs Vaughn, 'I have here your individual time-tables for the next two weeks. As you all know, it's mocks fortnight. You will each sit a series of practice exam papers, similar to those you will be sitting for the national examination boards in June. At the end, there will be full written reports, practice grades and your teachers' feedback, all of which will be determined by how you perform in the mock exams.'

Cameron nodded his head with the air of a doomed man. 'Now I remember.'

At exactly that moment, Kerry received a text message from Imogen:

OMG OMG OMG OMG OMG! We are fucked! Get passports 2gether ASAP. Fleeing to start new life in Buenos Aires now r only option!! xxxxxx

'The rest of the day will be spent in the study hall and libraries to give you the chance for some final revision,' said Mrs Vaughn.

'Oh God,' moaned Cameron, 'I really can't be bothered revising.'

'What's your timetable like?' asked Cameron as they sat round a table in the school library.

'Sad,' said Kerry. 'There are so many exams on it – one after another! And I have to come in on Saturday for English Lit in the morning and History in the afternoon!'

'My first exam is Physics,' sighed Cameron. 'How unfair is that?'

'God, I'm just so glad we forgot about these, otherwise they'd have completely ruined Christmas!' said Imogen.

'No drinking in the library,' said a prim voice from behind the main desk.

'Miss, are you joking?' argued Cameron. 'Without my Diet Coke, I'll die!'

'He's diabetic!' roared Kerry.

'A lie too far, Kerry,' muttered Meredith. 'A lie too far.'

'How are we supposed to revise Biology?' asked Imogen indignantly. 'Mr Corbett's such a crappy teacher. We don't have any notes! He so obviously doesn't care about our education.'

'We're screwed for Science in general, though,' said Cameron.

'What if we cram?' suggested Catherine.

'No!' barked Kerry. 'You know the rules – if the ship's sinking, we all go down with it. Secret revisers *will* be punishèd.'

'Well, maybe I'll just do some myself tonight,' said Catherine. 'Just to be on the safe side.'

'No!' said Kerry, angrily smacking her fist on the table. 'Didn't you hear what I just said?'

'But . . .'

'Don't question her,' commanded Imogen. 'Rules are rules.'

'But I –'

'Look, do you want a slap in the face?' threatened Imogen, raising her hand.

'No!' surrendered Catherine. 'I'll be fine.'

'Good.'

'We'll all be fine.' Meredith shrugged. 'They're mocks, not the real thing. Anyway, apparently for Chemistry we don't even have to take a written test – it's just a practical.'

'Oh, well, in that case,' said Imogen, 'there's no point even opening the textbook, is there? That would be a complete waste of my time.'

'Will the table at the back please keep it down?' asked the librarian.

'Power-mad bitch,' muttered Imogen.

'Psychopath,' hissed Kerry. 'Why is she oppressing us?'

'Like totally and stuff,' agreed Catherine.

Having discovered news of Imogen's infidelity, there was no denying that every boy on the First XV rugby squad was being pointedly cold to her out of loyalty to Stewart, but they had at least stopped short of shouting obscenities at her, which is undoubtedly what would have happened had Stewart not made it clear in the changing rooms on Monday that under no circumstances did he want anyone insulting her. With considerable bravura, Imogen affected not to notice the silent hostility oozing towards her from a dozen hulking lads every day in the corridor.

The group's dreaded run-in with Stewart did not actually occur until Wednesday afternoon, when the Physics exam took place in the school assembly hall. As the whole year filed in, Cameron was looking for his assigned seat, passing down each table until he reached the 'M' section. Thinking he must have arrived there by now, he glanced down at the table next to him and froze when he saw the name card:

PUPIL: LAWRENCE, STEWART W.
HOUSE: O'NEILL
TEACHER: MR N. ROSS

But before Cameron could move on, Stewart had arrived, right in front of him. 'Guess this is my seat?' he said.

'Yeah,' said Cameron, 'I must be just back over there . . .'

'Yeah, back there.'

'You know with the Ms and stuff.'

'Yeah,' said Stewart, keeping his head down.

'Well, I should probably –'

'Yeah.'

As Cameron moved off, Stewart turned back to look at him. 'Hey, Cameron?'

'Yes?'

'Good luck, mate.'

Far forward, close to the very front of the hall, Imogen sat across the aisle from Kerry, chewing on her pen lid as the papers were handed out. 'The exam will last two hours,' said the blond PE teacher who was supervising them. 'You may not speak to anyone else in that time.'

Imogen tutted. 'That's so rubbish!'

The teacher glared frostily and carried on. 'And, if you need extra sheets of paper, put your hand up and I will come down to you. All mobile phones must be turned off and handed in to the table at the front. You may only leave the examination hall at the end of the allotted two hours. You may now begin.'

Three minutes into the exam and Kerry's hand shot up in the air, only to start waving around when Mr Malcolms didn't notice her immediately. Finally seeing her, the teacher walked over and asked, 'Is something wrong?'

'Yes,' she said, 'I think you've made a mistake, sir.'

'Have I really?'

'Yes. You've given me the wrong paper, sir. It must be for another year or something.'

'You're Kerry Davison, taking GCSE Physics with Mr Jackson?'

'Yes.'

'Then this is your paper,' he said, beginning to walk off.

Kerry's hand shot out and grabbed his arm in a vice-like grip. 'Look! There *must* be some mistake,' she whispered hysterically. 'I've never seen any of this stuff before in my life!'

'Are you sure?' he said, trying to prise his flesh away from where her manicured talons were digging into it.

'I'm certain,' she said, nodding vigorously.

'Excuse me everyone,' said Mr Malcolms, 'but there may be a problem with the exam paper. Have any of you never seen the type of questions in the paper?'

Kerry, Imogen and Cameron put up their hands, while Meredith stared at Mr Malcolms as if she had no idea why he was talking. 'Oh dear,' he smirked. 'Looks like it's just a case of poor revision. I think you're going to have to sit through this one, Miss Davison.'

However, he had massively underestimated Kerry's ability to avoid work. Five minutes later, her hand pierced the air once more. Mr Malcolms walked over to her with a cocky grin on his face. 'What is it this time?'

'I have to leave, sir,' she mumbled tearfully.

'Oh, ho! I don't think so, young lady!'

'Sir, I have to . . . I don't . . . I guess I don't feel very well . . .'

'What's wrong with you?' he asked disbelievingly.

'I'd rather you didn't ask.'

'If you expect to leave a school examination, you'd better tell me.'

'It's . . . well . . . Sir, it's women's trouble. It's my time of the –'

'Yes!' he shouted, throwing his hands up in panic. 'Well, right, yes, indeed. Off you go. You can go. Go. Feel . . . better, not that there's anything wrong with that . . . Go. Just go!'

As Kerry triumphantly left the hall, the slow academic car crash of her friends was taking place. For example, one of the questions read:

At 12 noon, ship A is 20 km from ship B, on a bearing of 300°. Ship A is moving at a constant speed of 15 km/h on a bearing of 070°. Ship B moves in a straight line with a constant speed of 13 km/h. There are two possible times at which ship B can intercept ship A – giving your answer to the nearest minute, how long will the two ships take to meet for the first time?

Imogen had answered: 'I don't know. Sorry! xox'. Cameron had gone with: 'Surely, if they meet, the ships will collide and sink?' Catherine had scribbled a long and patently wrong equation, which had produced the answer: '4 hours, 6 minutes and 12.37 seconds', while Meredith had just left the entire thing blank.

The rest of the week didn't produce any better intellectual results. Kerry marched into the Spanish exam on Friday afternoon with no more knowledge than that which she could glean from her Shakira album and Imogen concluded the History essay, set on the Holocaust, with the masterful phrase: 'It was definitely not a good thing.' An underwhelming conclusion that could also sadly be applied to their academic performance over the last five days.

It was Saturday night and Meredith was coolly appraising the outfits during a rerun of *The Tudors*, while Cameron and Kerry inhaled ice cream beside her, when the doorbell rang. As Meredith rose from the sofa to answer it, the bell rang frantically a further four times.

Imogen was standing on the doorstep with her hair blowing about in the wind outside and a deranged look of panic on her face.

Meredith opened the door and Imogen barged straight past her and into the kitchen. 'Where's your wine?'

'What happened?'

Cameron and Kerry wandered out of Meredith's lounge and into the kitchen to find Imogen sitting at the table, looking as pale and traumatized as a victim of shell shock. Imogen still hadn't spoken, so they all sat down at the table and waited for a few minutes.

'Imogen . . .' said Meredith, tentatively taking her hand and trying again, 'what's happened?'

In response, Imogen just shook her head.

'Come on. Tell us,' Cameron urged.

'It was the date,' she said at last. 'The date.'

'Did Michael burp over dinner and now you have to dump him?' prompted Kerry.

'No. It wasn't him. It was me.'

Cameron and Meredith exchanged worried looks: for Imogen to even contemplate partially blaming herself, let alone accepting full responsibility for anything, it must have been *really* bad. After all, this was the girl who had once punched her little brother in the mouth and then complained that he had bitten her fist. 'What did you do?' asked Kerry, in a voice of awestruck fear.

'You have to remember that I've only ever been on one proper date with Michael before – you know, music, candles, wine, etc. Any other time I've done that, it's been with Stewart, so I've gotten into a certain way of doing things.'

'Oh my God,' sighed Kerry. 'One of your boobs popped out again, didn't it?'

'*Anyway*,' continued Imogen, 'we were looking at the dessert menu, when he said something really cute and so I said . . . I said . . .'

'You said?'

'*I love you.*' At the memory of it, Imogen bit her lip and shook her head again.

'Get her the wine,' ordered Meredith. 'There's a bottle of Pouilly-Fuissé over there.'

Kerry scuttled to get it and poured it into a glass that was about the same size as a toddler's head. She set it in front of Imogen, who began guzzling it back like it was the last drink she would ever have.

'What did he do?' asked Cameron.

'He drained of all colour, opened his mouth to say something three times, but no words came out and then we ate dessert in total silence. The only thing he said after that was about how nice the food was and the weather and then he shook my hand as I got in the taxi.'

'Oh dear,' said Meredith, not quite sure where to even begin comforting someone after such an epic multi-layered disaster.

'I didn't even mean it!' exclaimed Imogen. 'It was just a habit I got into with Stewart and now Michael thinks I'm a crazed bunny-boiler who can't wait to get married to him! Oh God, oh God, oh God! Why, God? Why!'

Swallowing hard against what she was going to say next, Meredith laid her hand on Imogen's shoulder. 'It's not too late to order some pizza . . . if all the cheese and carbs will make you feel better . . .'

'Really?' said Imogen.

'Sure. And there's some cheesecake in the fridge.'

'Why am I only finding out about this now?' squeaked Kerry, bustling over to the fridge.

'I'll get the *Sex and the City* box set,' said Cameron wearily.

'Let's go into the lounge,' suggested Meredith.

'Bring the wine,' commanded Imogen.

Imogen's nervous breakdown over her accidental confession of love lasted exactly ten hours and twenty-seven minutes, until she received a text message from Michael inviting her and her friends to party with him next Saturday. Bouncing into Deane's the next morning for Sunday brunch, she was determined that come hell or high water, she would be making everyone at the table come with her.

'No.'

'Meredith! We have to get to know his friends. It's *very* important. Don't you read advice columns?'

'Aren't a lot of Michael's friends quite indie?' asked Meredith. Kerry's head shot up and, bread roll still clamped between her teeth, she narrowed her eyes suspiciously at Imogen.

'I prefer to think of them as socially alternative . . . Ow, you bitch!' (Kerry had savagely kicked Imogen under the table.)

'I'm not going anywhere where the main drug of choice gives you the munchies,' said Meredith.

'Look, I am very lucky even to still have a boyfriend after my word vomit last night! Please come!'

'No.'

'Please!'

'Why should I?'

'Second year – History trip – France.'

'Oh God . . . fine. We'll take my car.'

A confused-looking Cameron turned to Meredith. 'What did you do to her on the History trip that was so bad we're now going to an indie house party in Downpatrick?'

'Dusted her bra with itching powder,' sighed Meredith. 'She's never let me forget it. So childish.'

'From the sound of things, this party's going to be much worse than some mild nipple irritation,' said Cameron.

'Oh, it wasn't mild,' answered Imogen. 'One of them ended up the size of a large grape.'

'Why am I being punished?' cried Kerry.

'We didn't want to leave you out,' soothed Imogen, provoking a pleased smile from Kerry, who feared being left alone more than she feared C-listers.

Between brunch and the party lay the horror of the second and final week of mock exams and by that time it was widely assumed that nothing could match the trauma of the Physics test, when Kerry had actually got up and walked out. However, Wednesday afternoon's Religion exam proved that this theory was rather like Catherine's taste in men – seriously flawed.

The countdown to the disaster began in the boy's bathroom twenty minutes before the exam started, when Cameron walked in to be confronted by the sight of Hector Colliner, Callum Quigley and Geoffrey Farnel. Hector and Callum were the boys of science-genius-smart and science-experiment-ugly fame, respectively. Geoffrey Farnel, like Hector and Callum, could generously be described as 'unfortunate'. With sandy-coloured hair, a pug nose, freckles and teeth like a beaver's, Geoffrey Farnel also had a constant cold and a fanatical love of *Star Trek* and pickles. Unsurprisingly, society had therefore not exactly been kind to Geoffrey, but he seemed blissfully unaware of both society and its displeasure. Callum Quigley, on the other hand, was close to bottom in the school's hierarchy and he felt it keenly. His (impossible) desire to be at the top had made him hopelessly bitter. When Cameron walked into the bathroom, Callum stopped talking and shot him a bizarrely half-patronizing, half-venomous look. Cameron rolled his eyes and stepped into the cubicle.

'See what I mean?' Callum whispered. 'What a stuck-up arsehole . . .'

Refusing to even contemplate talking while peeing, Cameron

decided to ignore them. With superb self-control, he managed to keep ignoring them, even when Geoffrey was standing at the sink next to him and blew his nose so loudly that Cameron jumped. He swiftly returned to the hall, still shuddering with disgust, and made his way over to his assigned desk. Since Religion exams were not sat in alphabetical order but according to house, Cameron's desk was across the aisle from Kerry's, and as the papers were being handed out the two of them fell into conversation about how criminally gross the three boys in the bathroom were.

'He sneezed right next to me,' Cameron said. 'It was so loud that it was like an elephant had taken a really bad line of cocaine.'

Kerry wrinkled her nose in distaste. 'That is vile. Don't tell me those kinds of stories. You know I can't handle . . . nasal debris.'

Imogen, who was sitting directly in front of Kerry, suddenly lifted her head from the table where it had been lying for the last two minutes and turned round to Cameron. 'Quick last-minute questions – totally off the top of my head. Who was the Roman Emperor when Jesus was born?'

'Augustus,' he answered.

'Fab. And when He died?'

'Tiberius.'

'What gospel does the angel come to Mary in?'

'Saint Luke's.'

'Super. And who replaced Judas?'

'What?'

'Who replaced Judas? You know . . . when he died, kicked the bucket, said *sayonara*, etc.?'

'Saint Matthias.'

'Hello all,' said a nasal voice behind them.

'Hello, Geoffrey,' murmured Kerry, who watched as he warily took the desk on the other side of her. 'What if he sneezes again?' she hissed at Cameron.

'No one's asking you to look in his tissue,' he answered.

'Good! Because I'd die. The sound is bad enough.'

'Greetings, delinquents!' boomed the voice of the same PE teacher who had covered their Physics exam a week earlier. 'In front of you are the Religious Studies examinations. I assume you all know the rules of the school's examinations by now. You may begin!'

As they turned over the first page, Cameron understood why Imogen's head had been so close to the table for five minutes and why she had asked those 'last-minute' questions. The first four questions in the exam were:

1. Who was the Roman Emperor at the time of Jesus's birth (*c.* 4 BC)?
2. Who was the Roman Emperor at the time of Jesus's crucifixion (*c.* AD 33)?
3. In which of the four Gospels is the visit of the Arch-angel Gabriel to the Virgin Mary recorded?
4. According to the Book of Acts, who replaced Judas Iscariot as an apostle after his death?

Imogen was busy scribbling furiously, before stuttering to a halt at question 5. Kerry had got off to a wobbly start after answering 'Julius Caesar' for question 1 and 'All of them' for question 3. About twenty minutes in, she was distracted from her incorrectness by the constant sniffing of Geoffrey at the next table. She was in the business of shooting him her best dirty look when, quite without warning, Geoffrey's head shot back as he let fly the most energetic sneeze in human history. Before Kerry's traumatized eyes, a straight projectile of snot shot from Geoffrey's nostrils and on to his desk.

And there it stayed – connecting Geoffrey's nose to the table.

For a split second, nothing happened. The aqueduct of snot remained and Kerry looked as if she was developing the first signs of post-traumatic stress disorder.

'Easy, Kerry,' whispered Cameron. But it was too late. Like a woman possessed, Kerry rose from her seat and began to half scream, half cry. She hopped up and down on the spot, flailing her arms in front of her, as if desperately trying to claw away the sight she had just seen, and her curls were bouncing along in crazed rhythm with their owner. Then she turned and ran out of the hall.

She was found two hours after the exam in Subway's, on her third twelve-inch sub and refillable Sprite. She had cried so hard that her mascara was now down to her chin.

'Hello, Kerry,' said Meredith, as they edged towards her. 'That's a very big sandwich.'

'You don't know what it was like,' she mumbled.

'The sneeze or the sandwich?' asked Imogen unhelpfully. 'Because if it's the sandwich, I actually got it on Saturday and if you get it with green peppers . . .'

'The sneeze!' hollered Kerry, banging her fist. 'I saw it happen. O dear Jesus in Heaven . . . I've never seen anything like it. There was so much of it that I thought his brain was trying to escape! You know nasal debris is my greatest fear.'

'I thought snakes were your greatest fear?' said Cameron.

'Greatest fear that I can actually talk about!' she roared, before instantly changing her tone to a whine. 'Pass the Doritos, please.'

On Saturday night, after spending about eight hours trying to find something to wear to an indie house party, Meredith, Cameron, Kerry, Catherine and Imogen stepped into the house Michael had given them directions to. Meredith, who had given up on trying to fit in six days before she had even arrived, looked like she belonged at a cocktail party on Manhattan's Upper East Side, not at a jamming session in a town twenty miles outside Malone. She looked vaguely panicked and suspicious, as if she thought she might actually have died at some point and ended up in Purgatory without anybody telling her.

Music sounding like angst-ridden, drowning cats was blaring from the stereo, joints were being passed around, beer and cider was spilled all over the floor and one spotty-faced youth was sucking face in the corner with some braces-sporting, hippie she-devil with three hickies and a bad case of acne.

'What is that music?' asked Kerry.

'It's them,' said Cameron, pointing to five guys who were energetically playing their latest 'composition' and six girls sitting cross-legged at their feet, singing along.

'Sweet Mary, Mother of God,' whispered Meredith.

'Imogen, hey!' It was Michael striding over, looking pleased to see her, but slightly startled by her outfit. 'What are you wearing?'

'Christian Lacroix.'

'It's beautiful, baby, but not exactly suited to this kind of party.'

'Oh,' said Imogen, who considered Lacroix to be a delight-fully avant-garde designer, perfectly suited to adventurous socializing. 'What should I have brought then?'

'A noose,' muttered Meredith under her breath.

'Come on, babes, what kind of bands are you into – Foals, Bloc Party, Soulwax, The Answer?'

'Sure,' she said, following him. Looking back on it, a silk-gazar Lacroix dress embroidered with crystals, and a pair of Louboutins, had probably been over-dressing a tad, but it wasn't as if she fitted in any less than her friends – given that Cameron seemed to have decided that Hell itself would host the Winter Olympics before he went indie and had instead turned up in a Ralph Lauren sweater and Calvin Klein jeans.

Imogen had been led over to meet Michael's friends when a couple of the other boys at the party had lurched over in Meredith's general direction. Why exactly they thought the girl who looked physically sick and was still clutching her handbag as if expecting/hoping to leave at any moment would be up for their banter was anybody's guess.

'Hey,' said one of them, 'I'm in a band.'

'You can't imagine our surprise,' replied Cameron.

'Why don't you come over with us?'

'Pardon?' asked Meredith in a voice so cold it could have made ice form over the infinity pool at the Esperanza resort.

'With us,' he slurred. 'Come over here and get to know us. You're hot.'

'And you have breath like a border collie,' she replied. 'Please leave.'

'That is you dinghied!' laughed one of the boy's friends. 'Paddle your dinghy.'

'I don't know what that means,' Meredith snapped, 'any more than I know why on earth your mother wasn't sterilized.' And with that she walked into the nearest abandoned bedroom, accompanied by Cameron, Catherine and Kerry.

Imogen in the meantime had wandered out to the back garden with Michael, who had put his arm round her. 'I've been thinking about what you said last week,' he said softly. At that mention of their last date, Imogen hadn't felt so sick to her stomach with fear since the day her father had opened her phone bill and saw that it went into four digits.

'Oh really,' she said, hardly daring to breathe.

'Yes. I was really surprised when you said it, but I've realized how cool it was, especially after how badly your last boyfriend treated you and all, and so, yeah, I love you too.'

'What?'

'I love you too, babe,' he repeated, leaning in and kissing her. 'It means a lot to me to be in a relationship that means this much to both of us, you know?'

'Sort of . . . I mean, yes!'

'And, well, I think we should prove how serious our love is.'

'I don't really do matching outfits,' she said.

'No,' he laughed, before taking her hand in his and staring deeply into her eyes, 'I think we should go all the way.'

'I think we should go,' said Meredith.

'We can't go,' said Cameron. 'We just got here.'

'What if we went back to the living room and saw if there was anyone there we liked? You know, make the best of the party and stuff?'

'Shut up, Catherine,' sighed Meredith.

Just then, Imogen burst into the room. 'There you are! I've been looking everywhere for you!'

'You've been looking for us?'

'Well, not really for you, Catherine.'

'Has something happened?' asked Meredith. 'Was it awful? Is it a disaster? Should we leave? I'll call the car.'

'No,' said Imogen, dragging her on to the bed. 'Michael wants to have sex.'

'Now?'

'No, not now! Or, at least, I don't think he meant now . . . God, maybe I should've been clearer on the general details of the plan. If he did mean now, then me running off to find you would have looked pretty rude . . .'

'When did he say this?' asked Cameron.

'Outside, just now,' she replied. 'He brought up what I said on Saturday night and said he felt the same way too.'

'He said he loved you?' asked Kerry.

'Yes!'

'Oh my God!' squealed Catherine. 'That's so beau.'

'You're still not using that word right,' Meredith snapped, before turning back to Imogen. 'So, he said he loved you and then what?'

'He said that we should prove our love by going all the way.'

'And what do you think?'

'Well, I don't know!' said Imogen in astonishment. 'How could I? I haven't spoken to all of you yet!'

'I think we need some drinks,' Meredith said, 'but I forgot my hip-flask. Cameron, can you go and get some from the kitchen, please? Anything that you think won't give us cholera would be great.'

Cameron nodded and went to the kitchen, inwardly hoping that Meredith would make Imogen see how suspicious Michael's timely declaration of love was.

8

THE SAINT VALENTINE'S DAY MASSACRE

Imogen was sitting at a table in AM:PM on Botanic Avenue on Sunday evening, waiting for the others to arrive before she ordered, when she saw Meredith arrive and hand her coat to one of the waiters. She sat down opposite Imogen and smiled. 'Sorry I'm late.'

'Not as late as the others,' said Imogen. 'Where are they?'

'They're not late. I told them to come at half six.'

'So we're half an hour early?' asked Imogen, looking at her watch in confusion.

'Yes,' said Meredith, taking a breath. 'I wanted to talk to you without the others.'

'What about?' asked Imogen, expecting a landslide of Grade-A gossip.

'Don't have sex with Michael. I know it seems like a good idea now, but, Imogen, he only said I love you, like, a full week after you said it to him and immediately after he said it he asked you to have sex with him. Doesn't that seem just a tiny bit suspicious?'

Imogen fidgeted awkwardly. 'But Michael and I have more or less been dating since September. It's almost been six months. He had sex with his girlfriend before me. He's been very patient, Meredith. I kind of feel like I should.'

'Imogen, don't be so stupid. It's only been serious for, like, the last month. You should never have sex because you think you owe it to someone. You don't owe Michael anything. He's already lucky enough to be going out with someone as fabulous as you! Sweetie, listen to me, I'm not being a prude or asking you to sign up to the Silver Ring programme – if you wanted to have sex with him and you were completely comfortable with the idea, then that's fine. But if you were really certain this was the right decision you wouldn't still be thinking it over – you would know that it was right, the same way you knew when you bought that pair of Sergio Rossi shoes. Pure instinct! Sex should be on your terms.'

'But . . .'

'Imogen, you're a spoiled, self-centred, megalomaniacal brat and now's really the time to use that to your advantage. Just tell him you need more time to think it over.'

'Maybe you're right,' said Imogen thoughtfully.

'I'm always right,' replied Meredith, 'and if he really does love you he'll be fine with waiting.'

'Michael dumped me.'

Meredith froze with the phone still held against her ear. 'What?'

'He. Dumped. Me. I went round to see him after dinner and I told him that I needed some more time to think through this whole sex thing.'

'And what did he say?'

'He said that if I really loved him I would be willing to show it and that he was a really sexual person and I wasn't considering his needs.'

'Oh my God.'

'So I said that he was putting me under a lot of pressure and then he said that having sex was a really important part of his personality, and that he probably couldn't be with someone who wasn't prepared to understand that!'

'Are you all right?'

'No, I am not all right!' she shrieked down the phone. 'I am furious! What a fucking tit-faced wanker! What kind of arse-hole dumps someone because they aren't ready to have sex? I am so furious right now, Meredith. In fact, I've got to that stage of rage where I just think – *fuck it*. You know, just fuck it! I mean, I can't believe I used to think he was so great and I spent all week worrying about this! He's not even worth crying over, seriously.'

'Why don't you come over?' asked Meredith, idly running her fingers round the edge of her frosted martini glass. 'Daddy's still in New York and I'm all alone.'

'What about Pauline?'

'I can't ask our housekeeper to do a sleepover with me!'

'Well, I would, but my dad phoned and said they need to talk to me ASAP. God, I wonder what they want. I hope it's not anything bad. After the day I've had, I will kill the next person who crosses me. I'll call you later. Bye!'

The line went dead and Meredith slowly replaced the receiver on the elegant telephone set which sat on the table in her closet. For a moment she sat considering Imogen's break-up with Michael . . . for someone who had a compulsive need for atten-tion, Imogen had been remarkably strong-willed. Many other girls would have caved in when the devastatingly handsome Michael gave them his bad-boy sex ultimatum, but then that was the thing Meredith had always loved about Imogen – her guts. That and her flawless alabaster skin.

For a brief second, she almost felt bad for what she had done to encourage Imogen into going out with Michael in the first place, but happily the feeling of guilt never materialized. Instead, a pleasingly familiar sensation of quiet superiority settled over her, helped by the fact that she was currently basking in her favourite place in the entire world. Picking up the remote control to her hidden sound system, she pressed PLAY and Nat King Cole began to croon 'Unforgettable', filling her softly lit and lusciously carpeted closet with his velvety tones.

Meredith gazed at herself in her dressing mirror, still running her finger round the rim of her glass. She was wearing Carine Gilson lingerie, a pair of Manolo Blahniks, Montblanc diamond earrings, a Bulgari diamond necklace and a 3.49-carat sapphire ring. The whole closet still carried the gentle smell of her favourite perfumes and of new purchases, of fresh leather and the crisp, reassuring fragrance of department stores. Rising from her seat, Meredith cradled her martini and strolled through her closet. She walked past her summer dresses, a wardrobe full of her coats, which sat opposite another one in which all her hats, gloves, shawls, pashminas, headbands and scarves were perfectly arranged. Next to them, her dozen sunglasses sat in a neat vertical row, awaiting summer or a particularly bright winter's day.

The closet was basically in the shape of a 'T', and most of the back wall was dedicated to Meredith's shoe collection. Her eyes stopped for a moment on a pair of Lulu Guinness heels that her mother had given her when she was twelve. She had worn them to her first ever Our Lady of Lourdes Ball. Had she turned left, she would have come to the section where her ball gowns and cocktail dresses were stored, along with a tiny area which was devoted to the religious *objets* her father had bought her – the white lace mantilla he had given her for her confirmation, the soft black mantilla worn to her grandfather's funeral two years ago, the silver and pearl antique rosary for her first Holy Communion and four small icons, all of them bought at auction, two of her patron saints – Elisabeth and Anne – and one of Christ and the Virgin Mary. Even Meredith's Christianity was couture.

She turned right and came to the side of the wall where her jewellery collection was kept. Nestling in their original boxes, or atop velvet cushions, they momentarily dazzled their owner and she let out a soft, slow sigh. There they were – her babies: the shimmering proof of her almost-perfect life.

Diamonds were her favourite – cold, brilliant, clean and flawlessly elegant; in many ways they reminded Meredith of herself. There were a few ruby pieces as well, including a necklace that her father had bought her for her sixteenth birthday, since ruby was her birthstone. The old rhyme said:

> *'The gleaming ruby should adorn,*
> *All those who in July are born,*
> *For thus they'll be exempt and free,*
> *From lovers' doubts and anxiety.'*

And it was true, thought Meredith smugly, she had never suffered from agonizing pangs of doubt about prospective boyfriends, perhaps because there had never really been any, but aloof glamour was part of Meredith's distinctive style and she wasn't exactly the first controlling woman to realize the utility of being a virgin queen. Slumbering in the jewel cabinet were her Levievs, her Cartiers and Breguets, of course (including a mesmerizing yellow- and white-diamond ring in gold and platinum, one of her personal favourites), a ring of Paraiba tourmaline – so dazzlingly blue that it never ceased to take Meredith's breath away, a David Morris rose-cut diamond necklace, the Asprey-cut cocktail ring, a Ritz diamond and ruby lace bracelet (from her fifteenth birthday), a stunning H. Stern diamond and noble-gold star necklace, a plethora of earrings and, of course, the diamond and emerald necklace she had received as a present from her father for Christmas. Those emeralds seemed to wink seductively at Meredith, subtly undulating shades of brilliant green in the light, and she very delicately traced over them with her perfectly manicured nails. Next to them were her ropes of pearls and all the other twinkling gorgeous accessories to Meredith Harper's relentless fabulousness.

Contentedly happy, she placed a Tiffany diamond and platinum Voile tiara in her glossy brunette tresses and spun around, finding herself facing the section where her handbags were kept. Walking back down the aisle, she paused and breathed in again. There, surrounded by her possessions, one of the richest girls in Northern Ireland knew that people who said money couldn't buy happiness were clearly either lying Communists or just plain stupid.

'Meredith?'

She turned round to see her housekeeper standing in the doorway. 'Yes, Pauline?'

'One of your friends has just called at the door asking for you. I left him downstairs in the library. Do you want me to send him up?'

'Who is it?'

'He says his name's Mark.'

Meredith paused for a moment, her face frozen in a look of disbelief and confusion. 'Pardon?'

'Shall I send him up?'

'No, no. That's all right. You're sure his name is Mark?'

'Yes.'

'Have you already told him I'm in?'

Pauline looked temporarily worried. 'Should I not have?'

'No, don't worry about it. No, it's all right. Leave him in the library. I'll be down in a minute.' She picked a dress from a nearby hanger. 'Could you zip me up?'

Mark was standing in front of the roaring fireplace in the Harpers' impressive Edwardian library. He was balling his fists unconsciously, anxiously awaiting Meredith's arrival. Truth be told, he had no real idea what he was doing here, only that he needed to see her. He wanted to speak to her. Having finally confronted his mother about the reasons for their divorce, he needed to know how Meredith had known about his father and why she had decided to tell him in the way she had.

Part of him was pleased to know that his unexpected arrival was bound to have unsettled her. It felt good to imagine her panic and confusion upstairs when she heard he had arrived and he hoped that those feelings might still be on her face when she arrived to see him. It was a pointless hope.

'Well, well, well, if it isn't living proof that evolution has a sense of humour.'

Mark turned to see Meredith standing just inside the doorway, in an elegant white dress and a pair of blue high heels with a glistening buckle upon them. There was not so much as a flicker of uncertainty on her face. She closed the door behind her and moved towards an oversized ottoman in front of the fireplace. She sat down and gestured for Mark to do the same on a nearby winged armchair. The flames from the fire bathed her in their light and they caught the diamonds in her ears, making them shimmer. Mark was temporarily flustered, before steadying his nerves by once again clenching his fists and sitting in the seat she had indicated.

'Why are you here?' she asked bluntly.

'I wanted to talk to you.'

'Do you mind if I ask why?'

Her eyes were watching him closely, but apart from a keen, calculating interest in what his next move might be, their expression was inscrutable. 'My father had an affair four years ago,' he said, with a lot less force than he had intended.

'I know.'

'That's why my parents got divorced.'

'Yes.'

'How did you know?'

Meredith shrugged nonchalantly and bowed her head temporarily, gently flicking an imaginary piece of lint from her dress. 'I know everything.'

'Your parents are divorced.'

'Yes. Five years ago.'

'Then why did you make fun of the same thing happening to me?'

'Because your misery amuses me,' she said with a careless smile. 'When are you leaving?'

'Once you tell me what I want to know,' he said, trying to sound firm. 'Why did you tell me those things, Meredith? Why do you hate me so much?'

'You hate me,' she answered, again in the same effortless tone.

'Not as much as you hate me!'

'That's true.'

'At least I have a reason to hate you! You're a terrible person. You actually take pleasure in bullying people. If you weren't so beautiful and so rich, *everyone* would hate you! You're vicious and you're selfish and you're cruel. But what have I ever done to you? Nothing! I've done nothing!'

'Your father had an affair with my mother five years ago.'

Mark opened his mouth to speak, but no sound came out. Meredith too remained silent, although inside she was furious with herself for having said that. It had not been part of Meredith's plan to tell Mark this, ever, but once she had done it, the only thing left to do was to carry on with it. 'That's why my parents got divorced. Your fat frump of a mother found out about it and came to the house to tell my father. So, yes . . . That's why I hate you: your father. And, of course,' she added, remembering how she was meant to feel about Mark Kingston, 'your noxious personality.'

Mark looked up at her and knew, instinctively, that she was not lying. He also knew, and he didn't quite know how, that she wasn't taking much pleasure in telling him this. There was none of the vindictive gleam in her eyes that he could remember from Cameron's birthday party, when she had first taunted him about his parents' divorce. There was obviously absolutely nothing amusing about this for her this time.

'So there we are, then,' she said. 'Now we're both ashamed of our parents – or one half of them, anyway.'

Mark stood up from his seat. 'I'm sorry,' he said. 'I should never have come here. I'll see myself out.'

He turned and swung open the heavy double doors, closing them behind him as he left. Meredith was left sitting on the ottoman, staring after him. His departure had been so sudden she hadn't even had time to think of a clever farewell. She shook her head, as if to banish the conversation from her mind, and made a mental note to tell Pauline that if Mark Kingston ever called again she was to say that Meredith had gone out for the evening. Something about him got under her skin and she did not like it. She couldn't afford to lose control like that again.

If anyone at school ever found out about their parents or, even worse, if they knew that Mark had called on her at home to find this out, it was bound to start the rumours about them again. Yet there was nothing she could do to stop Mark now if he decided to tell anyone; she would simply have to hope that he wouldn't and, in the meantime, take a leaf out of Cameron's book when it came to anything awkward or humiliating – and just pretend it had never happened.

Taking a deep breath, she stood and walked out of the library, turning out the lights as she went.

On Wednesday afternoon, Kerry was waiting for the bus home from school when she saw Michael and one of his friends walk past her. She humphed loudly enough for them to hear and Michael turned around. 'Hi, Kerry,' he said.

'Hello, Michael.'

'How're things?'

'Fabulous!' she replied defiantly. 'How's your sex addiction?'

'Cured now that I've got a new girlfriend,' he answered cockily. Kerry's mouth fell open in shock and it took her several moments before she could reply in her most self-righteous tone. 'I think it's disgraceful after everything Imogen went through for you. Don't shrug! She went to an indie party for you – indie! And you ruined Cameron's birthday by turning up uninvited, when you knew Stewart would be there and he'd cause a scene. We should have known then what a selfish troublemaker you were.'

'Grow up, princess,' he said, walking away. 'And I didn't turn up uninvited, either. One of your friends told me I should show up, because it would make Imogen's night if I did. Pity, 'cause Imogen never exactly made my night. Anyway, get your facts straight.'

As he walked away, a dumbstruck Kerry slowly fitted together all the doubts she had been harbouring for two long months about Meredith's involvement in that night.

And then she wondered what she'd look like in a beret.

Meredith did not mention Mark's unexpected visit to her house to anyone, especially Cameron, whose reliability on the Mark front was still suspect. She had a lingering suspicion that in retelling the story it might sound like she had lost control and that Mark had attained the high ground by walking out on her, rather than the other way round, and the more she thought about it, the more the policy of pretending it had never happened seemed like the best one. Indeed, the only one, unless Mark unexpectedly and fortuitously decided to emigrate. Mark, for his part, had also kept quiet, not wanting to answer any questions about why he had gone to Meredith Harper's home in the first place or tell anyone what he now knew about his father. The two of them had resorted to a policy of ignoring each other completely in the corridors of school, rather than their usual exchange of filthy stares.

The next time they ran into each other socially was that year's particularly fateful Saint Valentine's Day, which had quickly become the single most explosive topic of conversation in the clique. Having been dumped from two relationships in the space of two months, Imogen now seemed to regard it as a day that had been invented with the sole intention of upsetting her. She had already vandalized several romance-themed chocolates and had bought a packet of love hearts only to grind each one down into dust and then empty it vindictively into Catherine's pencil case. Fearing for what her behaviour would be like on the actual day, Meredith and Cameron had strategically arranged a large house party for Saturday night, in the hopes of distracting her. Unfortunately, Catherine could always be counted upon to wreck the best-laid plans and had invited Stewart, Peter and Blake, which meant that Mark might be dragged along as well, much to Meredith's fury. Discovering that they had been invited only when Peter's father mentioned it to her outside chapel after Mass on Sunday morning, Meredith could find no way of uninviting them and had to content herself with a particularly venomous rant at Catherine in English class on Monday afternoon.

Valentine's Day itself began quietly enough, as most Saturday mornings did when the group had no plans for brunch or shopping. Still feeling wounded about her newly single status, Imogen was curling up on her sofa to do some inspirational reading from Kimora Lee Simmons's book, *Fabulosity: What*

It Is and How to Get It, when her phone began ringing at half past twelve. Seeing that the Caller ID read *Kerry*, she decided not to answer. One of the benefits of being best friends with people is that it entitles you to be rude to them on this kind of level as often as you like. Kerry called back six times in quick succession and Imogen was beginning to get pretty ticked off, since Kerry's calls were coming so soon after each other that she didn't even have a chance to put her phone on SILENT. Finally, they stopped and a text message beeped through:

EMERGENCIA! EMERGENCIA!

'*Emergencia*' had been a word agreed upon a year earlier and which, if received, meant that the sender had to be contacted as soon as possible. No excuses, no delays. Imogen hit the '3' digit on her keypad and it speed-dialled Kerry.

'Hi. Sorry I missed your calls, I was in the shower.'

'Liar.'

'Fine. Sitting room.'

'Why lie, then?'

'I don't know. Good to keep in practice . . .'

'It's an *emergencia*!' snapped Kerry, raising her voice by a couple of decibels.

'What's happened?'

'Catherine's got a boyfriend.'

The idea that Catherine could possibly have got a boyfriend at a time when Kerry and Meredith were both still single and Imogen's love life had crashed and burned like the *Hindenburg* was a development only mildly less shocking than if Cameron had suddenly been appointed captain of the First XVs. The fact that it had happened on Valentine's Day only added insult to a totally unexpected injury.

By the time Imogen had recovered from the body blow that she, the acknowledged relationship queen of the group, had been overthrown by a girl who had the social finesse of an amoeba, Kerry had already phoned Meredith who had experienced some kind of massive wave of denial and was point-blank refusing to believe that the news *could* be true. It was firstly impossible that Catherine could have outmanoeuvred them all and, secondly, it was beyond horrifying to think that not only did Meredith not know everything as she so frequently claimed but that she hadn't even known of a scandal brewing inside her own clique.

'She's making it up,' she snapped. 'She has to be.'

'But she says she's bringing him to the party tonight.'

'Two hundred pounds says she cancels at the last minute and we never actually get to meet this mystery man.'

'I don't know, Mer . . .'

'Then why didn't she tell you his name?' came the shrill response. 'It's because he doesn't exist!'

True to form, Meredith regained her usual composure within a few minutes, but there was no denying that the ice queen had been ruffled and that was never a good sign. Kerry swiftly dispatched a text to Catherine full of sweetness and light, suggesting that she come to Meredith's an hour early so they could 'chat and stuff' about her new lover.

When Catherine entered Meredith's bedroom five hours later, wearing a halter-neck dress, the three girls began to panic even more. There was no denying that Catherine was positively glowing with happiness. Either she had actually found a boyfriend (and a good one at that), or she had finally gone insane and concocted a fantasy life in her head. With great difficulty, Meredith had to restrain herself from rattling off a silent Hail Mary, praying for it to be the latter. Cameron, sitting cross-legged in a navy sweater and Armani jeans on Meredith's giant bed, awaited the news with calm disinterest, since, as a boy, he had far less to lose in the competition stakes by Catherine's recent arrival in coupledom.

'So,' said Imogen, in her most convincing *let's gossip like besties* voice, 'who's the lucky guy?'

'Yeah,' added Kerry. 'Tell us *everything*!'

'Well,' said Catherine, 'we've kind of been texting and meeting up in secret and I didn't tell you guys because I didn't want to jinx it, but it got pretty serious and last night he asked me out.'

The smiles on everyone's faces remained intact, but all of them had gone strangely silent, apparently hoping that if no one asked another question then they could all continue to exist in a world where Catherine O'Rourke couldn't have a boyfriend if the rest of them didn't – a world that made sense. Finally, Meredith found the courage to proceed. 'And . . .' she said, walking slowly towards Catherine, 'who is it, sweetie?'

'Blake Hartman.'

Kerry gasped, Cameron looked shell shocked and Meredith stopped dead in her tracks. It was Imogen however who leapt up from her seat, as if she'd been electrocuted. 'What?'

'I know!' squealed Catherine. 'He's the hottest boy in school and he's so nice and so friendly and so cute and so keen and he's my boyfriend! Yay! I'm so happy.'

'And we're happy for you,' said Kerry, in a half-strangled voice.

'Yes,' answered Meredith, who turned back towards her beloved closet. 'He is cute. A bit stupid, but still . . . well done . . .'

The doorbell rang from downstairs.

'Could you go and get it, Catherine?'

'Yeah, sure!' she smiled, bouncing out of the room.

As soon as she left, Imogen threw herself on to the bed and began to cry. To have lost her own hot boyfriend, only to be ditched by the man she had replaced him with and then, finally, to be bested by the love life of a girl whom she considered to have the sexual charisma of a cactus was too much for her. Cameron sat staring at the wall. Kerry, delighted at any kind of crying, threw herself on to the bed beside Imogen and cradled her, singing 'Hush Little Princess' to the tune of 'Hush Little Baby'.

'Well,' said Meredith, standing over by the window, 'ain't that a kick in the head?'

Cameron nodded slowly. 'I can't believe Blake's going out with her. I thought he was . . .'

'Repulsed by her? Yes, we all did,' said Meredith.

'He should be!' screamed Imogen. 'I hate her. I want to burn all her clothes and dye her hair ginger. I want her dead. I want him dead! I miss Stewart!'

'Or do you miss Michael?' asked Kerry.

'I can't remember!'

Hoping to distract Imogen from her misery over Catherine's happiness and charged up with the self-righteous fury which occasionally came her way, Kerry waited until later in the evening to corner Imogen in one of the second-floor bedrooms and tell her what she had discovered about Michael's unexpected arrival at Cameron's birthday party back in December. 'Listen,' she whispered, pulling Imogen in close to her, 'I ran into Michael a few days ago and he said something that I wasn't sure I should tell you, but I think you have the right to know.'

'What was it?'

Kerry inhaled slightly before starting, weighing up whether it was a good idea to attack Meredith like this, but she figured that if anyone could take on Meredith in an argument it was Imogen. She also persuaded herself that it wasn't as if the group would break up because of this – it would simply pull Meredith down a peg or two if Imogen fell out with her for a couple of weeks. And that was a good thing.

'I yelled at him and said that you had put up with so much and had been a great girlfriend and stuff,' she began.

'Of course.'

'And then I said that you'd even smoothed everything over when he had turned up at Cameron's birthday uninvited and caused that fight with Stewart, even when he knew Stewart would be there and he was a really jealous ex.'

'I know. So selfish. I mean, we were lying about Stewart being my ex, but Fuckface Michael doesn't know that.'

'Exactly!' Kerry nodded. 'Anyway, he said he didn't turn up uninvited and that one of your friends had texted him and told him to come.'

'What?'

'I *knew* that's what must have happened. How else could he have known about it? It was Meredith!'

'She wouldn't.'

'She wanted to get rid of Stewart and Mark.'

'Mark?'

'When the whole you and Michael thing started, Meredith said that if it ever came out Mark was bound to blame Cameron for helping you and there would be a massive fight and their friendship would be over. Plus, she never thought Stewart was good enough for you. And you were supposed to decide in three weeks and you didn't. It had been going on for about three or four months and it didn't look like you were ever going to make up your mind about which one to keep dating, so I think Meredith decided to sort it out herself. You know what she's like when her plans get delayed.'

'But other people knew about the party,' said Imogen. 'There were, like, forty people there.'

'And how many of them knew about you and Michael? Cameron wouldn't have told him, neither would I, Catherine was in Prague and Anastasia doesn't even know him. It was Meredith.'

'No . . . no. She wouldn't go that far.'

'Of course she would! She's been getting away with this kind of stuff since first year!'

'But . . .'

'Just because she's our friend doesn't mean she can do anything she likes,' said Kerry, taking Imogen's wrist in her hand. 'Listen, I've been friends with her longer than you have and she's definitely capable of doing this. And, if you really think about it, you know she is too!'

'OK . . .' said Imogen, biting her lip in confusion. 'I'm already quite drunk and I've had a lot to deal with already this week. So we'll talk about it tomorrow, OK?'

Fidgeting at the prospect of losing the advantage of speed

against Meredith, Kerry nonetheless gave in since she was afraid of Imogen pinching her until she surrendered. 'Fine. Agreed.' At least the interim would give her time to work on Cameron, whose ability to back up Meredith in any situation was really beginning to irritate Kerry.

Cameron was emerging from the bathroom when he bumped into Mark. There was an awkward silence, which was broken when two girls passed them, giggling at some private joke.

Mark turned away, going into the bathroom that Cameron had just vacated. Standing where Mark had left him, Cameron was accosted by Kerry, who dragged him into a nearby alcove under the stairs. 'Don't tell anyone I told you this,' she said conspiratorially, 'but Meredith is the reason Stewart dumped Imogen.'

'I'm pretty sure Michael was the reason Stewart dumped Imogen.'

'No, no! Didn't you ever wonder how Michael ended up coming to Imogen's house on the night of your party, when none of us had ever told him?'

'I just assumed he had turned up to Imogen's on the off-chance and –'

'He knew it was your birthday!' interrupted Kerry, beginning to fear that her plan to isolate Cameron from supporting Meredith was backfiring.

'I was surrounded by a group of forty people singing "Happy Birthday" as I blew out sixteen candles on a cake,' said Cameron. 'I think he might have had a few clues.'

'I ran into him at the bus stop on Wednesday and he told me one of our very best friends had told him that the party was going on and that's why he showed up,' she answered triumphantly.

'What?'

'I know! Scandalous, isn't it? It must've been Meredith! Imogen is going to go crazy if it's true. Which it is.'

'And what good is that going to do anyone?' asked Cameron, annoyed at the return of Kerry's periodic resentment that Meredith was queen bee and she wasn't.

'Well, what Meredith did was really awful. You know why she did it, obviously?'

At the back of his mind, Cameron had always known it was Meredith but it was simply easier not to think about it and, as always, as much as he disapproved of her more extreme acts of manipulative meanness, there was still a very large part of his psyche that applauded what Meredith had done, because it was so brilliantly executed. Her bitchiness was so utterly monumental that all he could do was admire it for the work of art it was. On a more practical level, having seen how Mark had turned out to be everything Meredith had ever said – paranoid, self-righteous, demanding and petty – he didn't really care that she had happily trampled all over one of his longest friendships. After all, she had only done it in the pursuit of her friends' fabulousness. It was a compliment really – a twisted, vicious one, no doubt, but a compliment nonetheless.

'When's Imogen going to ask her about it?' he said.

'Tomorrow, I think,' said Kerry. 'But she's still not sure if it was her. I know it was, though. *Don't* tell anyone. Imogen will kill you if you do.'

'God, I wouldn't,' swore Cameron with sincerity. 'Hold on, I've got to go get another drink.'

In the kitchen, Meredith was sharing a couple of white-chocolate martinis with Anastasia, watching Blake with his arm round a besotted Catherine. Cameron walked over and leant in next to Meredith, whispering exactly what Kerry had told him. He then picked up a drink and walked back to where Kerry was waiting for him, making it look as if there had never been any time for him to alert Meredith.

'It doesn't seem right,' said Anastasia, looking at Blake and Catherine, shaking her head.

'It isn't,' agreed Meredith, her face betraying no sign that Cameron had even been near her, let alone spoken to her. 'First he became friends with Mark and now he's dating Catherine. I really, really expected so much more of Blake.'

'You know, apparently he said that before he came here from America he didn't even know Northern Ireland was a separate country.'

'Did he also ride the Special Bus in America?' asked Meredith.

'He then thought all Catholics were being persecuted by the Protestants,' laughed Anastasia.

'Maybe he's more suited to Catherine than we thought,' smirked Meredith, but the smile didn't extend to her eyes and she was now watching Catherine with cold determination.

9

TITTLE TATTLE

The next day was a Sunday and shortly after Mass Catherine received a text asking her to meet Meredith for lunch in the Apartment, a cocktail bar and restaurant opposite the City Hall. Deliriously happy at being invited to a one-on-one social event with Meredith and assuming that her relationship was the reason for this unexpected honour, Catherine dressed in her J. Crew finest and arrived five minutes early, prepared to discuss every detail of her newfound love affair with Blake Hartman. Meredith strolled in exactly on time, which was unusual for her and would have signalled to someone brighter than Catherine that this was no ordinary get-together. She kissed Catherine on both cheeks and sat down opposite her, ordering two Diet Cokes while they looked over their menus.

'So, Catherine, how are things going with Blake?' asked Meredith, carefully pulling her gloves off and setting them next to her on the table.

'Oh my God – so well. It's amazing, Mer-Mer. Like, we're just so, like, well suited and stuff. You know, I was thinking of organizing a dinner and stuff next week at my house, so you can all get to know him properly. Would that be fun?'

'Definitely. But before that can happen I need you to do me a favour. A huge one, actually.'

'Sure,' said Catherine as their drinks arrived. 'Anything!'

'Good. Well, where to begin? You weren't here, because you were hiding from disgrace in Prague, but you know all about Michael turning up unexpectedly at Cameron's birthday party back in December?'

'Yes. That was so bad and stuff.'

'The thing is there's sort of been a sequel to that unfortunate incident,' continued Meredith, running her fingers round the rim of her glass. 'Kerry bumped into Michael on Wednesday, apparently, and he told her the reason he turned up was because one of Imogen's best friends had texted him about it.'

'Oh my God!' gasped Catherine.

'And Kerry has got it into her curly little head that it was me,' said Meredith lightly, gazing down at her drink.

'That's so harsh of her!'

'Actually, she's right,' she replied, still looking at the glass, gently tapping the floating ice cubes with her fingers. 'I did text him. It was me.'

'What?'

Meredith shrugged. 'I don't pretend it was my finest moment. In fact, looking back on it, it was quite stupid and very risky, but it's done now and that's all there is to it.'

'But . . . I mean . . . What are you going to do?'

'Well, as we both know, Kerry is incapable of leaving anything alone for very long. She's already told Imogen, so it's only a matter of time before there's some kind of argument and when it happens it's certainly going to be a big one.'

'How big?'

'End-of-group big.'

'Oh my God . . . isn't there anything you can do?'

'No,' answered Meredith, looking directly at Catherine, 'but there is something *you* can do. I need you to go to Kerry and Imogen and tell them it was you who told Michael about the party.'

'But I didn't! I was in Prague!'

'Say you did it before you left. Basically, Catherine, it was either you or me that told him and you're the one that knows Michael's family, so it would be believable if you said you'd done it. It'll be much better for everyone if you take the blame.'

'What? Why?'

'It's like a game of chess: it's better to lose a pawn than risk the queen.'

'I'm not a pawn!'

'Now really isn't the time to start lying to yourself, Catherine. If Imogen and I fall out, the group is finished. No more shopping trips, no more days at the spa, no more fabulousness, no more group holidays . . .'

'Well, since I never get to go on them, that's fine!'

'Firstly, I don't like being interrupted, Catherine, so please don't make a habit of it. Secondly, you're right: you weren't invited on the group's first holiday and there's going to be so many more of them, none of which I had any intention of inviting you to – until now.'

'What?'

'I think I might have been wrong. You should come on the next group holiday,' said Meredith, removing a ticket from her handbag and setting it down on the table, pushing it towards Catherine.

'Our summer vacation is going to be in Mexico, at my cousins' five-star resort, and *this* is your ticket. All already paid for. And when I do the *Tatler* interview next week, I will be mentioning you as one of my besties. You'll finally be "in", Catherine. No more being a half-member of the group . . . All you have to do is tell Imogen you told him. She'll be mad with you, but it'll blow over.'

Catherine stared at the ticket in front of her. There it was: everything she had spent four years of social-climbing trying to get. 'No,' she said quietly. 'I don't really think this is fair, Meredith. I don't want it this badly . . . I don't need this.'

'Of course you do. What else do you have?'

'Blake,' she answered quickly. 'I have a boyfriend now.'

'And that's a replacement for your friends?' asked Meredith icily.

'At least he would never do anything like this to me! Blake is smart and hot and kind and sweet and generous. But you! You're trying to get me to save you by telling a lie that will make Imogen want to kick me out of the group!'

'Look at it this way: if you do tell Imogen it was you, she *might* try and kick you out but, if you don't tell her, then I *will* kick you out.'

'You can't do that.'

'Don't be stupid, Catherine, you know I can. If you don't do this you'll ruin the group, and if you do that I will take everything away from you.'

Getting up off her seat, Catherine looked at Meredith defiantly, for the first time in her life. 'Well, you can't take Blake away from me, Meredith.'

'I wouldn't have to,' said Meredith, just as Catherine was turning away. 'I could just get Cameron to do it.'

Turning back, Catherine looked too confused to speak for a moment. 'Pardon?'

'Oh, didn't you know?' asked Meredith sweetly. 'Cameron and Blake kissed at his birthday party.'

'No, they –'

'Yes, they did. Sorry. Cameron told me when we were in Dublin – the trip you didn't get invited to. Imogen and Kerry don't know about it . . . yet. The only four people in the entire world who know are me, Cameron, Blake and now you. And it sort of depends on you for it to stay that way.'

'You're making this up,' she said uncertainly.

'Think about it, Catherine: Cameron and Blake used to be so close and then after Christmas, they practically stopped speaking. Haven't you ever wondered why? Or why Blake suddenly became so interested in finding a girlfriend at exactly the same time? Now, I don't know if he's actually gay or just experimenting, but I don't think people at school would really be concerned with the technicalities, do you? You know how cruel gossip can be. So if you want people to carry on being jealous of you having Blake as your boyfriend, rather than seeing you as a joke, then I suggest you sit down, put the ticket to Mexico in your bag and get ready to run through the details of what you're going to tell Imogen.'

Catherine swayed slightly on her feet and, seeing her hesitate, Meredith leant towards her and spoke dangerously softly. 'Catherine, you're so close to being one of those girls who have everything. Don't blow it all over something like this. Think of it as the final exam. You've done the revision – now you have to prove that you can pass.'

*

'So Kerry ran into Michael last week,' said Imogen over lunch the next day in school, 'and he said something kind of weird – didn't he, Kerry?'

'Yes, he did.'

Cameron looked quickly at Meredith, but she was following the conversation between Imogen and Kerry as if it was all totally new information. Next to her, Catherine was staring down at her lap.

'What did he say?' asked Meredith.

'He said one of my besties told him about Cameron's b-day bash and invited him along, which means someone I trust set me up,' said Imogen.

'Oh my God,' said Catherine, 'I was hoping this wouldn't come out. I'm so sorry, you guys.'

All eyes then turned on the interruption. 'What are you sorry for?' asked Kerry.

There was a pause, before Meredith spoke in an interested, almost concerned, tone. 'Catherine, what is it?'

'I told Michael about the party,' she said quickly. 'I told him.'

'What?'

'I'm so sorry, Imogen. Please don't be mad. I just got so confused about the whole you-Stewart-Michael thing, that when I was talking to Michael, I asked him if he was going to Cameron's and I was in Prague before I realized what a mistake I'd made. And by then . . . well . . . the damage had already been done, so I thought it'd be better to just stay quiet about it.'

'How could you be so fucking stupid?' yelled Imogen.

Cameron was trying hard not to look too much at Meredith, in case it gave away whatever game she was playing. 'Really,

181

Catherine,' Meredith said patronizingly, 'that was kind of retarded.'

'What?!'

'Whatever,' huffed Imogen. 'Just forget it. Ugh, Catherine, I'm so mad at you!'

The rest of lunch that day was spent more or less in various forms of silence: Kerry was huffing because her beloved theory about Meredith had either been proved wrong or, worse, they had lost the advantage of speed and Meredith had somehow managed to pull off a coup in the short time between her party and the beginning of school on Monday. Even Kerry, however, couldn't quite see how she could have done it and she was therefore forced to grapple with the very unpleasant situation of having been wrong about gossip. Next to her, Imogen was silently seething about Catherine, while Cameron was wondering what the hell kind of a deal had been done and Catherine was trying to suppress her feelings of shame. It was only the apparently unruffled Meredith who kept up a steady flow of chit-chat, smiling and discussing pleasantries for the next half-hour.

'God, I hate Catherine,' snapped Imogen later, doodling over her Religion notes.

'I know,' agreed Meredith, 'I kind of regret inviting her to Mexico now.'

'Pardon me?' asked Kerry quickly. 'When was this decided?'

'Well, people were starting to talk about the fact that she's never invited along with us. It makes us look mean.'

'Meredith, we *are* mean,' reminded Cameron. 'Not inviting Catherine on holidays is one of the many advantages of that reputation.'

Meredith shrugged. 'Well, it's done now and she's already bought her ticket. The deal is done.'

Blake was sitting on the edge of Catherine's bed when she burst in with a magazine clutched to her chest. 'It's here!' she screamed. 'Oh my God! It's here!'

'Calm down,' he laughed. 'What's here?'

'The March edition of *Ulster Tatler*!' she answered, as if Blake had just asked her if the sky was blue. She sat down next to him and began flicking feverishly towards the lead article.

Every spring, *Ulster Tatler* ran a feature on the twenty most fabulous kids in the country. It was hardly a coincidence that every last one of them had a postcode that was either BT9 (Malone) or BT19 (Helen's Bay). To make the feature, it wasn't enough to be rich, you had to be fabulous, glamorous, an 'it' girl, a bright young thing, the daughter of a tycoon, the son of a major politician. You had to live in a certain place, attend a certain school, you had to be funny, attractive, clever and/or have some defining individual trait.

Meredith had first appeared in it when she was nine years old – a record – and her confirmation had earned a four-page spread two years later. Imogen and Cameron had premiered at fourteen and this year, for the first time, Cameron's sister Charlotte was appearing, posing in a Chanel dress inside the Grand Opera House. Naturally, there were those who weren't included: the touchiest exclusion being Kerry, who felt the humiliation keenly. She was one of twenty or so kids in Northern Ireland who always came close, but missed out by a narrow margin. Catherine had, of course, never been in it – or even close.

The article consisted of about fifteen pages of colourful

extravagance, with the teenagers dressed in couture, grouped in pairs or threes, smiling radiantly or looking sultrily broody. They had a paragraph describing each of them, their lives, likes, loves, pet peeves, schools and the all-important connections. At Mount Olivet Grammar School, the March edition of *Tatler* sold like hot cakes and never had Catherine O'Rourke read it with more tingling anticipation than this year – the year Meredith had finally promised to mention her.

Inside the magazine, Imogen was posing on the Giant's Causeway in a ball gown, with Anastasia Montmorency beside her. They had both gone for brooding, with the waves crashing over the rocks behind them and the wind fluttering their hair and dresses in a fabulously poetic way.

MISS IMOGEN DAWSON (16) *is the only daughter of English entrepreneur, Edgar Dawson, and his charming wife, Clarissa Gristwood-Dawson. Born at the family's home in London, Imogen moved to Belfast at the age of twelve when her father's business happily brought him to our shores. 'I adore Northern Ireland,' she enthuses, 'and I consider it my home. I feel myself to be the best of British – I'm as at home in London as I am in Belfast.' An avid charity fundraiser in her spare time, Imogen is an active member of the Our Lady of Lourdes Events Committee, helping to organize their annual ball, as well as her school's fundraising for the Royal British Legion's Poppy Appeal this year. An avant-garde leader in teen fashion among her peers and certainly the life and soul of any parties she attends, Imogen describes her personal style as 'eclectic, edgy, sexy-chic and personalized . . . I love accessories'. She is equally adventurous in her literary tastes, with her favourite television show being the risqué American series* Queer as Folk, *her favourite book is John Fowles's dark psychological*

thriller The Collector *and her favourite movie, the naughty but senti-*
mental romp that is The Secretary. *Her personal heroines are Argentine*
politician Eva Perón and American supermodel Kimora Lee Simmons,
who she greatly admires: 'They're very different, I know. But they both
manage to combine being a leader in their field with her own sense of
glamour and individual style. I really like that.' In her spare time,
Imogen likes to holiday with her schoolfriends and accompany her
mother on business trips to Japan, where she acquired her love of sushi.

Cameron had been posed in a designer jacket with jeans, next
to Anastasia's brother Sasha and another boy, Dominic, the son
of a wealthy liberal politician. The three boys were standing
against the white stone of Stormont Parliament Buildings, with
the gushing blurb about Cameron reading:

MR CAMERON MATTHEWS (16) *is the only son of businessman*
Alistair Matthews and his wife, Caroline Matthews, who is currently
President of the Saint John the Evangelist's Church of Ireland Ladies'
Charitable Society. The handsome and friendly young man is currently
at Mount Olivet Grammar School, taking his GCSEs, with his favour-
ite subjects being Religion and Drama. Does he hope to pursue a career
in acting? 'I'd love that very much,' he says, adding modestly, 'if I'm
good enough.' A fan of the television series Rome, *Cameron also likes*
to unwind with more classic cinematic choices, such as his personal
favourite All About Eve, *or by enjoying lunch at Deane's with his*
parents and younger sister Charlotte (overleaf) or dinner at AM:PM
on Upper Arthur Street with his friends. He recently celebrated his
sixteenth birthday there with a supper for his twenty closest friends,
before setting off for a long weekend in Dublin with confidantes, hotel
heiress Meredith Harper and socialite Imogen Dawson. He enjoys

clothes that are elegant and mix traditional masculine concepts with the new metro chic. 'Imogen [Dawson] bought me a lovely Armani jacket for my birthday,' he smiles, 'and I love it. I also couldn't live without Ralph Lauren, Calvin Klein, Gucci or Abercrombie. But I like to mix a lot of designers, because I think they all have something to offer . . . I definitely couldn't live without jeans or scarves, though. They're my major indulgence.'

Finally, sitting in the gardens of Hillsborough Castle, looking radiantly poised and confident, Meredith Harper, photographed on her own, had two pages devoted entirely to her. The title read 'The Girl Who Has Everything', the very phrase she had thrown in Catherine's face only a few days before.

MISS MEREDITH HARPER (16) *is the only daughter of hotelier and tycoon Anthony Harper and his former wife, American socialite Diana Weston. Currently taking her GCSEs at Mount Olivet Grammar School, her favourite book is* Gone with the Wind *and her favourite movie,* Dangerous Liaisons. *With a flair for languages, Meredith's favourite subjects are French and Italian. This elegant, beautiful and self-possessed young lady boasts such flawless style, in dress, complexion and manners, that one has every confidence in her future. Of course, being the sole heiress to the £295 million Harper family fortune must help? 'Oh, I don't think about money that way,' she smiles, 'I just feel incredibly lucky. In general, I try not to focus too much on the future either; I'm just enjoying the here and now.' And how does she enjoy the here and now? 'I like to travel, of course, but when I'm here in Belfast I like to surround myself with lovely things and my dearest friends – Cameron Matthews, Imogen Dawson, Kerry Davison and Catherine O'Rourke.' And what about the rumours that she and young Mr Matthews are more than just good friends? 'I would be truly lucky to have a boyfriend like Cameron,' she laughs, 'but, no, we're just good friends. That's what works for us. At the moment, there's no one special.' The gentlemen of Ulster must be breathing a sigh of relief!*

Lying on her bed, shaking as she read the magazine, Catherine O'Rourke let out a squeak of joy and sank back on to her pillow. Meredith had kept her word and Catherine had been mentioned. Every girl and half the boys in school would be reading this magazine and, for the first time, Catherine had been described as one of Meredith Harper's 'dearest friends'. She wasn't just a hanger-on any more; she was one of the club.

Forty-five minutes later, unable to take any more of Catherine's shrill excitement and alarmed at the number of calls she had received from her friends outside the group, all of them chirping along in happy jealousy, Blake kissed her goodbye and left to catch a bus home. At the Europa bus station he stopped off at a small newsagent's and bought a copy of *Ulster Tatler*, with a cover advertising the title of the main article, 'Ulster's Bright Young Bling'. Flicking to the page with Cameron on it, Blake read the interview over and over again as his bus sped home through the darkness to Carryduff, where he stepped off into heavy rain falling over the grey pavements, as the columns of commuter traffic slowly snaked their way out of Belfast, weaving their way round a roundabout, where a sodden Union Jack hung limply from a chipped flagpole.

10

AN UNEASY PEACE

The weeks immediately after the *Ulster Tatler* issue was released were probably the happiest of Catherine O'Rourke's life, so far. Meredith's inclusion of her in the interview had certainly clinched Catherine's membership of the group, at exactly the same time she had landed the hottest guy in school as her boyfriend. She was in heaven and there was no way she was going to let the truth about Meredith or Cameron get in the way of her joy. With astonishing abilities in self-deception, Catherine simply pushed the memories of her lie to Imogen and Meredith's revelation about Blake to the very back of her mind. Hand in hand with her new boyfriend – a tall, handsome American who seemed totally devoted to her – she walked the corridors of Mount Olivet, wallowing in the attention people were paying them.

Blake carried her books on the way to class, kissed her when they parted ways at the end of break or lunch and the half-envious, half-worshipful stares from the junior girls were always upon them. Much to Catherine's delight, a group of enraptured second-years had taken to stalking them at every available opportunity. Yesterday, one of them had been so busy staring at Blake in the cafeteria that she was pouring orange juice into her already-full cup for ten seconds before she noticed her mistake.

Everywhere she went in school, people were congratulating her on how well she looked, how cute her and Blake were together and asking about her impending birthday party with new interest. Delirious with happiness and enjoying the unexpected rush of attention, she began firing out invitations left, right and centre. By the end of the week, Catherine's birthday and her new relationship had actually managed to eclipse the Social Committee elections, which were ordinarily the biggest event of the spring term.

Her Saturdays were now mostly spent hanging out with Blake and the guys he had become friends with over the Christmas holiday – Mark, Peter and Stewart. When Blake first brought her along, Catherine had been so nervous that she was cutting off the circulation in his hand as he led her towards the bench outside City Hall where the lads were sitting and chatting. Horrible images of the nights she had made out with Mark and then Peter, before being rejected as a potential girlfriend by Mark, made her feel vaguely ill.

'Relax,' smiled Blake, kissing her comfortingly on the cheek. 'They all really like you. How could they not?'

Mercifully, the lads acted as if they couldn't remember their embarrassing encounters with Catherine and that was partially true, because to the guys it was in the past and therefore didn't really matter. After a few minutes, she forgot her discomfort and found that she fitted in rather well. With Blake's arm draped over her shoulder, she sat on the bench outside the gleaming white City Hall, laughing at the boys' crude, honest humour and as the weeks went by she got to see a totally different side of Belfast than the one she usually saw with her other group of friends. They had lunch at Burger King, Pizza Hut or KFC, shopped at Primark, HMV and Castle Court Shopping Centre, then they would go to the cinema or go back to watch a video. Once, they went a whole day without buying a single thing.

There was also the added benefit that Cameron and Meredith would never willingly come within a three-metre radius of the lads, which now suited Catherine perfectly. She was torn between wanting to show off how popular she was to her boyfriend and how happy she was to her friends, and there was no doubt that some day in the future she would eventually try to engineer a proper meeting, but right now, when either of them got too close to Blake, she had a very uncomfortable second where she remembered that there might actually be a problem with her perfect little world. However, since Death itself could not possibly have persuaded either Meredith or Cameron to stand anywhere near Blake or Mark, let alone talk to them, Catherine could breathe a temporary sigh of relief.

On the fourth Saturday after Catherine had taken to hanging out with Blake and his friends, they were once again sitting on a bench next to City Hall when Meredith, Cameron, Imogen and Kerry emerged from Apartment, just opposite, where they had taken a break from shopping for some martinis and nibbles. Spring had arrived and so too had the enormous sunglasses. Carrying bags from Clockwork Orange, Cruise, Harper and Calvin Klein, they sauntered past the City Hall, deftly avoiding the emos, goths, wannabe Satanists and hardcore indie kids who hung around there every Saturday. All of them waved in

Catherine's general direction, without necessarily looking at the boys they would rather not see – Stewart (Imogen), Blake (Cameron), Peter (Kerry) and Mark (Meredith).

Ordinarily, Meredith would have been furious at anyone spending so much time in the company of Mark Kingston and Blake Hartman when they could have been spending it with her instead, but the simple fact of the matter was that Blake's monopolization of Catherine's weekends was a godsend because the deal she had been forced to make could potentially have meant that Catherine's presence in their daily lives would suddenly have increased dramatically. However, because of Blake, the whole situation had resolved itself better than Meredith could ever have hoped. The *Tatler* interview and the ticket to Mexico had given Catherine the technical status as one of the core popular group, which was what she had always wanted, but her relationship with Blake meant that in reality she was spending less time with them than ever before. It was at moments like this that Meredith really knew she believed in God.

As Meredith's Mercedes pulled up in front of the statue of Queen Victoria and the four of them clambered in, she turned to smile and wave at Catherine one more time. Gratefully, Catherine waved back.

'She's being very friendly today,' said Stewart.

'Yeah, we're super-close now,' beamed Catherine. 'Meredith's, like, my best friend.'

Mark bit his lip and looked off into the distance, while Peter dived in to change the subject. 'Anyone want to hear me burp the alphabet?'

*

Dear Kerry,

*OMG! Maths class is so bad. Like, seriously, who's ever
going to need this in the real world? It's such a waste of time.
There's this thing nowadays called calculators!!! And Mr
Courcy is SO more annoying than a rash. He's moving
around the classroom like a manatee on land. I swear to God,
sometimes I look at him when he's sitting at his desk and I
think, Oh my God, maybe he's stuck there and Greenpeace
need to float him back out to sea. He's got all these moles
over his body as well. It's really gross. One of them is so big
it's probably got teeth or something. Yuck. I totally just
actually shivered thinking about it!! Also, he's got these
massive sweat patches under his arms and sometimes when
he's talking I think . . .*

'Cameron, is what you're writing Maths-related?' asked Mr
Courcy.

Cameron's pen froze in his hand. 'Yes.'

'Really?' asked the teacher. 'Because it doesn't look like it.'

'Well, it is.'

'Is it?'

'No, not really.'

'Can I see it, then, please?'

Imogen was sitting next to Cameron and he heard her exhale,
'Fuuuuuuuuck . . .' Weighing up his options, Cameron decided
that it was far better to run the risk of refusing to pass the note
forward than hand his Maths teacher a letter in which he had
been described as an obese, mole-ridden, sweaty sea monster
who could only move with the assistance of a large international

environmental agency. 'I'd rather not, sir, thank you,' he said, as if he were refusing the offer of a cup of tea.

It was so brazen that Mr Courcy had to cave in before the rest of the class were inspired by Cameron's defiance. 'I would like to see it after class, actually,' he said, turning back towards the board.

'Oh my God! *That* was closer than a fat lady's thighs,' whispered Imogen.

'Shut up and help me write a note that I can hand in to him at the end of class,' replied Cameron. 'Something that makes it look as if what I'm writing is really serious, so he'll feel really guilty for picking on me.'

'Eating disorder?' suggested Imogen. 'Family illness, religious conversion, self-harm, identity crisis or broken home? They're all winners.'

Handing in the note that strongly implied Cameron was trying to help an anonymous friend who was a compulsively bulimic, crack-addicted, homeless, gender-confused born-again Christian with leanings towards Kabbalah, Cameron and Imogen left the Maths department and sauntered into the cafeteria for lunch, taking their seats at their table next to Meredith and Kerry. Since Blake had choir rehearsal, Catherine was rejoining the group today.

'So,' asked Kerry, opening her Sprite Zero, 'how are things with Blake?'

'Really good. Like, really, really good and stuff! He's so kind and he's so understanding. Not like other boys.'

Meredith raised a perfectly arched eyebrow and smiled a catty, secretive half-smile at this statement, which made Catherine fidget uncomfortably before she decided to plough on with her rhapsody. 'What I mean is . . . you know, he doesn't put me under any pressure and stuff about *that* kind of thing.'

'Sex?' asked Imogen bluntly.

'Yeah,' said Catherine. 'He's never made me feel that I have to do anything.' Again, the same mocking, knowing smile danced on Meredith's lips. 'But I mean, we have done stuff!' finished Catherine defiantly.

'Like what?' asked Cameron, a tad more harshly than he would have liked. His tone definitely didn't sound as casual as it had in his head.

'Well . . .' said Catherine, '. . . nothing too far. Just, like, extreme kissing.'

Imogen looked at her with great impatience. 'Extreme kissing? You mean, blowjobs?'

'No!' squealed Catherine. 'No, God, no! Just like . . . really passionate kissing.'

'Catherine, you slut,' muttered Imogen sarcastically.

'Well, I'm definitely not ready to do *that*,' answered Catherine, 'and Blake understands that.'

'Ready?' asked Meredith irritably. 'You don't ever have to be "ready" for it, Catherine. Not everyone does it. I'm never going to.'

'You're *never* going to give someone a blowjob?' asked Imogen disbelievingly.

'No,' replied Meredith. 'Absolutely not.'

'But . . .'

'Look! I'm not going to do *that* for the very same reason I don't baby-sit – if it spits-up, it's not coming anywhere near my face.'

'Cameron, what do you think?' asked Kerry.

'I don't know,' he said. 'I guess I'm generally in favour of them. Yeah, I don't know.'

Sensing the awkwardness, Meredith swooped in to change the topic of conversation, but this wasn't the first time something like this had happened. The awkward and unspoken knowledge of Cameron's sexual confusion had now settled over the group's consciousness, creating more and more moments like this. Catherine and Meredith both knew about his kiss with Blake, while Imogen and Kerry knew there had been a kiss with a guy, but not who that guy was. Neither half knew that the other half knew anything about it and so there was no possibility to talk about it openly, even if they had been capable of frank, honest, emotional discussions – which they weren't.

As the conversation moved in the safer direction of school gossip, Blake entered the cafeteria, straight out of choir practice. He came over to their table, leant in and kissed Catherine on the lips. 'Hey, can I talk to you over here for a second?' he asked.

'Sure!' smiled Catherine. 'Two seconds, guys.'

Catherine followed Blake over to the wall of the cafeteria, where he put his arms round her and whispered something in her ear. She giggled and nuzzled up against him. Underneath the table, Meredith very discreetly took Cameron's hand and patted it supportively. Feeling his hand shaking slightly beneath her touch, Meredith finally began to suspect just how much the Catherine and Blake saga was killing Cameron and deep inside she felt a spasm of the emotion she hated the most: guilt.

'. . . and, anyway, now the psycho-bitch is completely raging at me and every time I speak to her she's in such a massive huff,' finished Imogen, explaining one of the many plots, schemes, fights and intrigues she was constantly involved in at school.

'What a psycho-bitch,' agreed Kerry.

'I know,' said Imogen. 'She's such a bitch.'

'And a psycho,' nodded Kerry.

'Come on,' said Cameron, standing up. 'Let's go. We have to vote in the Social Committee elections before lunch is over.'

In Friday morning's assembly, the election results for the coveted positions on the Mount Olivet Social Committee were revealed by the headmaster. It was the Social Committee's job to organize the final Leavers' Ball and all the fundraisers, parties, mixers, alumni reunions and dinners. The only students eligible to stand for it were the lower-sixth students, who would be in their final year after the elections.

And to anyone who thought the age of absolute monarchy had died out with the Romanovs, the Social Committee elections were proof that it was alive and kicking at Mount Olivet Grammar School. Every year, without fail, the queen bee wasn't so much elected President, as simply inheriting the job from her predecessor. The Vice-president was always her best friend and the Chairperson for Designer Events; the Treasurer and the Entertainment Manager were also inevitably part of her popular crowd.

This year, as always, the results went as expected – all of the heiresses in lower sixth got the jobs everyone knew they would get; Dr Stephenson announced that Tangela Henton-Worley was now Entertainment Manager, Natasha Jenkins was Treasurer, Mariella Thompson was Chairperson for Designer Events (an accolade a little tarnished for her when the request to change it to Chairprincess was turned down) and Lavinia Barrington was Vice-president.

Perched on the assembly-hall stage, listening to the results, was the current President, the pashmina-loving Cecilia Molyneux, the most popular girl in upper sixth, gazing disinterestedly at her replacements. With the air of a man who is woefully trying to make something tense and surprising, the headmaster held his breath before continuing, 'And now, I am very pleased to announce that your votes mean that the future President of Mount Olivet Grammar School's Social Committee is . . . Anastasia Montmorency.'

Applause filled the hall as the ever-beautiful Anastasia walked up on to the stage with all the poise and confidence of an empress, hugged Cecilia and went to stand with the other members of the committee. Sitting between Imogen and Kerry, Meredith clapped along with the same sort of serenity as Anastasia was displaying on the stage. This was the proper way – the way things had always been done at Mount Olivet. It passed from one queen to another, as far back as any of them could remember. Anastasia was taking over from Cecilia, who had taken over from Allegra Huntingdon-Bass, who had followed Natalie Trimble. Without doubt, Meredith would be next.

Cecilia had taken to the podium to give her farewell speech. 'Hi. So, I just wanted to thank everyone who's supported me on, like, the overwhelmingly stressful but totally rewarding journey that has been my time as First Lady of Mount Olivet.' Some eyebrows were raised at how Cecilia had transformed 'President of the Social Committee' into 'First Lady' of the entire school; Meredith and Anastasia nodded along in firm agreement.

'The whole committee's been really great. Well, most of them. Anyway! Big shout-out to all my girlies – Emily, Louise, Sarah-Jane and Olivia-Grace. It's been *so* beau and thanks to Meredith Harper for creating that word, which has totally become the mantra of my time as First Lady. Tickets are *so* now on sale for the Leavers' Ball, which is going to be so beau and fab, and we've managed to set aside twenty tickets for those outside our year who'd like to come. However, they're totally by application only, so if you could e-mail your request for a ticket to Olivia-Grace Wallace or Emily Rhys, including three good reasons why you should be allowed to come, they will notify you of our decision within absolutely seventy-two hours. Or whatever.

'I'd also like to say "Well done" on the decision to elect Anastasia to succeed me – *such* clever voting, you guys! She is going to bring the same level of commitment, party-planning brilliance and fabulousness that me and my committee brought. Well, most of them. Anyway, in conclusion, thanks so much, looking forward to the ball, congrats to Anastasia and all her girlies and see you at the ball. Well, some of you.'

'She's *such* a good speaker,' said Kerry admiringly, clapping as Cecilia left the stage.

That evening, Anastasia had organized a fabulous party to celebrate her election victory. The main festivities were being held at her house in Helen's Bay, which would begin with a supper at nine, so that her friends could watch the fireworks display over the bay, which her father had arranged to go off at half past ten. A couple of train carriages had been booked to take them from the gothic Helen's Bay train station into the centre of Belfast again, where all their names had been put on the list for Rain.

Meredith was standing in her closet picking out a dress to wear when she caught Cameron's face in the mirror behind her, looking like a picture of misery. 'What's wrong?' she asked. 'You don't like the dress?'

'No, no, it's not that.'

'Wrong colour? You don't think I should wear green? I was sort of thinking about going with lilac, but I've worn that quite a lot recently and I don't want people to think I have the same sort of limited fashion imagination as Kerry. Lilac will *not* become my pink.'

'Meredith, seriously, I like the green. It's not the dress.'

'Why are you still thinking about him, then?' she asked, turning back towards the mirror and running her fingers along her other dresses. It wouldn't be green or lilac, she decided.

'Who?'

'Don't do that,' she sighed with slight impatience. 'You know who – the *High School Musical* Abercrombie-and-Fitch looka-like closet-case who is currently dating a girl who makes Barbie look like a Mensa member.'

'It only happened once,' said Cameron, staring at his feet. 'It doesn't mean that we're . . .'

She looked back at him. 'What?'

'You know what! You know!'

'Yes, I know, Cameron, but do you?'

'It didn't . . . it doesn't mean . . . anything.'

'Tell me Blake Hartman doesn't mean anything to you, Cameron, and I'll believe you.'

'He doesn't.'

Meredith sighed. 'OK, I lied. I said I'd believe you, but I don't. You're quite clearly lying.'

Cameron growled suddenly and got to his feet. 'I'm supposed to get married! I'm supposed to have a normal, perfect life. I wanted to be the guy people wanted to be, not the guy they made fun of! This isn't supposed to be happening to me!'

'But it is.'

'Thanks, Meredith, that's really supportive of you.'

'Well, what do you want me to say? It's not going to help you if I start crying along with you like some big Gay Parade, Cameron. This is happening to you whether you like it or not and I'm just trying to make sure that you don't make a complete idiot of yourself like Blake has. I'm not even exaggerating when I say it would be my living nightmare if you turned out like him. He's so unutterably pathetic. Just look at him. He's run so far back into the closet that he's practically having tea in Narnia with Mr Tumnus.'

Meredith laughed a little at her last witticism and sat down at the mirror, applying a light sheen of lipgloss. Cameron looked up at her, catching her eye in the mirror and smiling at her ability to silently applaud herself even in moments of emotional crisis. Smiling back, Meredith continued putting on her make-up and chatting. 'Just promise me that if you discuss it with no one else, you'll at least be able to discuss it with yourself.'

Rising from the seat and ignoring that he had failed to respond, Meredith returned to her dresses and selected an elegant Dior number. She removed her dressing gown and slipped into the dress. 'Could you do me up, please?'

Cameron stood behind her, zipping her dress and then placing a small diamond necklace round her neck. As he fastened the clasp, Meredith held her hair out of the way and stared at their reflection.

'You know,' said Cameron sadly, 'you and I could have made a wonderful couple.'

'We already do . . . Now, come on!' she said, spinning round to face him and placing her hands on his shoulders. 'The car's waiting and you know what Anastasia's like about being on time; plus, Imogen and Kerry need to be collected on the way.'

'Catherine and Blake are going to be there, though,' he groaned. 'Can't we just stay in here?'

'In the closet? No, Cameron. Not for too long.'

11

THE FIELD OF DREAMS

The day after Anastasia's party, Kerry and Imogen were enjoying a day of R&R at the spa. 'Last night was so much fun,' said Kerry, as they received their massages. 'Anastasia invited a *very* entertaining crowd. So beau.'

'I know,' sighed Imogen. 'Although to be honest I don't really like Blake Hartman and I don't think Anastasia does either. Don't tell anyone I told you this, but she told me at dinner that she only invited him and Catherine because of what Meredith said in the *Tatler* interview. Christ, what was Meredith thinking? Why did she say Catherine was one of her best friends? Why? Now we're stuck with her and her teeny-bop boyfriend at every A-list party we go to. So irritating.'

'Well, I don't think the *Tatler* interview is that important,' said Kerry icily.

'It's important enough to get people inviting Catherine to parties she wouldn't necessarily have been at six months ago. And with her comes Blake, of course.'

'Yeah. He seems nice, but a bit . . .'

'Annoying,' finished Imogen. 'Maybe that's just when he's around Catherine, but they're definitely too much when they're together these days.'

'I know!' said Kerry. 'The way she's always draped over him is like a permanent PDA too far. It displeases me.'

'Catherine's whole life is a PDA too far,' Imogen replied. 'I mean, whatever happened to perfectly lovely PrADAS – *Private Appropriate Displays of Affection*? Blake and Catherine are like the anti-PrADAS. And I'm not only the one who thinks so – Cameron definitely hates them when they're together. He looked like he was going to be sick when they started making out at Rain.'

'He and Blake seemed to be good friends before this,' purred Kerry in contentment at her masseuse's brilliance. 'Thanks, Suzanne.'

'I know,' mused Imogen. 'They've totally drifted apart. I think Cameron ended up finding him quite annoying after a while. Who wouldn't?'

'Oh my God – do you think it was him?' asked Kerry suddenly, leaping up from the massage table, her face alight with gossip ecstasy. 'Do you think he was the guy?'

'Don't be stupid, Kerry. Blake's never shown any interest in Cameron that way, at all, and you'd have to be heterosexual to the point of compulsive to date Catherine.'

'I hope Cameron hurries up and comes out,' said Kerry excitedly. 'I can't wait to have a gay best friend.'

'Well, technically, you already do.'

'No, but I mean a proper Gay Best Friend. You know, one who's like *out and proud*. And then I can ask him all about gay sex. I'm very curious.'

'You might have to wait until he knows a bit more about it.'

'I know, I know,' she said dismissively, 'but how exciting! It's like the ultimate accessory and he can be one of my bridesmaids!'

'What?' asked Imogen, raising her head from the pillow in shock.

'When I get married, Cameron can be one of my bridesmaids! Yay! He'll be so pleased.'

'He'll be so insulted!' snapped Imogen. 'Never, ever, *ever* ask him that, Kerry. He's a man.'

'He's gay!'

'And?'

'So he shouldn't have a problem with it. He's one of my best friends, Imogen. He is *being* involved in my wedding!'

'Involved is fine, but don't you think it might be fulfilling a pretty vicious stereotype to have a gay man up at the front of the church filling a role that's usually taken by a woman?'

'Why should he care? You and Meredith will be there as well, and so will my sisters.'

'Me, Meredith, Helen and Victoria are all girls, Kerry. It's OK for us to be bridesmaids. It would be totally humiliating for Cameron to even be asked to do that!'

'Why are you getting so annoyed?' snapped Kerry.

'Because it's completely ridiculous!'

For a moment, Kerry was silent and then in a very cold voice replied, 'Fine.' She buried her face deep into the massage pillow and didn't speak again until their pedicures fifty-five minutes later.

Once a month, Meredith met with Anastasia Montmorency for a one-on-one meal; lunch if it was just a catch-up, dinner if it was something more serious. That March, Meredith asked Anastasia to meet her for supper at the Old Inn, a seventeenth-century hotel in the village of Crawfordsburn, in the plush district of

Helen's Bay, not far from Anastasia's home. Crackles came from the roaring log fire in the main restaurant as Meredith arrived at their table. Anastasia rose to kiss her on both cheeks and they ordered a bottle of white wine and two mineral waters while they looked over the menu.

'Francesco Modonesi sends his best,' Anastasia said.

'How lovely,' smiled Meredith, remembering the gorgeous Italian she had met back in November. 'How is he?'

'Very well and really quite smitten with you, but who can blame him? Now,' she said, becoming very businesslike, 'what's the issue this evening? Catherine?'

'How did you guess?'

'Something must have happened to make you mention her in *Tatler* like that. I couldn't believe it when I read it; I thought it must have been a typo!'

'No, there was no typo, although a mistake was made. The truth is I had to do a deal with Catherine and now I'm not sure what to do about it.'

'What sort of deal?'

'It's not just the deal that's tricky, Anastasia, it's the fact that I may have to try and get out of it. I don't have anyone else I can talk to about this, but if I tell you I need you to swear absolute and complete secrecy and not in the fake way we usually do. I mean it – it can't go any further than this table, not even to Lavinia or your brother.'

'If it's that serious, of course.'

'And no judgement?'

'Please!' said Anastasia. 'I didn't judge you when you planted a condom in one of the Christian Union girls' pencil case, I'm not going to judge you now.'

'OK. You remember when Michael Laverty turned up unexpectedly at Cameron's birthday?'

'Yes. That was the night Stewart dumped Imogen?'

'Yes. Well, Michael wasn't supposed to be invited to the party for obvious reasons, but I took his number out of Imogen's phone when she wasn't looking and I texted him from the dinner at AM:PM. I told him where the after-party was and said how great it would be if he could make it. I didn't sign my name at the end of the message; I just said it was one of Imogen's best friends. And luckily the moron didn't ever call back the number or check who it was. I knew it was a very risky thing to do, but Mark Kingston had said something at the dinner about how he was never going to get out of my life and I just thought, *Enough's enough*. I had to do something. I knew the only way to definitely get rid of Mark was to bring the whole thing between Imogen and Michael out into the open so that Stewart would have no choice but to dump her and Mark would get mad at Cameron. And as long as I got to Cameron first on the morning after I'd be able to drive a wedge between him and Mark permanently.'

'Which of course you did?'

'Of course – sealed with a Gucci sweater.'

'Nice touch.'

'Thank you. Anyway, Mark was out of the picture and Imogen was finally free of Stewart who was always so . . .'

'Average?'

'Exactly. I thought everything had worked out perfectly and then a few weeks ago, just before Valentine's Day, it all started to fall apart. Imogen and Michael broke up and, when she next saw Michael, Kerry threw all past complaints back in his face, including turning up to the party uninvited.'

'Oh God.'

'Yes. So obviously Michael told her that he *had* been invited, by one of Imogen's friends.'

'How did Kerry find out it was you?'

'She didn't, she just guessed. That's the thing about Kerry: she guesses everything. Sometimes they're wildly inaccurate like the time she thought Cameron and I were secretly dating and then other times . . .'

'Right on the mark?'

'Exactly. She told Cameron that she knew it must have been me, but before Imogen could confront me about it, I took Catherine out to lunch and offered her full membership of the group if she'd take the fall.'

'Oh, I see. It all makes sense now. And I take it Imogen was far less angry with Catherine for being stupid than she would have been with you for being . . .'

'A bitch? Yes.'

'Well played.'

'Not quite,' sighed Meredith. 'So, the deal had been made. I mentioned her in *Tatler* and so all of sudden she was part of the A-list. I gave her a ticket to come to Mexico with us in the summer and I managed to dissuade Imogen from killing her for what she had done with Michael. Plus, she was also going out with Blake Hartman, so actually she spent less time with us than before. Apart from having to bring her on holiday with us, it was the perfect solution.'

'But?'

Meredith paused before continuing. 'Something else happened that night.'

'The night of Cameron's birthday?'

'Yes . . . Blake Hartman's gay.'

The usually unflappable Anastasia stopped with her glass halfway to her mouth. 'Pardon?'

'He kissed Cameron.'

Setting the glass back down, Anastasia was staring at Meredith in temporary shock. 'Did you see them?'

'No, Cameron told me when we were in Dublin just before Christmas. He hasn't really mentioned it since . . .'

'And Blake's now going out with Catherine? Oh my God, it really does all make sense now. She's his beard! Does Catherine know?'

'Yes.'

'And she's still going out with him? I don't think I've ever heard of anything more pathetic in my entire life.'

'I told her about the kiss and said if she didn't tell Imogen she had been the one who texted Michael, I would make sure everyone in school knew her boyfriend was gay. That was the thing that finally broke her, actually. It doesn't matter to Catherine what the truth is, only that Blake's around her all the time and giving her the attention she's so desperate for. And for Catherine that's worth any price.'

'Oh my goodness,' said Anastasia, sipping her wine. 'And how's Cameron coping with this?'

'That's the real problem. At first, I thought he was fine, but when he puts his mind to it Cameron can fake it like a porn star, so it was only last week that I realized he's really not OK with this. Really, really not. Blake phased out their friendship as soon as the kiss happened, then he took Cameron's place in Mark's group and, to cap it all off, started dating a girl that Cameron has to hang out with on a daily basis.'

'What a bastard.'

'I know.'

'And now you don't know what to do?'

'Exactly. I do care about Cameron's feelings and, even if I didn't, it's obvious that he's going to lose it over this whole Blake/Catherine thing at some point and it's important that I manage how it all turns out. Imogen, Catherine, Michael, Stewart, Mark . . . it all sort of depends on the way Blake and Cameron end up resolving things. I have to stay in control of this, but I don't know what move to make next: I can't "out" Blake without outing Cameron as well and if I do, Catherine will tell Imogen about what really happened with Michael and then all hell will break loose. But, on the other hand, if I don't do something, Cameron's going to be totally miserable and have to sit there, day in, day out, watching Blake fake a relationship with someone who, thanks to my *Tatler* interview, attends every party we go to.'

'Well, I won't invite them to mine any more. I was only doing it because I thought you had changed your mind about her,' said Anastasia. 'It's not much, but it'll help a little and no one will know you had anything to do with it, but it's not going to be enough in the long term. The thing is, Meredith, you're right: you can't be the one that breaks Catherine and Blake up – it's far too risky. Imogen might forgive Catherine for *accidentally* ruining her life, but if she knew you had done it deliberately she would hunt you down and eat you.'

'I know.'

'However, what Blake and Catherine are doing is beyond tragic and wrong, especially if Catherine knows the truth. It's also completely unfair on Cameron and it can't be allowed to continue. Somebody needs to be punished for this.'

'I know. I can't wait for the punishing to begin.'

'Do Blake and Cameron speak now?'

'No. Not at all.'

'Have you considered suggesting that they do?'

'Of course not. Blake doesn't deserve to talk to Cameron. He deserves to be strung up by his heels and shot!'

'Maybe. But there's clearly something between them, Meredith. It wasn't just a kiss; otherwise Blake wouldn't have run into the arms of the first gullible airhead he could convince to go out with him. And I think we need to remember that in Blake's head no one else knows about their kiss apart from Cameron, right? Blake isn't dating Catherine because he's trying to convince other people, he's doing it to convince himself. If anyone can snap him out of this, it's Cameron, and if Blake is persuaded into "coming out" of his own free will, then Catherine can't blame you for it. I think it has to be Cameron who does this, sweetie. Like it or not, there's a connection between them which right now Blake is terrified of.'

'Cameron too,' said Meredith thoughtfully.

'I don't know why people make such a fuss about this gay thing,' sighed Anastasia nonchalantly. 'Shall we order?'

'Absolutely.'

'And what exactly are your plans for tonight?' asked Kerry's mother, as she drove her daughter towards Catherine's house.

'Just a sleepover.'

'And will her parents be there?'

'Yes!' snapped Kerry. 'God, Mum!'

'I was just checking, Kerry.'

'Yeah, well, there's also this thing called independence, which I quite like, actually!'

In fact, Catherine's parents were away visiting relatives that weekend and so Catherine had invited all the girls round for some drinking, facials and dancing. Kerry had manoeuvred her pink overnight bag into the car with considerable care, nervous that her mother would hear the clank of two bottles of peach schnapps, a bottle of rosé and a bottle of vodka. Thankfully, nothing happened and everything looked fairly normal from the outside of Catherine's house when Kerry's car pulled up into the driveway. As her mum drove off unsuspectingly, Kerry rang the front doorbell, only to be grabbed and dragged round the side of the house by Catherine.

'Hey! There's been a super-fun change of plan.'

'What?' asked Kerry, naturally suspicious of any plan which meant she had to be manhandled round to the side of the house rather than walk through its front doors.

'We're going camping instead,' smiled Catherine in a tone that suggested she feared how this suggestion would be received.

'No, we aren't,' said Kerry.

'Please, Kerry, please! It's my sister Orla's second anniversary with her boyfriend, Paddy, so they kind of need the house to themselves this evening!'

'So, where are we . . . camping?'

'Apparently, in the field over there,' answered a cold and unimpressed voice from the darkness. It was Meredith's, coming from somewhere next to the bright, glowing orange dot of Imogen's cigarette.

'Blake's sorted the whole thing out,' said Catherine. 'He's made loads of effort.'

'Yes, well, dating you he's probably used to it,' snapped Imogen. 'God, this is going to be so shit and we can't leave because we already lied to our parents about it.'

'It's not going to be shit,' said Catherine defensively.

'Do you think we could book rooms at Malmaison and just get a taxi there later?' asked Kerry.

'No!' squealed Catherine. 'No, guys, please. Come on! Just come and see it. It'll be fun and you'll get to spend time with me and Blake properly. Today I just realized that it's been way too long!'

'I've probably already seen something equally comfortable when I went on a tour of the trenches for second-year history,' answered Meredith.

Cameron, who had been standing by in silence, came up and linked arms with Kerry as they walked through Catherine's back garden into the field where Blake had set up the tents. 'You're so lucky you have a compulsive scarf and glove addiction,' said Kerry. 'Do you have any spare with you?'

'Of course,' he answered. 'Cashmere?'

Then they saw Blake, standing proudly next to the hearty campfire he had built up for their arrival, with three perfectly pegged tents nearby and a bundle of sleeping bags and a dozen or so chairs ranged around the fire. He was holding two packets of chocolate and caramel digestive biscuits, an enormous bag of marshmallows and a bundle of wooden skewers. 'So,' he smiled. 'Ever made smors before?'

'No,' answered Kerry. 'No, we haven't.'

'But they're like the most important part of the whole camping experience,' laughed Blake.

'Blake, I'm going to stop you in this merry banter right now,' said Meredith, holding up her hand. 'Do we really look like the kind of people who have any idea about the camping experience? Our idea of "roughing it" is the Travelodge.'

'That's cool,' he smiled determinedly. 'I actually really like the Travelodge, though.'

'Shocking,' muttered Meredith.

'Would anyone like a drink?' asked Kerry.

'Oh God, yes,' said Imogen, settling into one of the foldable chairs. 'With any luck, we'll have blacked out by midnight.'

Clearly disheartened, Blake looked around the campfire for someone who would support him. 'Cameron, you'll be up for it?'

Cameron deliberately looked down at his gloved hands, concentrating on keeping calm by admiring the beautiful cashmere. 'I don't think so.'

'Come on, I'll show you all how to make them when the guys get here.'

In perfect unison, the four heads of Cameron, Meredith, Imogen and Kerry snapped up to look in Blake's direction and Catherine plastered her face with a worried-but-pretending-everything-is-fine smile.

'What?' asked Imogen. '*What?*'

'The guys,' said Blake. 'Peter, Mark and Stewart are coming.'

'You invited PMS?' snapped Imogen.

'Catherine, can we talk to you for a minute?' said Kerry. 'Like, now?'

'Em, OK.'

Hearing a car pull up outside Catherine's house, Blake went over to greet the boys and as soon as he was out of hearing distance, the four friends fell on Catherine like a pack of hyenas upon an isolated antelope.

'I am going to cut you open and feed you to vultures,' growled Imogen. 'Firstly, you trick us into a camping trip and then you invite the one group of guys who every single one of us has a reason to hate!'

'Kerry doesn't hate any of them,' said Catherine, desperately clutching at straws.

'I don't hate anyone,' replied Kerry primly, 'but I hate Peter. Nobody is supposed to get over me.'

'What could I do?' said Catherine. 'They're Blake's best friends. He invited them. He loves to do things with the guys.'

'Oh, we know that,' muttered a supremely irritated Meredith.

Moving on quickly, Catherine continued to defend the evening. 'It'll be fun, guys, seriously. Let's just forget the drama for one evening.'

'Blasphemy,' hissed Kerry.

'The only thing we forget are morals and the basic rules of mathematics,' snapped Imogen. 'How dare you condemn us to an evening with Belfast's answer to the *Inbetweeners*!'

'Why don't we just try to make the best of it?' asked Catherine.

'Listen,' whispered Imogen, stepping in very close to her, 'if you don't drop this Hannah Montana act, I am going to tear you a new ho—'

'Hey!' called Blake. 'The guys are here.'

'Could you please tell Troy Bolton over there that this kind of never-ending enthusiasm of his is making me more nauseous than a seasick bulimic?' said Meredith, turning away and returning to her seat.

'Where's my drink?' asked Imogen.

'Coming right up,' said Kerry. 'I'll make it a double.'

'Oh, we're so past the point of using normal measurements,' said Cameron.

The atmosphere around the campfire was initially so divided it looked like someone had built the thirty-eighth parallel down the middle. As the guys sat bantering with their lagers, beers and ciders, the clique simmered on the other side of the fire, with their entire attitude being summed up by the chain-smoking Imogen, pouting in absolute fury at this social ambush, and Meredith, sitting in her fur coat, with enormous sunglasses (despite the pitch-black night), sipping a bottle of Dom Perignon out of a straw. Blake and Catherine had kept up a steady stream of conversation, but it was only when Cameron, now slightly tipsy and incredibly bored, finally agreed to make smors that things began to thaw a little.

'Let's play Never Have I Ever,' suggested Peter. 'It's always good for a laugh.'

'O Sweet Jesus, what have I done to deserve this?' prayed Meredith.

'I'll start,' said Peter. 'Everyone got enough to drink? Right. Never have I ever cheated on a test in school.'

Stewart and Catherine drank. Cameron, Imogen and Kerry all downed their drinks and Meredith took a hearty sip from the straw still bobbing at the top of her Dom Perignon bottle. 'Does that time in Biology count as cheating?' asked Kerry.

'Yes,' answered Cameron.

'What happened in Biology?' said Blake.

'Well, we had a test and Kerry said she had actually revised for this one. Of course that meant we had to freeze her out as punishment, but when the test started we all copied off her anyway. Unfortunately, the only word she could remember was "synapse", so the four of us ended up answering "synapse" for all thirty-three questions.'

'I remember that,' laughed Stewart. 'We had to pass the tests round to mark each other's and I got yours.'

'I don't think I even ended up spelling "synapse" right, either,' said Cameron.

'You really didn't,' said Stewart. 'There's no x in it.'

'Never have I ever, um, shoplifted,' said Blake. Catherine, Kerry and Stewart drank. Kerry, who was already quite drunk by this stage, threw her head melodramatically into her hands. 'It was a pick 'n' mix,' she confessed. 'I was seven. I wanted a Milk Dud. I've never told anyone that before.'

'Never have I ever been promised a sleepover but actually found myself forced to sleep outside in the field like some dirty moo-cow,' said Meredith, taking Catherine's go. Imogen, Kerry and Cameron knocked back their drinks.

'Never have I ever had a crush on a teacher,' said Imogen. Everyone except Blake, Catherine and Meredith drank.

'Never have I ever kissed anyone around this campfire,' said Kerry, feigning innocence, but secretly reckoning that it was a good way of trying to see if Cameron's mystery kiss was here. Everyone around the fire, except Meredith, drank.

'Who've you kissed Cameron? You sneaky fucker!' laughed Peter.

'Me,' answered Imogen quickly. 'We did it as a dare ages ago.'

Cameron turned to Imogen and looked at her, suddenly aware that she must know about him and Blake. He had drunk instinctively, before he had even thought about the consequences, and Imogen had swept in immediately to get him out of trouble. Meredith too was staring at Imogen, raising her sunglasses on to her head and then catching Cameron's eye. How she knew, neither of them had any idea, but amid the panic it was at least a relief to know that, despite being left out of the loop, Imogen still remembered whose side she was supposed to be on.

'Never have I ever had sex,' said Cameron, quickly plucking the most obvious proposition from thin air. Peter drank, of course, but slightly more surprisingly so did Catherine and then a shamefaced Stewart. Meredith and Kerry both sucked air through clenched teeth, aware of how badly Imogen would react to this; Imogen, cigarette frozen halfway to her mouth, looked as if she had been hit in the face with a shovel.

'Who?' she asked, totally forgetting to play it cool and letting the cigarette fall from her hand.

'Just this girl at New Year's,' he said, not meeting her eye.

'Right. Yeah. No. Good. Whatever. Great. OK. I need more to drink.'

Kerry made her a concoction that was fifty-fifty peach schnapps and lemonade, hurling the schnapps into the glass in a wild hurry, as Meredith placed a fresh cigarette in Imogen's mouth and lit it.

'Never have I ever passed out drunk,' said Mark, changing the subject to spare Stewart any further embarrassment, but secretly enjoying Imogen's obvious indignation. Stewart, Mark, Cameron, Kerry, Peter and Imogen drank.

'You have to down your whole drink, mate,' said Peter. 'If you propose and you did it, it's a boast. Down it, down it, down it! And then you have to tell how it happened.'

After downing a can of beer, Mark confessed. 'The first time, I was fifteen. We did, like, four shots on the school football tour and I blacked out in the hotel corridor.'

'What a fascinating story,' said Meredith sarcastically. 'Can I please record it and use it as my ring-tone?'

'I'll tell you what you can do with it,' snapped Mark. 'You can –'

'Oh, please don't try to be witty, Mark. It would be pathetic beyond the point of funny.'

'Never have I ever had a wank on a plane,' said Peter.

'Classy,' whispered Meredith to Imogen. But Imogen didn't hear her; she was still too busy fuming at Stewart's revelation. Mark, Stewart, Blake and Catherine all drank.

'Catherine, what are you doing?' asked Cameron. 'That's biologically impossible.'

'I know,' slurred Catherine. 'I haven't done it. So . . .'

'Oh my God,' sighed Meredith. 'You propose something you haven't done, but you drink if you have! Why do you always forget the point of this game?'

'I don't know,' smiled Catherine drunkenly. 'You're pretty.'

'You are lucky we figured this out, Catherine. For a moment there I thought you were a kleptomaniacal slut.'

Blake, who had a relatively low alcohol tolerance, had now sunk into maudlin, faux 'deep and meaningful' drunkenness and did what all people like that do to a game of Never Have I Ever – he dragged it down. 'Never have I ever contemplated suicide,' he said slowly. Meredith rolled her eyes. No one except Blake drank, which was staggeringly uncomfortable for everyone else involved.

'Never even contemplated it, Mark?' asked Meredith sweetly.

'I wouldn't want to give you the pleasure, Meredith.'

Just then, Catherine threw up over herself.

'Good,' said Imogen savagely.

'Maybe we should put her in the recovery position?' asked Kerry.

'Or just see how it plays out?' suggested Meredith.

'We should probably get her changed,' said Stewart. 'Do any of you have a spare top she can borrow?'

'No,' lied Kerry, Meredith and Imogen in unison.

'Well, we can't leave her here covered in sick,' said Stewart.

'Why?' asked Meredith. 'It helps cover up that hideous top she's wearing.'

'I'll go and get her a sweater from her bedroom,' sighed Imogen.

'But what about her sister?' asked Kerry.

'I won't go into the dining room or her bedroom and I'll be quiet. Plus, I need to pee.'

'Wait for me and I'll come with you,' said Stewart. 'I don't want you tripping over on the way to the house.'

'No, that's not necessary, Stewart. I wouldn't want to get in the way of you having sex with some random tramp.'

'What?'

Picking up a roll of toilet paper, Peter began to move away over to the bushes. 'Well, I have a call of nature to take too. I'll be right back.'

'Hold on, mate,' said Mark. 'I'll come with you.'

'No, mate, that'd be a bit weird.'

'Shut up, it'll be just like using a urinal.'

'Not that kind of call,' laughed Peter. 'I'm going to bend a fresh biscuit over there.'

'Fair enough, I'll meet you back here.'

Peter's horrifyingly graphic description of what he was about to do settled over the group's consciousness. True to form, Meredith did not betray one flicker of a facial reaction, which is what she always did when she heard something unpardonably gross. Cameron rolled his eyes and returned to his drink, while Kerry looked perplexed. 'Bend a fresh biscuit? I don't even know what that . . . MEANS!' She screamed the last word and covered her face in horror, finally realizing what had been discussed.

As Peter walked off chuckling, Imogen stormed towards the house to fetch a coat and sweater for the vomit-clad Catherine, who had now slumped on to a rather unimpressed Blake. Stewart chased after her. 'Imogen, are you annoyed about me having sex?'

'No!' she snapped, skidding to a halt and spinning round to glare at him in magnificently self-righteous fury. 'Why would I be? We broke up.'

'Because you cheated on me.'

'Oh! So this is all my fault?'

'Yes.'

'What a typical man! Look, Stewart, if you were happy enough to throw your virginity away on some perma-tanned, short-skirted, lager-swilling, happy-slapping slut, then that's your decision. I just don't think I should have to hear about it.'

'Firstly, Amanda wasn't like that −'

'Oh! It has a name!'

'Secondly, at least you only heard about it and not saw it happen in front of you at your best friend's birthday,' shouted Stewart. 'You broke my heart and now you're trying to take the moral high ground. Too far, Imogen. Even for you.'

'I just think you should be aware that . . . um . . . eight out of ten teenage girls in the UK have chlamydia. It isn't safe.'

'I've only had sex once. And that statistic is clearly untrue.'

'Well,' answered Imogen prissily, 'I'm sure you'd know more about STD statistics than I do.' She flounced off towards the house and Stewart followed after her.

Back at the campsite, Blake had stood up and looked fairly shaky himself. 'I think I need to go for a walk,' he said.

'Cameron will go with you,' answered Meredith quickly. 'I'll take care of Catherine.'

'That'd be really nice,' nodded Blake, looking at Cameron hopefully.

'Thanks, Meredith,' said Cameron, in a *very* false cheery tone.

As the two boys wandered off, with Cameron's back ramrod straight as they departed, Mark, Meredith and Kerry were the only ones left at the campfire who had the ability left to speak. Catherine's head was lolling all over Meredith's shoulder and Meredith was struggling to hide her expression of deep revulsion.

The mood was so incredibly awkward between Meredith and Mark that Kerry almost pounced on Peter when he returned. 'Peter, let's go look at the stars!' Clearly thinking he had scored for the evening, Peter winked at Mark and walked off with Kerry on his arm.

Mark continued to stare down at his beer bottle, picking off the label, before looking up to see a semi-comatose Catherine propped up on an indifferent Meredith's shoulder. Sensing his surprise at what he obviously thought was a charitable move on her part, Meredith quickly shoved Catherine off on to the ground.

Mark's glare of disapproval merely earned him a smirk.

Blake and Cameron had ended up standing beneath a couple of trees, next to a broken-down stone wall. 'Well, this is awkward,' said Cameron.

'I missed you.'

'No, you didn't.'

'Cameron, listen . . .'

'No, Blake. It's been four months since my birthday. You've ignored me, you've ended our friendship, you've taken my place with the guys and you're now dating one of my friends. Why the hell should I listen to anything you've got to say?'

'I was frightened. I was confused. I didn't know what to do,' said Blake, finally looking at Cameron's face. 'I don't know what to do or even who I am when I'm around you.'

'Well, that isn't my fault.'

'No, I know,' he said, in a fraught tone. 'But I . . . Cameron, I don't . . . I'm afraid.'

'And you think this has been totally easy for me?'

'No! That's not what I meant.'

'You don't know what you mean, Blake. You're such a pathetic loser!' snapped Cameron, suddenly overcome by anger towards him. 'You just don't get it, do you? To Catherine, you're this perfect guy, the perfect boyfriend, but really you're just using her to make yourself feel better. And she doesn't deserve to go through that, because believe me, Blake, no one should have to lie down alone in bed at night and go over and over in their head how they could've been so wrong about you!'

'Since when have you ever cared about Catherine?'

'Excuse me?'

'Don't get so self-righteous with me, Cameron. Remember, I know what you really think of Catherine. You told me you have no idea why you're still friends with her and it's probably because she's too stupid to realize how much you all secretly hate her!'

'That's not what I said and that's not the point!' retorted Cameron. 'And even if we aren't very good friends to her, what gives you the right to even say that to me? Do you really think you've been such a great boyfriend that you can criticize how other people treat her?'

'I've made her happy,' said Blake helplessly. 'I've tried to. And . . . and, well, I never meant to hurt you, Cameron.'

'You didn't? So, what . . . you're just retarded?'

'Hey, hold on a minute! This worked both ways, Cameron. This worked *both* ways. You didn't come to speak to me, either. You didn't say anything to me when I started dating Catherine and you haven't once given me any sign that you were upset or sorry about any of this! Am I supposed to be some kind of magical mind-reader and just guess what you're feeling? You decided that rather than make any effort and risk being rejected, you'd just do *nothing* instead. So, why don't you shut up and stop yelling at me for something that isn't my fault?'

At that moment, the heavens above them opened and it began to rain. 'Oh, great!' yelled Cameron, flinging his arms up in frustration. 'This is just what I need. Not only am I standing in the middle of a fucking field with the person in the world I hate the most, but now I'm also getting soaked. Just great, God. Thanks a lot!'

'You hate me?' Blake looked at Cameron in devastated shock, oblivious to the torrential rain now soaking them both.

'Are you an idiot?' Cameron hissed. 'Are you actually missing a chromosome? Of course I hate you! There is no one in the entire school I hate more than you, because there is no one who has ever done to me what you did! And it was *your* fault!'

'Look, I'm sorry, OK? For whatever you think I've done, I'm sorry! It wasn't easy for me, either, Cameron. I missed you. I wasn't lying about that. I missed you – and I meant what I said the first night we had dinner together. I'm so, so glad we're friends.'

'*Were*, Blake, *were*. At least get the tense right, you moron. It's *were*, not *are*.'

'Cameron . . .'

'Friends? Don't touch me!' Cameron threw off the arm Blake had stretched out towards him. 'Whatever we were, Blake, you threw it all away over a kiss, which obviously meant nothing!'

'It didn't mean nothing, Cameron.'

'Well, it did to me,' lied Cameron.

'No. It didn't,' said Blake, pulling him by the scruff of his sweater and kissing him again.

Back at the campsite, Meredith decided to run for the shelter of the trees, forgetting that poor Catherine had slumped back against her, as the unfortunate girl flopped forward with her skirt up over her waist.

'U-um . . . those are her pants,' Mark stuttered awkwardly.

'Yes, Mark, those are her pants,' muttered Meredith sarcastically, hiking Catherine's skirt back down with the heel of her shoe. 'You can tell they're hers by the fetching Winnie-the-Pooh design.'

'Just help me get her under that tree,' said Mark gruffly. 'Otherwise she'll get soaked.'

'Yes, well, if she had planned the party inside then maybe this wouldn't be happening.'

'Just help me.'

Mark put Catherine's arm over his shoulder and Meredith technically did the same, but she certainly wasn't carrying any of the weight. Once they had deposited her under the tree, Mark and Meredith stood under its shelter, watching as the rain became torrential. Mark desperately tried to ignore the huge knot in his stomach at being left alone with her. He had imagined a moment like this a thousand times since that evening in her library, but when it came to it, it turned out that the Mark in his head was a good deal sterner and far more eloquent than the real Mark, who simply stood tongue-tied and strangely bereft of the desire to take advantage of this perfect opportunity to upbraid Meredith for what she had said.

He glanced over at Meredith; the wind and rain had left her usually perfect, shiny and smooth hair all tousled and wind-swept. She looked almost normal. Still utterly beautiful, certainly, but now he found that all he could think about was her words, back in her library: *Now we're both ashamed of our parents.* Mark tried to fight the overwhelming sense of feeling protective towards her – after all, he had only had to deal with this for a few months; she'd had to deal with it for years.

Meredith sensed his gaze. 'Yes?' she said, turning to regard him, scowling, as if he was responsible for the weather.

Mark desperately willed his brain to come up with something he could say to her that would disguise the fact that he had been thinking only about the person who was meant to be his arch enemy for the past five minutes. 'Er . . . well . . . You have a twig in your hair.'

'What?'

'A twig . . . in your . . . Hold still.' He reached out and extracted a small twig. It could have been his imagination but he thought he saw Meredith tense. 'There.' Not sure what to say next and lost for words again, Mark looked straight ahead and shuffled. *What was wrong with him? Why was he acting like such a girl?*

Meredith regarded him with some confusion for a second and then decided she was uncomfortable with the strange feeling Mark's action had caused. 'Your fly's been open since you got here.' And with that, she turned her back to him and fished her BlackBerry out of her handbag.

Damn it! thought Mark. Shuffling away from her slightly, he pulled up his zipper with what little dignity he had left. *Next time, I'm getting those jeans with the buttons on them.*

Further awkwardness was mercifully prevented when, from the gloom, Kerry came into view, piggybacking on Peter's shoulders, squealing, 'My curls. My curls! Frizz alert, frizz alert! *Emergencia!*'

Seeing Kerry return so unexpectedly, Meredith inhaled in sheer panic about what Kerry and Peter might think if they returned to see Mark zipping up his fly. Luckily, Mark had executed the task more quickly than she had anticipated, but he felt the change in her body language and saw the fear in her face.

'It's OK,' he said reassuringly. 'They didn't see anything.'

'Thank you,' she muttered, before turning her body towards the approaching Kerry and acting as if she could no longer see or hear Mark Kingston in any way.

*

In the warmth of the nearby house, Imogen sat on the floor of a darkened corridor outside the bathroom with one of Catherine's hoodies in her hands. Stewart sat next to her. 'I'm sorry you had to find out about the girl,' he said. 'It didn't mean anything and it wasn't what I wanted. If it makes you feel any better, it was awful . . . just awful. It should've been you.'

'But it wasn't,' said Imogen quietly, 'and I've only myself to blame for that.'

'Maybe I wasn't a good enough boyfriend?'

'No, Stewart, I'm just not a good enough person.'

Stewart took her free hand. 'Well, it's over now, Imogen. Maybe some day, we'll . . . I don't know.'

Footsteps came down the stairs and Catherine's pretty seventeen-year-old sister, Orla, appeared in front of them. 'Oh my God, are you guys the only ones who've come in?' she asked.

'Yes,' said Imogen. 'Catherine got sick, so we came to get her a top. The others are still out there.'

'She's so silly,' tutted Orla. 'Go and get everyone! There are plenty of spare rooms and sofas. Just . . .'

'Don't come into yours?' smiled Imogen. 'Thanks, and happy anniversary!'

'Thanks,' giggled Orla. 'I can't believe it's been two years!'

'We'll go grab the others,' said Stewart, rising from the floor.

'There's an umbrella just there by the door,' said Orla as she returned upstairs. 'Night!'

'Actually, you stay here,' said Stewart to Imogen. 'I'll go and get them myself . . . I just totally wasted my breath saying that, didn't I?'

'Yes. There is no way in hell I'm going back out there.'

Stewart chuckled and stepped out into the freezing night,

looking around him for the others. The campfire had been totally extinguished, making it much harder for him to see clearly, but some light was coming from the windows of Catherine's house, so that was something at least. Preparing to clamber over the stone wall at the back of the garden, Stewart saw two of his friends a few metres ahead of him. He was about to call out, when he realized they were both kissing – and that it was two guys.

Shocked, he immediately turned his back and moved further away, climbing over the wall when he got there.

'Stew!' It was Mark's voice, calling from a tree in the middle of the field. Running over to it and ducking his head against the rain, Stewart arrived under the swaying branches to see Catherine slumped against the trunk, Kerry cuddling up to Peter while simultaneously trying to reinvigorate her curls, Mark leaning against the tree waiting for the rain to stop and Meredith maniacally waving her arms around trying to get a signal on her mobile, presumably to call Malmaison and book a room.

'Where are Cameron and Blake?' asked Stewart. Immediately, Meredith's eyes flickered over him, quickly scrutinizing him before her face became impassive once again. 'Blake didn't feel well, so they went for a walk,' she answered. 'They must be by one of the trees over there.'

'Orla's told us to come on in and spend the night. I think you could call Cameron or text him,' he said, looking directly at her. 'Tell them to meet us back in the house.'

Meredith held his stare for a split second and then, accepting she now wasn't the only one who knew, nodded. She tossed her fur to Kerry to make sure it didn't get wet. 'Fine. I don't have any signal, but I'll go and get them. The rest of you can go back to the house.'

Putting up her umbrella, Meredith trudged across the field, trying to figure out the chain that had led to both Stewart and Imogen knowing the truth about Cameron. Judging from Stewart's look just now, he had seen them together somewhere in the field and they were presumably kissing again – or more. But she still couldn't work out how Imogen knew. And, more importantly, had she told anyone else?

Just ahead of her, she saw the two of them, apparently oblivious to the rain, very close to one another and for a moment, Meredith stood watching them, a feeling of the deepest irritation shooting through her body.

At that moment, the wind caught her umbrella and turned it inside out above her head, snapping two of the spokes. God, even Burberry was trying to sabotage her tonight! She tossed the umbrella to one side and walked over to them, tapping Blake on the shoulder. The noise of the rain had muffled her steps until the very last minute, so both of them jumped when they realized someone was next to them.

'We're going into the house,' she announced. 'Orla's said we can. Thank God. Let's go.'

Blake nodded and looked at her, trying to gauge exactly what she knew. Meredith's face gave him no answer; Cameron's too seemed to have settled into one of cryptic impassivity and Blake shrugged his shoulders, making to follow after Meredith as they moved towards the house.

'How much does she know about us?' he whispered to Cameron, as they walked along together, side by side.

'She knows everything,' Cameron answered. 'She always does.'

When they arrived in the house, they could hear Imogen screeching from upstairs. 'Oh for God's sake! Just put her in the recovery position and leave her and . . . oh my God, stop being sick on my shoes, you drunken bitch!'

'What if she dies in the middle of the night?' asked Kerry, in a voice that came very close to sounding like it cared.

'Then it's God's Will for what she's done to us tonight and . . . Catherine! For fuck's sake! There's a bowl – right there! My shoes are not your target!'

'You're right,' Kerry agreed far too easily. 'And, anyway, I need to wash my hair and get it recurled. I've got tongs in my bag . . .'

'But it's two a.m. We need to get to bed,' said Imogen.

'There isn't time for sleep!' Kerry squealed. 'We are on the verge of major frizzdom and . . . CATHERINE! Bowl!'

The doors to Catherine's bedroom closed and their voices were drowned out. 'I should go and sort this out,' said Meredith wearily. 'Wait here.'

Emerging from a door on their left, Stewart stood still for a moment, looking at the two boys. There was a tense silence as Stewart took measure of the situation. Then he stepped forward, wrapped Cameron in the biggest bear hug imaginable and walked off, nodding at Blake as he did so with a smile.

Cameron smiled at Blake.

But Blake didn't return the smile. 'Stewart knows too?'

'Apparently,' Cameron said quickly, looking at Blake and feeling slightly confused. 'But I didn't tell him. Is it a problem? It's just Stewart – you know him.'

'No, I know you didn't . . .' Blake nodded slowly. He took Cameron's hand and led him down the hall. 'Ignore me, it can wait until the morn–'

'Right, all sorted,' said Meredith, swiftly reappearing from Catherine's room where terrifyingly deafening silence now reigned. 'Cameron, you're coming with me.'

'No, we're cool,' said Blake.

Meredith raised a perfectly plucked eyebrow and smiled coldly. 'Cameron, you're coming with me.'

'Am I?'

'I think it would be best. After all, this is Catherine's house,' she said authoritatively. 'You're sleeping with me tonight.'

Cameron gently disengaged himself from Blake. 'She's right,' he sighed. 'It would be better if we didn't stay in the same room, especially in this house. I'm sorry.'

Blake rolled back his head and sighed. 'That's fine. But come see me in the morning.'

'OK.' Cameron smiled. He was about to kiss him again, but he was suddenly conscious of Meredith standing next to them and became sheepish.

'You think I'm going to tell you to kiss him goodnight and express your feelings,' she said, 'but you're wrong. Let's go.'

Mark's temporary bedroom was decorated with one or two religious pictures and an awful lot of Disney merchandise, which led him to assume it was the bedroom of Catherine's ten-year-old sister, Caoimhe.

His jeans were soaking and as he struggled out of them he lurched backwards into a chest of drawers, knocking over a statuette of the Virgin Mary and a Sharpay Evans Barbie doll. Laying his sodden clothes over the back of the chair and on the radiator, which mercifully had been switched on by a kind-hearted Orla, Mark glanced at the photographs lining the wall. There was one of Caoimhe at her first Holy Communion, dressed all in white like a tiny bride, next to another of Catherine and Caoimhe at a pony-club competition. Mark's smile faltered slightly when he saw one of Caoimhe smiling amid a group of Catherine's friends. The photograph had obviously been taken downstairs in the O'Rourkes' dining room, some night before the girls had headed out into Belfast. Caoimhe, still dressed in her school uniform, was posing with a grin on her face between Catherine, Imogen, Kerry, Cameron and Meredith. Even at the age of ten, Mark reflected, this girl had obviously caught the dangerous bug of wanting to be part of the 'in' crowd. If Caoimhe had any sense, she would see what it had done to her sister's self-esteem and stay well away.

Mark's eyes lingered on the photographic Meredith – her hair perfectly styled, her skin luminously pale and her smile confident. This was the Meredith that everyone knew – cold, perfect, aloof. The Meredith who, however in the right Mark knew he was, still managed to get a rise out of him every time they spoke. But tonight Mark had sensed something else – something more. The combined effects of wind, rain and fatigue had given Meredith a vulnerability that Mark had only ever glimpsed once before – that night of their heated exchange in the library.

Much to his annoyance, Mark's heart flipped as he wondered whether he was the only one who'd ever seen Meredith's Empress of Winter crown slip. Why him of all people in her life? Exasperated, Mark ran his hand through his hair and sighed. He was probably being an idiot and reading too much into the whole thing. Was there anything he could think about these days besides Meredith Harper?

He climbed into the bed, yanking up the pink-and-white Princess Jasmine sheets that Kerry would have found utterly delightful, and tried to get some sleep. If he could only be certain that Meredith wasn't having similar thoughts right now, perhaps he could just forget about tonight and put her out of his mind. But, as ever with Meredith Harper, Mark didn't seem to be able to control his thoughts, no matter how hard he tried.

Pulling the pillow over his face, Mark groaned with frustration at himself, at Meredith and the whole situation. He stayed like that for most of the night, with a face full of Disney, trying to blot out the fevered screams of Kerry Davison as the maniacal deployment of her hairspray can echoed softly from the far corners of the house.

In one of the guest rooms, Imogen had changed into her pyjamas, taken a huge drink of water to stave off a hangover and climbed into bed. The door opened and Stewart stepped softly into the room. 'Can I stay with you tonight?'

Imogen nodded and Stewart removed his soaked jumper, T-shirt, socks and trousers. He climbed in next to her wearing only his boxers – a pair of Calvin Kleins Imogen had bought him months earlier.

'Whoever got you those must have had some seriously classy good taste,' she said.

'Yeah,' smiled Stewart, spooning her. 'She was pretty great.'

The rain was pounding against the windows as the two of them snuggled against one another contentedly. The pain of Imogen's betrayal with Michael seemed to be forgotten, but at the back of her mind Imogen still knew that they weren't ready to get back together again. Stewart certainly wasn't, as much as he clearly loved her, otherwise he wouldn't have spent the best part of the last four months avoiding her. After sitting with him in the hall below and remembering how much she missed being near him, how comfortable they had been together and how well he knew her, she regretted more than anything that they hadn't had a better ending to something that had – at times – been a wonderful relationship. Still, she could change that, because tonight could be a goodbye, a sort of fond farewell and acknowledgement of how happy they had been for over a year, before she had ruined it for the sake of her own vanity and entertainment.

Lying with Stewart's arms round her once more, Imogen could finally appreciate just how badly she had behaved and how her friends had encouraged her. Every last one of them had been prepared to feed her comforting lies, rather than awkward truths. And now, she thought, they were repeating the same cycle with Cameron. All of them, bar Catherine, knew that Cameron was gay. She had seen it tonight in Meredith's face when Cameron slipped up and drank during the game of Never Have I Ever. Meredith had known, for God knows how long, presumably from Cameron's own lips. And what were they doing about it? Nothing.

Cameron's drink narrowed it down to only four people – Blake, Mark, Peter or Stewart. Sheer logistics dictated that it couldn't have been Stewart (leaving out that Imogen knew better than anyone that he wasn't gay) because he had left the birthday party in December before the kiss had happened; Peter, who was admittedly so wild and badly behaved that it was hard to say what he would find funny to do when drunk, had still been in the kitchen, as far as Imogen could remember, which meant it had to have been either Mark or Blake. Had the fight been about more than Mark's parents and Imogen's affair? Had Cameron and Mark fallen out because they had kissed, then panicked? Or was Kerry right – had it been Blake? Was Blake's totally unexpected relationship with Catherine some sort of desperate cover-up? There were so many questions, none of which any of them had apparently bothered to try to answer. Instead, they had spent four months either ignoring the problem or selfishly trying to prevent somebody else knowing more about it than they did. Kerry and Imogen had both taken the decision not to tell Meredith within twelve hours of the kiss happening and Meredith had been more than happy to cover the whole thing up herself without ever asking for the advice or help of her two girlfriends.

'What are you thinking about?' asked Stewart.

'Where's Cameron sleeping tonight?'

Stewart's arms tightened round her. 'The fact that you asked means I'm guessing you know where.'

'How did you know?'

'I saw them kissing outside, just now,' he answered. 'I take it it's not the first time?'

'No,' said Imogen. She knew Stewart too well; if she revealed she didn't know who the other guy was, then he would be far too honourable to tell her. She had to keep on pretending she knew all the major details. 'It's not the first time, you're right . . . So, where's everyone else sleeping tonight?'

'I'm not sure. I'm pretty sure Meredith is taking the parents' bedroom, Kerry's going to take Joanne's room but she's washing her hair or something . . .'

'Curl crisis,' said Imogen. 'It's massively urgent. She'll look like Simba in the morning if it's not fixed immediately.'

Stewart laughed. 'Peter's taken a sofa downstairs, I think, Mark's in one of the other bedrooms, and Cameron and Blake are obviously in the attic bedroom upstairs.'

'Yeah,' said Imogen thoughtfully. 'I suspected they would be.'

A comfortable silence settled over the two of them, broken only by the sound of the storm outside. The weather had been a lot like this the night they had broken up, she remembered. She had run out of her house from Cameron's birthday, trying to catch up with Stewart, but he had already vanished. Her thoughts shifted to Cameron and Blake and what an unholy mess the whole thing had turned into. In her head, she cursed Blake for dragging Catherine into the situation and wondered how Cameron had possibly managed to cope with watching them together, more or less every day since Valentine's Day. Repression over honesty again, she thought. And it was Meredith and Cameron who were chiefly responsible for it.

After all, in their entire friendship, the only time Imogen had ever seen Meredith cry was when she had a migraine so severe that her vision had actually started to falter. Even when her mother had left, Kerry had told her that Meredith kept the whole thing bottled up. At her grandfather's funeral two years ago, Meredith had appeared looking immaculate, with the only sign of her grief being how pale she was. Cameron, so free with so many of his emotions, drew a firm line at revealing anything that might make him look vulnerable, careful to the point of paranoid about appearing weak. Even Kerry, who cried at the drop of a hat and shared every tiny, petty emotion that popped into her head, had never once discussed any deeper feelings. Of course, Imogen didn't exactly want to be one of those hippy freaks with dirty fingernails who lolled around on bean bags endlessly discussing their neuroses, fears and deep, oh-so-impor-tant emotions, but given the carnage that the group's policy of Fabulousness Before Feelings had wreaked on her private life, as well as Cameron's – not to mention Catherine's, by the look of things – maybe it was time that they took the risk of telling each other unpleasant truths once in a while, and not about things like hair, shoes, make-up and clothes. Well, not *just* about things like hair, shoes, make-up and clothes.

Stroking Stewart's arm as she pondered her newfound wisdom, Imogen felt unexpectedly sorry for her ex. She knew how much he regretted losing his virginity to a random girl at a drunken party. That kind of thing just wasn't who Stewart was; it was who Peter was, sure, but it wasn't Stewart. She shuddered as she thought about the close escape she had had with Michael the Odious Immaculate Heart Sex Pest.

Stewart was right – their first time should have been with each other, but that could never happen now. Stewart had slept with someone else and Imogen had hurt him so much that getting back together was never going to be an option, at least not for a very long time. This realization hurt, but in the spirit of looking life in the face, Imogen decided that there was only one thing she wanted to do. It would be the perfect goodbye. She turned round to face Stewart and smiled. His eyes had closed and he was dozing contentedly. Imogen gently stroked his cheek and he slowly opened his eyes. 'What is it?' he asked softly, smiling at how beautiful she looked, with her blonde hair complementing her pale skin.

'I love you,' she answered, leaning in to kiss him and wrap-ping her arms round his neck.

*

The morning dawned cold and clear; Catherine had assumed the foetal position in her bed and was moaning in agony at her hangover. Orla was still curled up in bed with her boyfriend; Peter was passed out snoring on a sofa in the living room and Kerry was sleeping in a guest bedroom, her curls restored, wearing her sleeping mask reading *THE PRINCESS IS SLEEPING* in pink diamanté. Cameron woke early in bed next to a slumbering Meredith and he moved quickly, quietly, so as not to disturb her. Hurriedly pulling on his jeans, he slipped down the corridor, trying desperately to fix his hair as he moved up the narrow staircase to the attic bedroom. He paused outside the door and breathed deeply, steadying himself, before knocking softly and slipping inside.

The bed lay in front of him, unmade and empty. At the back of his mind, he could feel the panic building, but a tiny glimmer of hope made him think – even pray – that he was wrong. He turned round and walked back down the stairs again, where he almost collided with a hungover Mark, making his way to the bathroom.

'Have you seen Blake?'

Even through the pain of post-beer brain, Mark looked taken aback at Cameron speaking to him after four months of ostentatious silence. 'Ehm . . . no. Sorry, I mean, yes. Yeah. He left about an hour ago. He said he had to get back to Carryduff for church. Why?'

'No reason. Did he leave a message?'

'Just for Catherine. He said he'd call by to take her out for dinner later.'

For a moment, Cameron felt as if he had been punched in the stomach and every single function of his body, right down to breathing, had stopped. Blake was gone. He had left. And there was no good reason to explain why he had – except the worst.

'Thank you,' he said, turning away from a puzzled-looking Mark. He made his way back up to the attic and sat on the edge of the bed, still in a state of utter shock. For a few moments, Cameron simply stared down, unseeing, at the floor, as all the things Blake had said to him last night resurfaced in his mind. Swiftly, suddenly, the numbness had gone and a bolt of pure rage shot through Cameron so fiercely that he leapt up from where he was sitting. He could actually feel his muscles twitching and reacting to how angry he was. The door was pushed open to reveal a curious Meredith, still in her negligee, casting her eyes imperiously around the room, only for them to flicker with the realization that Blake had left. Seeing it written all over his friend's face, Cameron hurled a punch at the wall. There was a horrible thud as his fist hit the wall and Meredith stood there, her mouth hanging open slightly in shock, as Cameron grabbed his bleeding knuckles and turned away from her.

Meredith walked down to the room Imogen had occupied for the night. Knocking on the guest-bedroom door and entering, she saw Imogen perched on the window seat, with a businesslike look on her face.

'I saw Blake leaving earlier. I take it that loud smack on the wall was Cameron?'

'Yes, he's very upset.'

'I see. So, when do we start ruining Blake Hartman's life?'

Meredith smiled at her friend's question and closed the door behind her.

*

Later that afternoon, after they had left a mostly silent Cameron back home, Meredith and Imogen sat in the back of the Harpers' chauffeured Mercedes, sipping two Diet Cokes they had bought from the garage at the top of the Malone Road.

'So, when did you know?' asked Meredith.

'Kerry saw them kiss at Cameron's birthday party,' said Imogen, 'but she didn't know who it was. She ran into Cameron at the bottom of the stairs during the black-out, so she could never figure out who the other guy was. She still hasn't. When did you find out?'

'Cameron told me just before we came home from Dublin. I didn't tell you because . . .'

'You didn't trust me,' finished Imogen, 'and you wanted to be the only one to know. It's OK. I was the same.'

'So, when did Stewart find out?'

'Last night. When he went outside to bring everyone in, he saw them kissing. That's how I found out it was Blake. Before Stewart let it slip they were together I was pretty convinced it was Mark.'

'And you don't think he'll tell anyone?'

'No, definitely not. You know Stewart. He's too good to gossip.'

'I.e. too boring.'

Imogen continued, ignoring the jibe. 'So that's everyone who knows: you, me, Stewart, Blake and Cameron . . .?'

'And Catherine,' said Meredith.

'What!'

'I told her when they started going out. I wanted to warn her and spare Cameron the pain, but she just wouldn't listen,' lied Meredith. 'And there's a lot of other very complicated reasons, which I promise I will explain to you later once we've thought this thing through. But swear you won't tell anyone I told her? It would only humiliate Cameron even more if he knew one of his friends had gone out with Blake, knowing the truth.'

'I swear.'

'Swear to Mary,' demanded Meredith, knowing that Imogen's Catholic guilt was a powerful but little-used weapon in the gossip wars.

'I swear to the Virgin,' replied Imogen, crossing herself piously to prove the point. 'And you're sure we should wait a week before sabotaging Blake?'

'Yes,' ruled Meredith, nodding decisively. 'A lot can happen in a week. It'll give him a chance to fix things, in case this morning was just a momentary spaz, and, if he doesn't, we have a week to decide what to do.'

'Ugh. He's too weak. He won't fix things,' said Imogen knowingly.

Meredith smiled and stared out of the window. 'Then let the games begin.'

12

The Curious Incident
of the Birthday Piñata

As Imogen and Meredith were busy scheming in the back of the Mercedes, Kerry crawled into her house and plunged into a steaming hot bath. She then pampered herself shamelessly before snuggling down on her sofa to watch the only movie she knew would recharge her fabulousness after the horrific experience of last night's camping – *Marie Antoinette*. As she saw Kirsten Dunst get her new shoes while surrounded by a mountain of cakes, Kerry was also keen to forget the rather unpleasant moment last night when she had kissed Peter, again, despite that vile biscuit comment of his earlier in the evening. Thankfully the rain had rather conveniently interrupted them even though it did involve a Simba-hair crisis.

The Duchesse de Polignac had just burst into the Royal Opera Box when Kerry's pink phone began to ring. It was Catherine. Painfully aware that her favourite shoe-and-hair montage was about to begin onscreen, Kerry contemplated not answering, but her need to hear how much hangover agony Catherine was in temporarily outweighed her love of period-designed Manolos. She hit PAUSE.

'Hello?'

'Hi,' came a fragile voice from the other end of the line. 'I think I might be dying.'

'Yeah,' said Kerry.

'Is everyone mad at me?'

'Well, I don't think last night's going to go down as your finest performance ever.'

'I didn't know it was going to rain!'

'It was the camping that was the problem and then inviting the boys. You were lucky, Catherine. You got so drunk you passed out and you didn't have to camp any more! It was completely hideous.'

'I'm paying for it now and I think I'm having an FIB too.'

Kerry pursed her lips in an unimpressed fashion. Since when had it been OK for Catherine to claim she was even capable of suffering a Fabulous Induced Breakdown? Had the whole world gone completely mad? Also, didn't she know that you couldn't have an FIB when you were hungover? The whole point of an FIB was that you were feeling so overwhelmingly, terrifyingly fab/glam that you went into total meltdown. You couldn't do that if your head felt like someone was operating a pneumatic drill inside it and your tongue tasted like carpet. It really didn't sound as if Catherine was taking the whole nature of an FIB seriously at all.

'I'm freaking out about my birthday party,' Catherine continued. 'I haven't got anything planned and I've just looked at how many people are coming. There's so many of them, Kerry. I'm in such, such deep trouble. If I don't pull off a good party, it'll be like Meredith never said anything in the *Tatler* interview. I'll be on the A-minus-list again!'

'Probably more like B,' said Kerry. 'But that might not happen. Unless you ordered a clown. That could ruin you.'

'I don't know the first thing about actually planning a party,' squeaked Catherine hysterically.

'That's because you've been a hanger-on for so long that you've never had to host,' said Kerry sympathetically. 'Now you're one of the real popular girls, so everything's different. I hope you appreciate how much hard work it is being fabulous?'

'Sort of . . .'

'Good. Don't worry. I'll help you with this one,' said Kerry, becoming excited at the idea of being a party-planner again. 'I mean, do you want this to be lusciously themed or traditional?'

'What's the difference and stuff?'

'Well, a luscious theme involves enormous amounts of planning, some sort of dramatic centrepiece, costumes, theme-appropriate food and at least four Fabulous Induced Breakdowns.'

'And what about the traditional?'

'Order in a lot of alcohol, dress nice, play games, get drunk and congratulate each other on how fabulous we are.'

'I think I'd like a theme . . . Maybe.'

'You have to commit to a theme! You can't say *maybe*. It's very important, because you can't change it halfway through. Especially,' Kerry said accusingly, 'since we only have two weeks to plan this and get theme-appropriate invitations out and RSVPed to as well.'

'Couldn't we just use Facebook?'

'Maybe, but it doesn't look good for a major b-day party. Right, first things first: theme?'

'Me?'

'No.'

'Em . . . America?'

'No, because some boy will then think it's funny to turn up

as a Ku Klux Klan member or something equally politically incorrect, because boys are stupid and unfunny. Or some secret slut will use it as an excuse to come as a Playboy bunny.'

'Right . . .'

'Think!'

'Well, what about Mexico and stuff?' suggested Catherine. 'Because of, like, you know, the holiday.'

Kerry sat in a silence for a few moments, musing. 'Yes. That's . . .' Catherine waited with bated breath for *the* word, the word that she had longed to hear about one of her ideas for four long years: '. . . fabulous,' finished Kerry.

'Oh my God! Yay!'

'Right,' said Kerry. 'Let's get my notepad and start brainstorming. Oh! I mean mind-mapping. I'm *so* politically correct.'

'You're such a good person, Kerry.'

'I know, right?'

The boys' locker room was practically empty when Cameron entered it after school on Monday afternoon. Blake's locker was the one right next door and he looked temporarily panicked to see Cameron standing next to him, blazer in hand and schoolbag on shoulder, as he put his Spanish textbooks away.

Cameron stood next to him for a minute, in a silence that felt like it lasted for ten. 'Hi,' he said finally.

'Hi,' replied Blake, not taking his eyes off the books he was moving in and out of his locker.

'Are you seriously just going to ignore me?'

'I'm not ignoring you,' Blake snapped, turning to face him. 'I just said hi, didn't I?'

'That's a lot more than you said on Sunday morning – and a lot less than the night before.'

The look of panic swept over Blake's face again and he glanced nervously around to see if anyone was nearby. 'Keep your voice down!' Then he turned back and began rifling through his English books, focusing excessively on finding his copy of *Macbeth*. Cameron reached out and put his hand on the open locker door, blocking Blake's access with his arm.

'Are you really doing this to me? What's changed since that night of the party? You seemed fine when it was just you and me.'

Blake didn't turn to look at him this time, but just kept staring at the arm that stood between him and his locker. Cameron was pleased to see a mortified blush beginning to spread across Blake's face as he clenched his jaw in an effort to keep calm. 'I'm not doing anything to you. Look, what happened on Saturday was a mistake, OK? If you want everyone to know that you're *that* way, then that's fine, that's your choice. I don't have a problem with it, if you want to be that way, but I'm not the same as you, OK? I'm not.'

Cameron's hand stayed where it was, but his eyes glazed over slightly and his head sank down, no longer looking directly at Blake. He didn't speak and after a few seconds Blake turned to look at him, his face a perfect cross between anger and anguish. 'I didn't mean to hurt you, Cameron. I really, really didn't. Please don't look like this. You've no idea how bad I feel. But I can't do this. I'm not . . . y'know . . . like you . . .'

At that moment, the door behind Cameron swung open as a fourth-year boy sauntered in. The door would have hit Cameron squarely on the back of the head if Blake's hand hadn't shot out to stop it.

'Hey!' he shouted instinctively at the fourth-year. 'What the hell, dude? You could have hit his head! Watch where you're going, OK?'

The boy mumbled an apology and walked on as Blake turned his attention back to Cameron, pulling him in slightly.

'Would you come away from the door?' he snapped. 'Next time you'll get hit when it opens.'

Cameron had never heard Blake use any word stronger than 'damn'. Under normal circumstances, it would have seemed as strange as Kerry turning up in a Kappa tracksuit, but right there and then Cameron really didn't care. He remained standing, his face completely drained of all emotion.

Blake stared at the plasters and cuts on Cameron's hand. 'What happened to your hand?'

Cameron just shook his head. 'I thought you were wonderful. But I was wrong.' Then he turned and left as quickly as he could.

Cameron did not go in to school on Tuesday, nor did he go in on Wednesday. He spent most of his time lying on his bed and lying to his father. Luckily, Cameron's mother had gone to spend two weeks with her sister and it is always much easier to lie about your health to your father. By Thursday, the feelings of mortification and embarrassment – how, how could he have been stupid enough to believe Blake had wanted the same things as him? – had been replaced by a sort of dull, empty feeling. All he wanted to do was stay in his bed, thinking of nothing. On Friday, emotional repression gave way to a sense of heart-break so strong it made Cameron feel physically ill. He spent hours trawling through Facebook, looking at every picture of

Blake he could find. Each time he reached one of him with Catherine, he had to close the laptop. Cameron could not even take any pleasure in knowing that, as far as Blake was concerned, the game was up. No matter what he did from now on, there was absolutely no way he could outmanoeuvre the juggernaut of Meredith's vengeance against someone who had twice trespassed the boundaries of her group.

'Let's punch him in the penis.'

'No, Imogen.'

Imogen tossed her empty coffee cup into the bin on the first-floor Languages' corridor at Friday lunch-time. 'It's been a week! Clearly, he's not breaking up with Catherine. It's punishment time. We agreed!'

'The agreement was not that we'd wait until the end of the week then punch him in the genitals.'

'I think it's a super idea.'

'It wouldn't solve anything.'

'It would make me feel better – a quick thump to the testicles would teach him a *very* valuable lesson.'

Meredith sighed. She was bored with this line of conversation and Imogen eventually relinquished the idea of a crotch-crushing to review more realistic avenues of vengeance. 'So, tell me what the *exact* situation is with the whole Catherine–Blake–Cameron thing again, please.'

Meredith inhaled, preparing to give yet another virtuoso performance in lying. 'When Cameron told me Kerry thought it was me who told Michael about the party, I panicked and I knew Kerry wouldn't let it go until the whole thing was dragged out into one big mess. You see, I thought Michael had made the invitation thing up just to get back at you after you were so brave and walked away from him about the whole sex thing, but by that stage the truth really didn't matter because you know what it's like when Kerry gets an idea into her head and . . . well, I didn't want any more stress for us after everything that had happened, so I told Catherine to take the blame for it and after we negotiated it for *ages*, with Blake's secret and Mexico as the bait, she gave in.'

'But now you think she actually did tell Michael and was just using you?'

'I don't know,' Meredith sighed. 'Maybe . . . or maybe Michael was actually lying to Kerry and we all fell for it. Either way, if I look like I'm ruining her relationship with Blake, she'll tell everyone I did the same to you and Stewart.'

'And they'd think I was a fool for staying friends with you!' Imogen realized. 'So what can we do?'

'Catherine knows he's gay – at the very least, bisexual – and a liar,' Meredith continued, 'but, as much as she hates being used or lied to, she still loves the attention it's brought her a lot more.'

'Well, then we need to find a way of ending the attention, don't we?'

'Yes. We need to chip away at the only part of their relationship that's still working – the public side of it. We can't do anything to the private side, because of what she might do, and we can't run the risk of people finding out that they broke up because he's gay. At least, not yet. Not until Cameron's ready. If we start to make people think there's *something* weird about them as a couple or even just him on his own, all the good kind of attention they're getting will stop. Blake's only using her to increase his respectability and take attention *away* from his love life and she's only using him to make herself feel better. There's no *way* they'll stay together if all this stops. As long as Catherine never discovers it came from us, we'll be fine.'

'If she breaks up with him, though, what happens if she tells Cameron that you told her about their kiss?'

Meredith shook her head worriedly. 'We just have to hope she isn't that stupid. She couldn't be. Could she? I mean, if she tells him, then she'll basically be admitting to dating Blake even though she knew it would hurt Cameron all along and if she knows Cameron at all she'll be smart and keep her mouth shut.'

'Yes – *if she's smart*. The only problem is that Catherine isn't smart. She's an idiot.'

'Yes, but she's also terrified of people being angry at her,' Meredith reasoned. 'She won't tell him.'

'I suppose we can threaten her with a beating if she even suggests the idea,' Imogen said happily.

'You can. And in the meantime we just have to make sure that the reason she breaks up with Blake has nothing to do with Cameron, me, you, Michael or Gay-gate. She can never even suspect that whatever rumours we start about her and Blake came from us.'

'I know exactly when we can do this,' said Imogen triumphantly. 'Sports Day. Every popular girl in senior school will be in the same place at the same time. All we need to do is start a rumour and it'll be all over the school in hours that Catherine and Blake are hiding something. No one needs to know we're the ones who started it and there'll be no way of stopping a rumour that's started by every popular girl in Malone, is there?'

Meredith smiled and linked arms with her friend. 'That's

perfect, Imogen! We're not going to break them up; the whole school is.'

That Saturday afternoon, Cameron was lying on his bed, in his pyjamas, with his eyes puffy and exhausted. He looked up with surprise and embarrassment as Imogen and Meredith walked into his room, carrying a couple of bags in each hand.

'Imogen knows everything,' Meredith began. 'We've had a long chat together about the whole thing and we've been scheming for the entire week.'

'We're not talking about Blake, or what has happened or what is going to happen,' said Imogen. 'We don't give a fuck. Fuck him, Cameron. You're so overwhelmingly too good for him.'

'But . . .'

'Don't interrupt,' said Meredith decisively. 'We are here to be the best friends possible. We're not talking about him, it, or anything unpleasant.'

As Meredith sat down on the edge of Cameron's bed, Imogen continued to outline their plans. 'We're going to be foul. Today is a day of total self-indulgence; there's going to be no effort of any kind. Not even about being fabulous. It's going to be greasy and disgusting and naughty and wrong.' Then she held up a massive KFC Bargain Bucket, a large Pizza Hut box and two tubs of Ben & Jerry's Caramel Chew Chew.

Meredith placed four bottles of Diet Coke and the box set of *Rome* on the bed.

'This is how much I love you,' Imogen continued. 'Fuck the diet. Fuck calories. We're going to sit here with you, for the rest of the day and the night, if you want. And we're going to pig out and veg. We'll get as fat as you like and we're going to watch

Rome from the first episode until we physically can't take it any more.'

'We're going to splurge so much we hit a food coma,' said Meredith, popping disc one into Cameron's DVD player.

Tears welled up in Cameron's eyes. 'Thanks. I really appreciate this.'

'Appreciate what?' said Meredith, curling up next to him, as Imogen joined them on the other side. 'This is so much fun for us. Atia's my role model.'

Giving Cameron a comforting kiss on the cheek, Imogen nodded. 'Good food, good friends, good ancient orgies, killings and general all-round naughtiness. Fab-o-rama.'

'Oh my gosh!' said Meredith. 'Pass me the bucket! I haven't had fried chicken in years. Sometimes I think that this is worth being fat for. Then I remember that Chanel don't do kaftans.'

Sports Day at Mount Olivet took place on the large rugby fields and sports tracks that sat at the back of the school. Medals were awarded for each individual event, with Gold carrying ten points, Silver seven and Bronze three to the house of each medallist. At the end of the day, one of the school's four houses – Antrim, Chichester, O'Neill and Stormont – would be declared winner, with an end-of-year party for the victorious house being thrown for them in the school grounds. Those members of the school who weren't participating got to come down in non-uniform and watch the day's proceedings, cheering on their fellow housemates and cultivating some school spirit.

At least that was the theory.

The popular kids used it as an excuse to come to a summer garden party, which was occasionally spoiled by some cheering and other non-elegant noises from those around them. This year, Sports Day turned out to be a beautiful day and the upper-sixth queen bee Cecilia Molyneux could be seen holding court as the rest of the queen bees and their posses in the latest summer-season attire dutifully orbited her. It was tradition that the upper-sixth, lower-sixth and fifth-year popular girls all sat together on Sports Day, while the fourth-year popular girls sat alone, knowing (or hoping) that they would be included in the 'ladies who lounge' circle this time next year, unless they did something stupid like got fat, became a slut or joined the Young Farmers' Club.

Cecilia, Anastasia and Meredith sat gazing out across the fields, enjoying the warm weather and the cool breeze. Meredith's long brown hair hung loose down her back today and it fluttered in the wind, momentarily swirling around her pearl earrings. She reached up and delicately guided it back into its proper place. As ever, she looked perfect and her outfit's colour was beautiful, although it had required lengthy nego-tiations last night with Kerry, who felt it was her colour. Meredith had turned up in an elegant pink-and-cream dress with a pink skirt and cream-and-pink top half; she had also brought a matching parasol, determined to preserve her freckle-free, ivory-white complexion at any cost. Imogen, who was equally pale, had donned an enormous hat with matching sunglasses. Conceding defeat on the dress but not the refresh-ments, Kerry, whose outfit was a purple number by Derek Lam with a pair of Miu Miu shoes, was placing jugs of iced pink lemonade, pink-topped cupcakes and a careful pyramid of Mikados on the rug. Surrounding the queens, the members of their clique had merged to form some sort of conglomeration of popularity – Emily, Louise, Sarah-Jane, Olivia-Grace, Tangela, Natasha, Mariella, Lavinia, Imogen and Kerry.

'It's such a totally lush day. Lush-o-licious,' sighed Cecilia, letting her summer pastel pashmina dangle from her elbows.

'I know,' agreed Anastasia in her dulcet aristocratic tones. 'If it wasn't for all the sports, it would be perfect. I don't know why they have to make so much noise.'

'Where's Catherine?' asked Tangela, a question which momentarily brought a slight arch to Anastasia's left eyebrow since Tangela was very much the Catherine of *her* group.

Meredith, Imogen and Kerry exchanged glances with one another, with Meredith apparently refusing to say the words, which meant Imogen had to answer from beneath her hat. 'She's competing.'

Ten perfectly coiffed heads snapped in her direction. 'She's what?' asked Olivia-Grace, mouth open in horror.

'She's competing, all right?' snapped Imogen. 'Yes, we're very ashamed, but she only sprang the news on us this morning!'

'In what?' asked Natasha, pouring herself an enormous glass of pink lemonade.

'The women's hurdles,' replied Kerry. 'I don't know why. She's got no natural rhythm. I'm worried she might kill herself at the first leap.'

'How could you let one of us compete?' asked Cecilia, in a tone that wasn't so much angry as just plain confused. 'It's Sports Day. We don't *do* Sports Day. It's like the half-off bin. We just don't go near it, babes.'

'Also, this is the one day of the year that the rest of the school gets to be better than us,' said Sarah-Jane. 'We shouldn't take that away from them.'

'Or at least they think that they're better just because they run, jump and throw,' murmured Anastasia. 'Gorillas can do the same. I don't know why anyone gets excited about it. On the plus side, at least it means that Catherine won't be sitting with us all day. She did rather ruin Mariella's birthday picnic. I've never seen anyone spill quite so much in such a short period of time.'

There was a tense silence as most of the girls looked expectantly at Meredith. No one had insulted Catherine openly since the *Tatler* interview, because Catherine was now 'in'. However, Meredith's face didn't register even the vaguest flicker of a reaction to Anastasia's comment. Instead, she merely dusted a tiny piece of dandelion off her skirt and said neutrally, 'Of course, I love Catherine, she's obviously one of my best friends, but she's not herself nowadays. Something's up. I think her boyfriend is the problem. There's something . . . weird . . . about him and their relationship. Maybe I shouldn't have said that.'

Instantly, Kerry watched for any sign of eye contact between Meredith and Imogen. She was absolutely certain that some kind of plan was being hatched. Blake had never been publicly bad-mouthed before, certainly not to every single senior popular girl in the school and never to the extent of being described as 'the problem'. Whatever Meredith was doing was something new and something very, very deliberate.

Imogen continued to deliberately stare out across the grounds, with an air of polite indifference, but inwardly she was delighted that this was the beginning of the end of Blake Hartman. And, as Kerry watched and Imogen feigned normality, Meredith's carefully timed dropping of the word 'weird' had set the popular girls into a flurry of gossip, just as Imogen had predicted. No matter what they thought, or didn't think, knew or didn't know, Meredith's use of the words 'weird' and 'problem' had effectively given permission for a fevered session of theorizing and character assassination. From the moment the word 'weird' had been deployed, Blake Hartman was finished.

'How do you mean *weird*?' asked Tangela. 'Like it's a lie and stuff?'

'Do you think they're not really going out?' gasped Mariella. 'Oh my God!'

'I don't know,' murmured Meredith demurely. 'I mean, they're probably definitely a real couple. At least, I think so . . . oh, I don't know . . . *something*'s just not right. I'm probably wrong or just worrying too much. I hope so! Am I the only one who's noticed it?'

'No!' chorused three of the girls, who had never noticed anything unusual about Catherine and Blake, beyond his beauty and her klutziness.

'I've always thought there's something really secretive about him,' announced Sarah-Jane, adjusting her own pashmina. 'And didn't you think it was really weird they were going out in the first place, Cee?'

Cecilia nodded authoritatively. 'Totally. I've thought that there's something weird about them from the beginning, haven't I?'

Emily, Louise, Sarah-Jane and Olivia-Grace hastened to agree with her. 'Yes,' said Louise. 'You knew right from the beginning, Cee.'

'It's like they're trying to prove something,' said Lavinia, eager to be included.

'I know,' said Tangela. 'Like the way they're all over each other all the time, right?'

'Exactly!' said Cecilia. 'It's a total permanent fake PDA.'

'Maybe he's gay?' suggested Lavinia.

Kerry saw Imogen's back stiffen with surprise, but Meredith again stayed expressionless, gazing down at her fluttering pink skirt with a face so serene it would have shamed a saint. *Oh my God*, Kerry thought feverishly, *Blake is gay and the other two know about it! He was the guy at Cameron's birthday. And Imogen has somehow found out but hasn't told me! That treacherous little she-beast! This is clearly supposed to be some sort of weird punishment for my totally innocent bridesmaid comment.*

Kerry knew enough to keep silent and never to interrupt an attack launched by another member of the group, but inside she was fuming – particularly at Imogen. She expected nothing less from Meredith.

'I don't really get a gay vibe from him, though,' said Tangela. 'Do you?'

'Not really,' said Mariella slowly. 'I mean, has there, like, been a guy he's ever even, like, flirted with?'

'I don't really know him,' said Olivia-Grace, picking up a cupcake. 'But I'm sure there is something weird about him. I've always got that impression.'

'It's even weirder that he's not gay,' continued Mariella. 'It's like he's trying to prove something, but nothing's really there. That's even weirder, right?'

'Right,' agreed Cecilia and Louise at exactly the same time.

'So weird,' said Lavinia.

'So weird,' sighed Natasha.

*

Over at the running track, Mark had just taken Gold in the 400 metres for Antrim and was laughingly taunting Stewart, who had come in three seconds behind him, winning Silver for O'Neill. As the hardcore kids prepared for the 1,500 metres, Catherine was busy stretching for the hurdles, while Blake was catching his breath after failing to win a medal for Chichester in the 400. After a few minutes, he went over to congratulate Mark and Stewart on their performances. Mark beamed and clapped his hand on Blake's shoulder. 'Cheers, mate,' he laughed, 'and better luck next year.' Stewart simply nodded cold acknowledgement and wandered off to talk to some of the lads from his form class, leaving Blake with a tightness in his chest that had nothing to do with the 400 metres.

'Oh my God!' said Imogen. 'Catherine's about to do the hurdles.'

'This is going to be a disaster,' said Sarah-Jane happily as they all turned to look at the running track where Catherine was currently psyching herself up.

'Oh my God,' whispered Lavinia. 'Look! Blake hasn't even come over to see her before she runs. Isn't that weird?'

Meredith suppressed a smile. The starting pistol went off and Catherine shot out of the blocks. She cleared the first hurdle, but her foot caught on the second one and so she ended up head-butting the third, careering under the fourth and skidding to a painful halt just before the fifth. Some of the girls inhaled in sympathy at Catherine's obvious pain – others, namely Imogen, Tangela and Sarah-Jane, had to repress their giggles. Louise and Emily lost the battle completely and dissolved into a fit of hysterics, only pulling themselves together as Catherine was brought hobbling over to them with an ice-pack on her head.

'That was really sore and stuff,' she said, wincing as she sat down. Olivia-Grace looked like she was about to faint at the sight of someone – blood and grit-splattered – sitting on her picnic blankets, but she reckoned that refusing a seat to a cripple might make her look like a bitch, so she kept quiet.

'Oh my God,' said Meredith. 'Coral Andrews is about to do the long jump. Talk about defying gravity.'

'She's indie, Mer-Mer, not fat,' laughed Cecilia.

'Yes, but she is a witch,' replied Meredith, regarding the figure of Coral with sizzling dislike, especially as the girl sailed through the air to win first place and received the cheers of the sporting clique.

'Catherine, what are we going to dress you in to cover that cut on your forehead?' demanded Kerry, oblivious now to everything but the fear that Catherine's thoughtless decision to skid face-down through gravel was going to ruin the beautiful vista of fabulousness she had planned for tomorrow's birthday. 'It is *not* theme appropriate.'

'I know! There's so much to get done,' said Catherine. 'What should I do first?'

'Eyebrow plucking,' answered Meredith swiftly. 'Unless you're planning to go as Frida Kahlo, although I suppose that *is* theme appropriate. Kidding!'

Catherine smiled, pretending to understand the joke. Her thoughts about the mysterious Frida Kahlo, Blake and tomorrow's party were interrupted by an apparently casual Cecilia. 'Catherine, Blake didn't win anything in the 400 metres. Or the relay.'

Catherine moaned. 'Really? He's going to be in such a sulk for the rest of the day. I don't know what's wrong with him at the minute, but he's been in a real mood and stuff with me for the last few days. I really hope he's not like this at my birthday tomorrow.'

All of the girls exchanged looks with one another – what *was* Blake's problem?

Kerry picked up her phone as it began ringing. 'Hello. Yes, this is Kerry Davison, party-planner for Catherine O'Rourke's Sweet Sixteenth. No, no, no. We only want *one* big piñata. It's our centrepiece! And it has to be pink . . .'

Pink piñatas were far from everyone's mind in the boys' changing rooms late that afternoon, after Sports Day.

Having won first place in the 400 metres, Mark was in fine form and left on a high to go home early to help his mother with decorating their new house. Peter left ten minutes later, rushing to make it home in time to get ready for a date that evening with a girl from Immaculate Heart. But despite taking Silver in the same race and Gold in the javelin, Stewart seemed quiet and preoccupied. Since he had no plans for the evening, he hung back and allowed others to use the showers first. Emerging from the changing room alone sometime after most boys had left, dressed in a navy T-shirt, jeans and flip-flops, Stewart was surprised to see Blake in the locker area, searching for something.

'I've lost my locker keys,' he explained, seeing Stewart's puzzled expression, 'and I really need to get my Spanish books out of here for the weekend.'

'Sometimes they open if you do this,' said Stewart, strategically tapping the locker with his elbow. It popped open and Blake smiled back in gratitude, reaching in to get his books. Stewart simply turned and walked away.

'Are you going to Catherine's on Saturday?' asked Blake.

'Yeah. Are you?'

'O-of course,' stammered Blake, struggling to remain calm. 'Why wouldn't I be?'

'Don't do that,' commanded Stewart, in a very quiet but very firm tone. It was the first time they had spoken since he had seen him on Cameron's arm and he wasn't impressed. 'Don't try and shit around with me the way you have with everybody else. Catherine and Cameron don't deserve what you're doing to them. I used to really like you, Blake. I thought you were a good guy, but I guess I must've been wrong.'

'No, Stew, you don't understand. What happened on Saturday night . . .'

'I'm not annoyed about what happened on Saturday night. I'm annoyed about what happened on Sunday morning, Blake. Don't worry, I'm not going to "out" you. It's up to you to sort this out, if you ever have the balls to. But don't try and be matey with me after what you've done.'

'Stew, don't you think –'

'Stop. Fucking. Talking. Or else I'm going to lose my temper with you and I really don't want to do that. Maybe I don't know the ins and outs of this; maybe I don't understand what happened with you and Cameron or what it's like to feel the way you do, Blake. I'm sure this *is* incredibly hard, but a lot of people are . . . are . . . gay, Blake, or bi, or whatever, and they deal with it better than you have. Much better. And, like I said, I'm sure I don't know how difficult and confusing it is, but all that I do know is that I'd much rather be friends with a gay guy than a liar. I'll see you around.'

Cradling a half-empty Pimms and lemonade and wearing a beautiful green cocktail dress, Meredith was admiring the spectacular sunset over the bay from Anastasia's veranda. All the popular girls had been invited back to Anastasia's for a post-Sports Day supper party. It should have been fabulous, but for the fact that she couldn't quite figure out why Kerry kept throwing her filthy yet pained glances every five minutes or why she had been so cold with Imogen for the best part of the evening.

Imogen, sporting a sexy navy-and-white number, was standing next to her smoking. 'Christ, the view's beau, isn't it?'

'It really is,' said Meredith. 'What's wrong with Kerry?'

'I don't know. Time of the month?'

'No, we all get it at pretty much the same time, don't we?'

'God, that's horrifying.'

'She's kind of annoying me tonight.'

'Yes, she's quite good at that. How's Cameron?'

'I don't know,' answered Meredith irritably. 'The same as he was yesterday and the day before and the day before. It's getting ridiculous.'

Glancing behind her to check none of the other girls were too close, Imogen lowered her voice and leant in closer. 'Listen, Mer, I've got something to tell you.'

Meredith turned to look at her, her eyes sparkling at the prospect of gossip. 'Oh?'

'I had sex.'

A light gust of wind off the bay tousled Meredith's hair. 'With who?'

'Stewart, of course!'

'At Catherine's?'

'Yes.'

'Oh.'

Meredith turned back towards the sunset and took a sip of her drink.

'Aren't you pleased?' asked Imogen.

'Is it something to be pleased about?'

Not expecting this reaction, Imogen faltered slightly. 'Do you think it was a mistake?'

'I didn't say that.'

'Do you think it was the right thing to do?'

'I definitely didn't say that.'

'Well, what, then?'

'Don't snap at me just because you're beginning to realize what you've done,' Meredith commanded. 'It takes years to build up a reputation and one rumour to destroy it, especially if you're a girl. You should know that.'

'I haven't turned into some massive slag!'

'I know.'

Imogen stood in silence for a moment, before trying to explain herself. 'It was one time, with a boy I used to be in love with. It was special.'

'Yes. And a risk.'

'How?'

'It won't do your rep any good if people find out about this.'

'How will they find out?'

'The same way they always do.'

'People would only find out if I started making a habit of it,' Imogen snapped.

'Well, then don't make a habit of it.'

'I'm not going to!'

'Good. I'm going to get another drink,' said Meredith. 'I love your dress.'

The day of Catherine's birthday party dawned bright, breezy and beautiful and Catherine was delighted that it couldn't have been more different from the storm that had plagued her last party, two weeks earlier. Kerry arrived at her house shortly after ten a.m. to prepare everything for the party's six p.m. starting time. A forest of green, white and red streamers and bunting was being hung from tree to tree in the garden, the beautiful (pink) piñata had been suspended from the largest tree at the centre, icons of Our Lady of Guadálupe were dotted across the house and the caterers had done a spectacular job, with twelve tables set for Catherine's seventy-two guests around a large central buffet section.

Since the weather was so hot and the party was being held outside, Meredith was dressing in an embroidered white silk-chiffon 1950s-style Robert Cavalli dress, with the floral design in fetching purple, when her phone beeped with an incoming message.

Hey. Really sorry, Mer, but not feeling up to Catherine's today. Still not feeling good. Love Cam xoxo

Dressed in her Cavalli finest, with an enormous pair of Chanel sunglasses in her hand, a white Fendi bag on her right arm and Catherine's gift-wrapped present on her left, Meredith swept into Cameron's bedroom twenty minutes later with an unimpressed look on her face.

'Don't be mad,' Cameron began. 'I just can't, Meredith.'

'No, Cameron, you *won't*. There's a difference. This has been going on for almost two weeks and now you're missing a birthday party because of it! Do you really think Blake Hartman is special enough to spend this long moping over him? I don't! Look at yourself, Cameron! I can't even begin to imagine how embarrassed you must be. Or should be. Now, pull yourself together! I've been patient, I've done the good-friend routine, I even ate fried food for you, but enough is enough and it's tough-love time! You are not heartbroken, you are not in love with him; you couldn't be – you haven't known him long enough and he's so not worth it! This is just a confusing crush that's gone badly, badly wrong. I know that you're upset, but I'm just not putting up with this any more. Either pull yourself together or don't get in contact with me again until you do.'

Cameron's eyes filled up with tears again, shocked that she had turned on him so unexpectedly and so viciously. 'Meredith . . .'

'Your job is to be fabulous, Cameron, not badly kept and pathetic. So fix it. I'm not friends with losers and that's what you're turning into, and all because of some bambi-eyed transfer student!'

But rather than inspire him, Meredith's words only seemed to have crushed Cameron further and he lay back on the bed, rolling over, away from her furious gaze. A tiny part of him wanted to yell at her that she had been the one to keep them apart that night, that maybe, if he had stayed in that room, Blake wouldn't have left in the morning, but he wasn't entirely convinced about that argument himself and he couldn't bear to hear the scorn and vitriol Meredith would pour on the very idea.

He heard the swish of her dress as she spun round and left him alone. He picked up the remote and clicked PLAY on the DVD player, returning to the movie he had been watching, one of his and Meredith's favourites, actually – *Gone with the Wind* – one they had not tired of watching since they'd first discovered it at the age of thirteen.

By this stage in the movie, Scarlett O'Hara had just returned home and was trudging wearily up the hill of her family's plantation. Broken by hunger and exhaustion, the spoiled Southern belle, who had been used to a life of luxury and privilege, and of always getting her own way, collapsed on the soft earth and began to weep. She was staring into a future that was now shaped by war, defeat, famine and ruin. Then, in an iconic moment of cinema history and one of the campest, most melodramatic and yet most magnificently wonderful speeches of all time, Scarlett stumbled to her feet, raised her clenched fist to the sunset and, with the tears still on her face, she vowed: 'As God is my witness . . . As God is my witness, they're not going to lick me. I'm going to live through this and when it's all over, I'll never be hungry again – no, nor any of my folk. If I have to lie, steal, cheat or kill, as God is my witness, I'll never be hungry again!' And the music swelled to a crescendo, leaving Scarlett standing, defiant and alone, against a painted sky, before blackness swallowed her up again. Cameron clicked the OFF switch on the controls and stared at the blank screen.

Imogen and Meredith were met by Catherine's mother at the front door on arrival and she threw open her arms to greet them. 'Girls, it's so lovely to see you!' she beamed, hugging them each in turn.

'Thank you, Mrs O'Rourke. The party looks amazing,' smiled Meredith. 'Where's the birthday girl?'

'She's out in the back garden with Blake and all the other guests. And how many times have I told you, Meredith? Call me Mary!'

Meredith blushed charmingly. 'Sorry. Here's our present for later.'

'You really didn't have to,' said Mary O'Rourke. 'You've already done so much for Catherine this year with the holiday and everything. I don't know what she would do without you girls. I just know she appreciates it so much.'

'We feel the same about her,' simpered Imogen.

'I believe it's you we have to thank for Blake? Catherine says you introduced them.'

'Well, actually, Mrs O'Rourke, Blake's far closer to Cameron than he is to us,' said Meredith. 'It's pretty much because of him that Blake and Catherine are dating in the first place, although I'm sure he'd be far too modest to say anything about that himself.'

'Really? And what's Blake like in school?' asked Mary.

'Just as nice as he is outside of it,' answered Imogen.

'That's such a relief. We like him so much and he's been so good for Catherine's self-confidence,' said Mary. 'I just wanted to make sure he wasn't trying to cover up his bad points in front of the girlfriend's parents. You know what boys can be like.'

'And so does Blake,' said Meredith.

'Is he a popular fella in school, then? I imagine he must be, given how nice and how handsome he is. Is he a bit of a ladies' man?'

'Blake? No, not at all!' replied Meredith. 'Well, we should go say happy birthday to the lovely lady herself.'

'Ach, yes! Have fun, girls!' called Mary O'Rourke, reflecting on what good friends Meredith and Imogen had been to her daughter.

Surrounded by her guests at the centre of the garden, Catherine looked lovely, with a Brooks Brothers headscarf placed decorously over the cut on her forehead and with Blake's arm dutifully round her waist. She smiled happily as Imogen and Meredith leant in and kissed her on the cheek, wishing her happy birthday. 'Oh my God, guys. It's all turned out to be *so* beau.'

'It looks lush,' said Imogen. 'Fab party.'

'Where's Cameron?'

'He didn't feel very well,' Meredith answered.

'Well, I hope he's OK,' Catherine said politely, but looking slightly relieved. 'Oh well. Poor him. Oh! Natasha's here! I'll be right back.'

As Catherine bounced off to say hi to Natasha, Meredith and Imogen turned their backs on Blake without addressing a single word to him and went over to get two margaritas from the caterers.

'Is Cameron still . . .' Imogen began.

Meredith nodded. 'Yes. He is. I'm not pleased.'

Imogen sighed. 'Meredith, there's something else I wanted to talk to you about . . . That thing you said yesterday really upset me.'

'About how your brother Richard kind of looks like the baby from *Family Guy*?'

'No! When did you say that?'

'Um . . . never.'

'No, I mean what you said about the sex thing.'

'Oh.'

'Look, I need you to understand something. I'm not saying that it was perfect . . . in fact, you were right – it was kind of a risk. But it wasn't attention-seeking or pathetic. I didn't do it to get some boy to like me or make myself feel worthy – if I felt that way, I could have had sex with Michael the Immaculate Heart Rapist when he asked. But I didn't. I did it with Stewart because it should have been him all along and I don't think the opportunity's ever going to come again. We were careful and it meant a lot, Meredith. Please don't ruin it and make me feel embarrassed about it. I'm not saying this is the right decision for you. I know you've decided not to and I respect that, so please respect my choice. I have absolutely no intention of having sex again for a very long time. There's obviously no one who's good enough even for a kiss from me right now. But, anyway – I'm happy with my decision.'

Meredith scrutinized Imogen for a moment and then casually nodded her head. She accepted her friend's point, but, as ever, would be damned if she would verbally admit it.

Imogen smiled. 'Thanks. I –' But she suddenly stopped speaking and began looking over Meredith's shoulder. After a few seconds, she pointed in that direction and Meredith turned round to see Cameron stepping out of his father's car and walking up the garden path towards them. He looked amazing. Freshly showered, clean-shaven and wearing a Howick green rugby top, Armani jeans, Kurt Geiger shoes and the Rolex his father had given him for his sixteenth birthday, he removed his sunglasses and kissed Catherine on the cheek. 'Sorry I'm late,' he said.

'I thought you weren't coming? Meredith said you were still sick.'

'I just felt a bit tired after being ill all this week, so it took me a bit longer to get ready. Happy birthday!'

'Thanks,' she said with a smile, although as always Catherine felt a twinge of panic if Cameron showed up when Blake was around. Thankfully, Blake was over talking to Mark now, which meant Cameron wouldn't be going anywhere near him, she reasoned. She breathed a sigh of relief as he walked over to Imogen and Meredith, who were regarding him with quizzical smiles.

'Well, well, well,' said Meredith as he approached.

'Sorry I'm late,' he said, leaning in to kiss them both on the cheek. 'I wasn't feeling very well, but I'm totally over it now.'

'Really?' asked Meredith. 'Because I don't want you to catch the same thing again.'

'I won't,' Cameron replied. 'My immune system's pretty invincible now.'

'I'm glad to hear it, but I hope you've come to terms with the condition that made you susceptible in the first place?'

Cameron nodded. 'Yes. I have. And that condition isn't going away and it doesn't make me sick – it's just part of the way I'm made up. Unfortunately, it did leave me open to my recent brush with . . . um . . .'

'Mental influenza?' suggested Imogen.

'Exactly, but I'm over the flu now and I've come to terms with the original . . . condition. I'm back!'

Meredith broke into a warm smile, before replacing it with a look of cool indifference. She took a drink. 'You know, Cameron, I do rather love you . . . Please don't make a fuss.'

'So do I,' said Imogen.

'All right. That's enough feelings for one day,' snapped Meredith. 'Let's move on.'

'So what brought about the rather miraculous recovery from the flu?' asked Imogen.

'I was watching *Gone with the Wind* and I decided if Scarlett O'Hara can get through war, famine, disease and disaster and still look amazing, I can certainly get over a couple of kisses. Also, I'm far too young and popular to give up.'

'So . . . let me get this straight. You got out of bed because Scarlett O'Hara yelled at you?' asked Imogen. Cameron nodded and she threw back her head and roared with laughter. 'That is the gayest of gay things I have *ever* heard!'

Cameron smirked and as Imogen doubled over, Meredith burst into laughter too. They only stopped when Kerry skidded to a halt next to them. 'What's so funny?' she asked in a harassed, belligerent way – clearly under the impression that if she was swamped with organization her friends should not be having fun without her.

'Nothing, Kerry, I'll tell you later,' said Cameron breathlessly.

'You probably won't,' she snapped.

'Oh, he will,' snorted Imogen as her laughter began again. 'As God is his witness, he will!'

Meredith started laughing again and even Cameron struggled to suppress his giggles, wary of how they would be received by Kerry, who flounced off to supervise the arrival of the birthday cake. The other three went to get some food from the buffet table and then took their seats at their assigned table to wait for Catherine's birthday speech.

'Now, Cameron, make sure you eat up everything. You don't want to be hungry again – no, nor any of your folk.'

'Ha ha, yes, I made a major life decision based entirely on the words of Scarlett O'Hara. It's all very funny.'

Kerry tapped her glass with a knife as Catherine stood up to speak.

'Hello? Hi! Um, I just wanted to say thanks to everyone for coming to my totally awesome b-day fest and for all the presents. Yay! I really have to thank my bezzy Kerry for being the world's greatest party organizer and planner and stuff, because she planned and organized, like, everything. Like, seriously. Also, to Mummy and Daddy for being so nice and paying for everything and getting me such lush presents and being, like, so loving and kind and great. And, um, also, I have to thank my boyfriend, Blake Hartman – he's been really sweet to me all day and great and I'm so lucky to have such an unbelievable amazing boyfriend!'

'Oh my God,' muttered Meredith, 'what's that smell? Ah yes, the cloying stench of desperation . . .'

'Really?' said Imogen. 'Is that what that is? I always get it so confused with bullshit.'

'I know, they're very similar, aren't they?'

'So, in conclusion, I just want to say thanks to everyone,' said Catherine, 'and I really hope you all have an amazing time and stuff. Thanks!'

People clapped and began to sing 'Happy Birthday' as the cake was wheeled out and Catherine stood in front of it, flanked by Blake, her parents, grandmother and two sisters.

With her task now finished and still sulking at being excluded from the others' joke, Kerry knocked back a margarita, a shot of tequila and asked the bartender to whip up her favourite cocktail – a cosmopolitan. Since she hadn't eaten all day due to the stress of party-planning, it took about forty-five minutes until she was well and truly hammered. Excusing herself, Kerry tottered upstairs to find somewhere to lie down. Her feet, however, had rather different ideas and she went over on her stiletto, sinking down on to the carpet as a wall of pink fabric from her dress billowed up around her face. *Hmmm*, she thought, *this doesn't feel like a bed. Oh, wait, it isn't; it's the floor.*

Just then, Mark Kingston emerged from the bathroom next to her. 'Kerry, are you all right?' he asked, stooping down to help her.

'I'm fine,' she smiled. 'I'm on the carpet. And it's very comfortable actually. Carpet. How are you?'

'I'm fine. Let's get you somewhere to lie down properly,' he said, gently placing her arms round him and getting her back on her feet. 'Let's try in here.' He navigated her into Catherine's bedroom and tried to get her to lie down on the bed.

'No!' she hollered. 'I've changed my mind. I'm the party-planner! Party-planner's never quick.'

'You mean quit?'

'That's what I said,' she slurred, pointing a finger at him and winking cheekily. Unfortunately, her right eyelid somehow forgot to come up from the wink and instead chose to remain closed, so Kerry was now regarding Mark beadily with one eye.

'Maybe you should just lie down for a bit?' he said gently. 'I'll get you a glass of water.'

'I'm bloody fine! Jus' a li'l bit too drunky. My head hurts ... pink ...' Then her head flopped forward and she started staring intently at the twinkling pink diamantés on her shoes. She then moved one of her feet and watched it, entranced.

'Are you sure there's nothing I can do to help?'

Kerry shook her head with exaggerated seriousness, before mumbling, 'I'm sorry I thought it was you who was gay.'

'What?'

'Gay, gay, gay,' she trilled happily, throwing herself backwards on to the bed. 'I thought it was you that Cameron kicked at his birthday.'

'Pardon?'

'Kissed. I mean kissed. You knew that,' she snapped, jabbing an accusing finger in his direction, but accidentally stabbing her chin with it instead. 'Ow, I hurteyed my chin. And I only have one . . . Yes, yes, yes, Cameron kissed a guy. A guy, a gay. Isn't it funny how there's only one difference between them? You know, only one letter that's different. One little "u" turns into an "a" and suddenly a guy becomes a gay. Maybe that's why so many gay men are guys. And so many guys are gay men. The letters . . .'

Mark was standing over her, clearly stunned. 'Cameron kissed a guy?'

'Yes,' giggled Kerry, kicking her heels into the air and enjoying the sound her skirt made as her legs moved. 'Yes, yes, yes. I thought it was you because you've always been a bit weird and really possessive, but it wasn't. It was Blake. I know that. Even though some people think I don't. Oh, they think that, yes, yes, yes, they do, but I do, not don't. So they're wrong about me being wrong, and we're both right, but I'm right about everything and they're only right about him not me. Ha ha. And Meredith knows and Imogen knows and Cameron knows and Blake knows and I don't know if Catherine knows and you know and Cameron's gay but he can't be my bridesmaid because Imogen's a bitch and my head really hurts and I don't even really like Mexican themes and I wonder why I did this and I

274

think it's maybe because I feel really sorry for Catherine because she's dating a gay guy or maybe it's just because I'm a good person. I'm a good person, aren't I? Yes, yes, yes. Oh, why did I kiss Peter? I don't like toilet humour at all and I don't even really like him and I think pink is my only real friend and . . .'

'Cameron's gay?'

Kerry sighed melodramatically and slapped the quilt with her hands. 'Duh!'

'I'll go get you some water,' said Mark quietly, slipping out of the room and walking down the stairs, where he almost collided with Meredith and Imogen who were walking up in search of Kerry. 'Congratulations. You've finally turned him into what you want.'

Meredith wasn't sure what he meant, so just to be on the safe side she threw him a filthy glare as he walked away, before she continued up to Catherine's bedroom, where she and Imogen came across the wreckage of Kerry Davison, who was lying on the bed gently singing 'Believe' by Cher to herself.

'Kerry?'

At the sound of Imogen's voice, Kerry suddenly gasped in realization and squeaked, 'I did a bad thing.'

'Were you sick?'

'No. I'm not Catherine! You see I know what you think I don't know, but I do.'

'What?' asked Meredith.

'About Cameron,' she mumbled tearfully, 'and Blake. I guessed. I knew. I've always been the one who knows and feels and guesses and sings. And I know, but . . . but . . .'

'What have you done?' asked Imogen, sitting next to her on the bed as Meredith watched her suspiciously.

'I told Mark,' she said as she began to cry. 'He tricked me. I hurt my chin.'

'One day, I'm going to have to kill you,' said Meredith.

'What a fucking bastard!' roared Imogen. 'That must've been what he meant when he spoke to us on the stairs.'

'What?'

'He thinks we turned Cameron gay! What an ignorant troll!'

The story of how Mark Kingston got mild concussion that night varied depending on who you were talking to. Meredith Harper always swore it was an accident, but several eyewitnesses – Imogen and Cameron included – maintained that they had seen her look in Mark's direction and clock exactly where he was standing before being blindfolded and handed the stick that she was supposed to hit the piñata with. It was also noted by some that instead of striking the stick upwards, to where the piñata was hanging from the tree, she had actually swung it up and then sideways, bringing it down into direct contact with Mark Kingston's head. It was also curious that instead of seeming surprised by the fact that she had bludgeoned a fellow party guest, Meredith simply removed the blindfold and said, 'Oops,' in a light, breezy tone, before handing the stick over to a terrified-looking Blake.

As Stewart and Peter helped Mark upstairs, Meredith was heard to remark, 'Oh, don't worry, I'm not that upset. I didn't even really want any sweets anyway.'

'Cameron, could you grab some ice for the poor guy's head and bring it upstairs?' asked Peter. Irritated at being asked to help Mark when they were still technically on non-speakers, but reluctant to look like he was refusing medical aid to some-

276

one who had just been pummelled on the forehead, Cameron went into the kitchen and retrieved a bag of ice from the freezer, then he walked upstairs where Mark was sitting on the edge of the bath looking furious. 'Fuck, that hurt,' he hissed. 'Fuck, I hate her.'

Stewart nodded sympathetically, knowing that now was not the time to challenge Mark on this kind of sentiment. He looked up to see Cameron standing in the doorway, from where he passed the bag of ice, without stepping in.

'Hope he feels better.'

As he walked across the landing, he bumped into Blake, who had come up to check on Mark. Cameron felt his entire stomach tighten at the sight of him and it felt like someone was sitting on his chest. 'Excuse me,' said Cameron, attempting to get past him.

Blake grabbed his arm and placed himself in his way. 'Cam, wait.'

'Blake, let go of my arm.'

'Can we please just talk?' he whispered.

'Blake, we really don't have anything to say to each other. Remember, you're not like me.' And with that Cameron Matthews gently pulled his arm out of Blake's grip and walked down the stairs without looking back.

13

EMERGENCIA

Mark sat with Stewart in the school gardens on Monday as they ate their lunch. The good weather had continued and it was a hot May afternoon, so most of the students were also outside doing the same.

In the distance, Meredith was sitting on the lawn with Cameron, Imogen and Kerry. Imogen had obviously just made some joke and the other three were laughing; Mark sighed in frustration at the fond smile that appeared on Stewart's lips as he watched her. He decided to distract him and change the subject to what had been on his mind for the whole weekend anyway. 'Stew . . . Kerry said something kind of weird at the party on Saturday night.'

'Oh?'

'Yeah . . . she said . . . She said that Cameron was gay.'

Stewart took a drink of water before responding. 'Oh?'

'You don't sound that surprised.'

'That's because I'm not,' Stewart admitted.

'You already knew?' Mark asked, shocked.

Stewart nodded.

'For how long?'

'Since that night at Catherine's.'

278

'She said he kissed Blake way back in December.'

'So it happened more than once . . .'

'What?'

Stewart looked at Mark for a minute, as if weighing up whether to continue, but there seemed no point in holding back now and he was sure Mark could be trusted. 'They pulled again at the camping trip at Catherine's.'

'And then Blake ran off first thing in the morning?'

'Yep. Pretty shitty of him.'

'Pretty shitty of Cameron to do that to Catherine,' said Mark. 'At her own party, like.'

'That's also very true.'

Mark fell silent and stared over at Cameron before speaking to Stewart again. 'I really thought I knew him.'

'You do, mate. I think this is something no one knew about for definite, not even Cameron.'

'I bet *she* knew. I bet she's known all along and kept it secret.'

There was no need for Stewart to ask who 'she' was and he stood up in irritation, grabbing his schoolbag. 'Come on, Mark: not this again! You're always giving off such stink about how the whole school's obsessed with Meredith Harper, but there's no one who thinks about her more than you do. Your best friend, the guy you've been mates with since you were kids, has just realized something that's changed his whole bloody life and all you can think about is how Meredith must've known about it before you did! She has *nothing* to do with it, Mark. I'll see you in Chemistry.'

Mark sat in a grumpy silence in class. When was he going to learn not to mention Meredith to anyone? He never came out of any conversation about her looking good. He either sounded like a madman with a grudge or a crazy stalker.

Still, it was not OK for Stewart to talk about Mark's friendship with Cameron like that. It had definitely been uncalled for – as if Mark didn't have enough to stress out about after finding out Cameron was gay. He also hadn't liked the implication that he didn't care about Cameron any more. Angry with Stewart, Cameron and with himself, Mark spent most of the day moodily brooding over the whole messy situation.

He was still huffing when the fifth-years were herded into the assembly hall, where the headmaster was standing at the front, waiting to speak to them. 'Good afternoon, students,' he smiled. 'You have been summoned here today for a formal and very important announcement. Today is the first day of your study leave. You will all now be allowed to remain at home to commence private and individual study for the forthcoming examinations, which start in three weeks' time.'

'Damn,' hissed Imogen under her breath.

'You should all go now to the school office and pick up your individual examination timetables, and . . . Quiet at the back, please! I really can't stress how important it is for you to have these and pay close attention to them. And now, go with God and with good luck. I am sure you are all going to do this school very, very proud.'

Over the next few weeks, the beautiful May sunshine meant that Meredith, Imogen and Cameron spent more of their time at each others' houses, relaxing outside with their books open on the table next to them – more for show than anything else. Meredith was currently on the sun-lounger reading the 'Poor

Little Rich Girl' column in *Tatler* and nodding at every other sentence. 'God, it's so true,' she sighed. 'It is *so* true.'

Lying next to her in a crêpe de Chine dress by Chanel with star-shaped sunglasses, a plethora of rings, bangles and a Marlboro Light for accessories, Imogen was mentally debating whether to go Brazilian or Hollywood for the group's forthcoming holiday to Mexico, and Cameron was drinking a cold Diet Coke and pondering what it might be like to actually want to work on a day like this.

'What are your plans for revision, Imogen?' asked Cameron, taking another drink of Diet Coke.

'Saint Jude,' she replied. 'Well, I mean, it's sort of staggered really. I'll start off with Saint Giuseppe and Saint Thomas Aquinas, but I think in the end it's all going to come down to Saint Jude.'

'Oh, he's very good,' said Meredith.

'Really?'

'Oh yes. I've used him before. He really comes through. He's very efficient.'

'What kind of levels of efficiency are we talking about?' asked Imogen.

Meredith paused to think. 'Saint Teresa.'

'Not as good as Saint Anthony?'

'No, but then, he's the best, isn't he?'

'He's fabulous,' said Imogen, lighting another cigarette. 'I think he's absolutely tremendous. I love his work. He's like the Ronseal saint – does exactly what it says on the tin.'

'Well, as long as you both have a plan,' sighed Cameron lazily.

*

On the morning of the first exam, Catherine had got so nervous she had rushed to the toilet three times already. Sitting in one of the cubicles, she heard the voices of Anastasia, Natasha and Tangela, as they arrived to reapply their lipglosses at the bathroom mirrors. 'Did you see him?' asked Natasha.

'I know, right?' said Tangela.

'I told you,' sighed Anastasia. 'He's weird.'

'He's just so rude recently and I seriously don't understand why Catherine's still with him,' Tangela said. 'I mean . . . she can't be *that* desperate.'

'Obvo she is,' said Natasha as she puckered her lips. 'Everyone's talking about how moody and angry and weird he is and how she doesn't even seem to notice.'

'Because she is *that* desperate. Obviously.'

As the three girls walked out, still gossiping about her and Blake, Catherine had to put a hand on her chest to try and steady her breathing. What had happened? What had Blake done that had made the whole school change their mind about him – about them? And why had no one said anything to her? Maybe it was just Anastasia's group that felt that way? After all, Anastasia had always thought he was kind of stupid . . . maybe that's what they meant? With great difficulty, she put their comments to the back of her mind and tried to ignore what she had just heard – the very same policy she had employed with Blake for the last three months.

As she returned to wait outside the assembly hall before the exam started, Catherine was distracted from her worrying by the sight of panic-stricken students all around her. Kerry was holding an unblemished copy of *Macbeth* in her right hand and was digging her nails into the arm of a terrified-looking, well-prepared Patsy Harris, hissing: 'What do you mean she kills herself? I thought her hands were just dirty!' In a corner, Imogen's lips were moving in furious, rhythmic prayer. She had just finished rattling through Saint Thomas's prayer for a student and she had now embarked on another round of Hail Marys. The only person who seemed calm, of course, was Meredith, who hadn't even bothered with last-minute revision cards. With twenty minutes still to go before the doors opened, Catherine sat down to have one last read of her *Macbeth* notes and Cameron wandered off down the corridor to use the bathroom.

When he pushed the swing door open, Cameron was confronted by the sight of Mark Kingston, with his hands placed on either side of the sink, ashen-faced. Turning to see who it was, the relief was palpable on Mark's face. 'Cam . . . Cameron, I'm so worried. I forgot I got like this at exams. I . . . I need to do well.'

Cameron went over to him and put one hand on his shoulder and another on his arm, patting it reassuringly. 'Mark, it's OK. It's fine. You always freak out and you always do well.'

'Cameron . . . I have to do well. Doing well. It's important to me. I can't . . . I can't fuck them up.'

'You won't.'

'You don't know that!'

At that point, a bullet-shaped third-year walked in and saw the two of them. He looked at Mark's face for about five seconds before Cameron snapped. 'Why don't you take a picture? It'll last longer!'

'What's your problem?'

'You, obviously.'

'There's no need to be so gay about it all.'

'Why don't you get out?'

'Why don't you fuck off?'

'Because I'm older than you and I'm better than you. So, off you trot and try not to make a mark on the door with your hooves as you leave.'

As the third-year slunk off muttering angrily to himself, Cameron returned to comforting Mark. 'Listen, you'll be fine. You're smart and you'll definitely have done enough revision. Mark, if someone like you isn't going to do well in these exams, then what chance has anyone else got? I *promise* it'll be fine. Just like it always is.'

Mark nodded and took a big gulp of air to steady himself. 'Thanks, Cameron. Thanks.'

With normality more or less restored, awkwardness settled over them as they remembered the tensions of the last five months. 'I should probably get back to the hall,' Mark muttered. 'Thanks and . . .'

'Yeah. I'll see you around,' said Cameron. 'Good luck.'

'Thanks,' said Mark, walking away. 'Yeah, thanks and . . . good luck.'

By and large, the GCSEs passed without any real incident, apart from the frankly horrifying moment when Kerry realized there was coursework for Business Studies that she had never handed in; Cameron's total inability to recall how to say anything in his Spanish Oral that wasn't in the present tense; and, of course, the unforgettable terrified squeak from Imogen at the beginning of the History exam, when she had opened the first page to see the title THE ENGLISH CIVIL WAR before realizing that their module – WEIMAR AND NAZI GERMANY

– was actually listed three pages later. For a split second, she'd thought that she had paid such poor attention in class that she'd revised for the wrong country and wrong century. Her eyes had shot heavenward, with an accusatory glint in them, but after turning more pages she breathed a sigh of relief and then looked up again with an apologetic smile.

And so it was on a blisteringly hot summer's day in the middle of June that the last GCSE exam took place for that year at Mount Olivet. Walking out into the sunshine in his school uniform, Cameron breathed a happy sigh of relief and was about to call Meredith to see what the plans for that night were, when Mark walked up behind him. The two hadn't spoken since the day of Mark's ritual pre-exam panic in the boys' bathroom, almost three weeks earlier.

'Hey. What'd you think of the exam?'

'It was OK,' answered Cameron. 'Although I don't think they could've asked any more questions on *Blood Brothers* if they'd tried.'

'Yeah, I know! What are your plans now?'

'Em . . . nothing definite,' said Cameron, wary of mentioning Meredith's name.

'You probably have plans with Meredith and the girls later on?'

'Yeah.'

'That's cool,' answered Mark, in a tone that sounded friendly, if slightly forced.

'OK. Well . . . I hope you have a good night. Em . . . bye.'

'Cameron, wait! I thought you might fancy catching the bus to Newcastle and going for a walk up to Tollymore Forest. It's a good day and we used to do it all the time.'

Cameron looked totally startled at the suggestion. 'Oh . . . God . . . I don't know.'

'Or anywhere, really. It's important. I've got a lot to say, Cam – honestly. Please.'

Cameron hesitated, but he could read the look of sincerity and urgency on Mark's face, so he nodded. 'Tollymore it is, then.'

14

EVERYTHING THAT REALLY COUNTS

For most of the bus ride, Cameron and Mark managed to stick to slightly strained but neutral topics of conversation – the exams, their teachers and any plans for the summer. It wasn't until they passed under the stone archway and began to walk down the tree-lined entrance avenue at Tollymore Forest Park that Mark finally decided to say what was on his mind. 'Listen, Cameron, there's something I need to say to you and I should have said it to you a long time ago.'

'OK.'

'I'm really sorry that I yelled at you so much and for all the things I said to you on your birthday. It wasn't cool and I'm sorry.'

'Well, I'm sorry too. As much as the girls are still amazing friends, what I did to Stewart definitely wasn't right. I know that. I think I knew it at the time. I didn't give you any reason to trust me.'

'Thanks. That means a lot . . . so are we cool?'

'Yes,' Cameron smiled. 'Definitely cool.'

'Good . . . because I was wondering if there was anything else you wanted to tell me?'

'What do you mean?'

'Cameron, are you gay?'

They had reached the small obelisk that stood on top of a hill, and all around them the rolling fields and tree-topped Mourne Mountains shimmered in the sun.

Cameron turned to look at him and then turned back, gazing up to the mountains. 'Yes. I think so.'

'Are you OK with it?'

'I think so. I will be.'

'OK.'

'Are you OK with it, Mark? I thought you might be weird about it . . .'

'I'll get used to it,' Mark replied as he sat down next to him on the stone. 'I did freak out a little when I found out . . .'

'How did you find out?'

'Kerry got rat-arsed at Catherine's birthday and started telling me how she thought I was the guy you'd pulled at your party, but now she realized it was actually Blake and . . .'

Cameron threw his head into his hands. 'Oh my God. She saw us?'

'You didn't know?'

'No!'

'Crap. Sorry . . . Anyway, when Kerry told me, I kind of panicked, but mainly because I thought I must have been a rubbish friend if you'd told all the girls something this big before you told me. But Stew sort of made me see how much of a prick I was being and I just really wanted to see if you were OK.'

'Thanks.'

'I don't think the thing with Blake was right . . . I mean, I don't think it was really fair on Catherine. I know she's really annoying, but still.'

Cameron laughed. 'She is – that's true, but, yeah, it wasn't my shining hour.'

'What Blake did was worse, though.'

Cameron bit his lower lip and looked at his friend. 'I don't really like to talk about him any more.'

'Because he dumped you?'

'He didn't dump me!' gasped Cameron, instinctively appalled at the very idea that someone in his group could be dumped by anyone. Apart from Catherine, obviously – she was pushing eight, and counting.

Mark laughed at the sheer horror in Cameron's tone and the aghast look on his face. 'Well, he's a dick . . . Are you going to tell Catherine?'

'No, I don't think it would help anything or anyone right now.'

'Fair enough . . . maybe the less you get involved the better.'

'That's what I think. Anyway, it's all in the past.' Cameron took a deep breath, feeling a weight drop from his shoulders now that he didn't have to lie to one of his best mates any more. 'Do you wanna go get some ice cream?'

'Definitely.'

'Wait. Before we go, I have to ask you something else. Something else that needs to be in the past.'

'OK?'

'The thing with you and Meredith . . .'

'What thing?' Mark asked, a trifle too quickly.

'It can't go back to the way it was before,' Cameron replied. 'You can't constantly be fighting over me. It was getting exhausting.'

Mark fidgeted slightly. 'Well, just because she's your friend doesn't mean she has to be mine.'

'Oh, I don't think you want her to be your *friend*,' smirked Cameron. 'I think that's probably the wrong word for how you feel.'

'What? I don't get it . . .'

'OK,' said Cameron, with an infuriating shrug. 'And, by the way, the next time you want to convince someone you don't have a crush on her, you might want to work on your blushing.'

'Shut up!'

'Oh my God, I can't believe that's what it was about all along!'

Mark glared over at Cameron and decided to even the playing field a little by firing an awkward question back at the insufferably smug jackass standing before him. 'Cam, since we're being honest with each other . . . I need to ask you one more thing.'

'I don't know what Meredith's favourite type of flowers are, sorry.'

'Ha. No. That's not it,' Mark replied drily. 'I need to know – have you ever fancied me?'

'Um . . . no,' Cameron laughed. 'Conceited, much?'

'Really?'

'No, of course not.'

'What . . . Not even a little bit?'

'No.'

'Why not? What's wrong with me?'

'OK, we're not having this conversation.'

'Cameron, come on. Like . . . seriously. Look at me. Do you think Blake's better-looking than me?'

'Shut up!'

*

With the Leavers' Ball only five days away and the exams finally over, a frenzy of organization had gripped those who were attending. Cecilia's twenty tickets for non-leavers had been snapped up pretty quickly and, of course, she had made sure that most of them went to Meredith and Anastasia's cliques.

Imogen, Kerry, Catherine and Meredith were currently in a boutique on the Lisburn Road, trying to pick their dresses for the occasion and Catherine had just emerged in a strong yellow number by Dior. 'What do you think?'

'Oh my God,' gasped Imogen, 'that's actually beau. How do you pull off that colour, Catherine? It always makes me look like I have hepatitis.'

Meredith looked at Catherine and, finding nothing wrong, she simply nodded and turned back to Imogen, who was standing in front of a set of mirrors trying on a Balenciaga gown, with Ermanno Scervino, Chanel, Alexander McQueen and Oscar de la Renta numbers waiting for her to sample next. Kerry was close to crying about whether to choose one by Prada, Dior or Narciso Rodriguez, and the salesgirl was bringing a black Jonathan Saunders gown to Meredith, along with a beautiful, flowing number by Marchesa. 'Oh my God,' she gasped. 'They're both *amazing*. My life is so hard!'

The bell above the door tinkled as Cameron walked into the shop. 'Hey.'

'Hello, lover,' smiled Imogen. 'You look tanned.'

'Do I? I've been at Tollymore all afternoon, but I didn't think it was long enough to get some colour.'

'Who were you at Tollymore with?' asked Meredith as she inspected the Jonathan Saunders dress.

'Mark.'

'Oh really?'

'Yes. Can I talk to you for a minute, Mer?'

'Sure.'

As Meredith and Cameron retreated to one of the sofas in the corner, Imogen, sensing horrific fallout, made a panicked face at Kerry and asked to try on the McQueen. Catherine ran back to the changing rooms to step out of the Dior to avoid what she also thought would be Meredith's bitch-fit from hell.

'Listen, Meredith, Mark and I kind of sorted things out today and I'm pretty sure he's going to be back in my life like he was before my birthday and I need to know you're OK with that?'

'Are you sure you're going to be able to cope with that? How much does he know?'

'Everything.'

Meredith sat in a thoughtful silence for a few very tense moments. 'Is he OK with everything?'

'Yes. Better than OK. He was great about it.'

'Oh. And did he apologize for how awful he's been to you over the last few months?'

'Yes and I've apologized too.'

'Well, I don't see what you had to apologize for,' she said huffily.

'Meredith, I really don't want things to go back to the way they were before. I need them to be a bit calmer with you two . . . a bit more civil.'

Meredith sighed. 'All right. If it means that much to you, then . . . fine. I can be civil. It's the best, *the very best*, that I can do.'

'That would be great, Meredith – really, really great.'

'Then civil it is. By the way, it may take some time before I can stomach you talking about him to me, but when that irritating face of his is actually in front of me I'll be totally fine.'

Cameron laughed. 'OK. Thanks. I really appreciate this.'

With a great effort at dignity, Meredith rejoined the other girls. 'Mark's back "in". We're making an effort. I don't want to talk about it. Ever.'

'What'd I miss?' asked Catherine as she emerged from the changing room.

'So very much,' sighed Meredith.

Set atop a hill reached by a mile-long avenue, the spectacular white stone Parliament Buildings of Stormont were the impressive venue for the Mount Olivet Leavers' Ball – it was Cecilia Molyneux's ultimate social coup in securing it. As the cars began driving up the Mile at half past eight on the night of the ball, Stormont was bathed orange and purple in the evening sun, the stone turning a cool, crisp, floodlit blue when the sun finally disappeared.

Shortly before nine o'clock, the Harpers' Mercedes stopped at the entrance steps and Cameron exited the car first. He was followed by his date for the evening, Imogen, in a lush Oscar de la Renta dress of champagne tulle with her mother's earrings sparkling on her ears; seconds later, in the willowy blue-grey Marchesa gown from the shop with glistening earrings by Michael Beaudry, Meredith slipped out of the car with all the exquisite poise of an aristocrat.

Inside the building, the students mingled in the beautiful marble entrance hall beneath a fabulous gold-plated chandelier that had once belonged to the last Emperor of Germany. Canapés and champagne were circulating among the guests and every girl had made an effort to look as glamorous as the location. Unfortunately, there were some girls who had inevitably overdone it on the fake tan and looked like an Oompa-Loompa in faux couture.

Five minutes after Meredith and Imogen had arrived on Cameron's arm, Cecilia Molyneux entered the room with an even more dramatic first appearance. She had no date; she stood alone, shimmering in an Elizabeth Emanuel gown and a ton of jewellery, with her backcombed hair hovering around her head like a nimbus cloud. Behind her, arranged like loyal ladies-in-waiting, were Sarah-Jane, Louise, Olivia-Grace and Emily in Nicole Miller, Nina Ricci, Isaac Mizrahi and Zac Posen. Anastasia, Meredith, Imogen and Cameron began to clap and soon all the other guests joined in.

It was true enough that Cecilia was so monumentally dim in most areas of her life that she had once been fooled into believing that 'Chode-o-slovakia' was a real country, Roald Dahl was a woman and that tsunami was a place, but the girl certainly knew how to organize a party. This was what all the queen bees of Mount Olivet did so well; this is what made them necessary and earned them their applause. Cecilia moved through the crowd, accepting congratulations and throwing smug, self-satisfied looks at those people in the year who were either badly dressed or hated her.

Standing at the foot of the staircase, next to Catherine, a tuxedoed Blake Hartman watched the whole scene unfolding around him. The more he saw, the less he felt that he belonged in this world. He barely recognized himself from this time last year and he was disgusted at what he had become. He had never imagined himself to be a 'bad guy', but there was no way to deny that his treatment of both Cameron and Catherine had been pretty shameful. By his own emotional standards, right now, he was a failure. He had also finally confronted the fact that it was inevitable that his relationship with Catherine would come to an end. For the last few days, she had definitely been acting strangely around him and, one way or the other, Meredith, Cameron or Stewart were bound to tell her eventually. Even if they hadn't told Catherine – yet – the sensible part of Blake's mind told him that it was highly unlikely that they wouldn't have told somebody else and in a room surrounded by the popular cliques of three successive years Blake felt dozens of eyes watching him, appraising him, judging him. From where they were standing, he could see two of Anastasia's friends, Lavinia and Mariella, looking in his and Catherine's general direction. He was sure they were talking about him and there was a suspicious, vindictive gleam in their eyes. He felt short of breath and instinctively glanced over at Cameron, hoping for reassurance of some kind from him. Cameron eventually caught his eye, but he held his gaze for less than a second before coolly turning back to his conversation with Meredith, Imogen and Anastasia.

Kerry, who had been mingling, appeared at their side in the Narciso Rodriguez silk dress and a cosmopolitan clamped firmly in her hand. Rather unexpectedly, she had brought Peter as her date and he was now standing next to her, having cleaned up rather nicely in his rented tux. '*Don't ask*,' she mouthed at Imogen, whose quizzical smile had been replaced by a knowing raise of the eyebrow and a wink in Kerry's general direction.

By the time everyone began to move into the chamber where dinner was being served, Blake decided he needed to get away soon. He wasn't sure what had bothered him more – the gossipy, penetrating stares of Lavinia and Mariella, or Cameron's bored indifference. In the seat next to him, Catherine was keeping up a steady stream of chatty conversation with everyone at their table and the sound of her voice had never irritated him more.

Excusing himself, Blake carefully slunk out of the dining hall and wandered up the staircase, turning left down a corridor and entering a darkened, abandoned committee room. The only light came from the beams that had been set up outside to floodlight the building. Exhausted and shaken, he sat down on a table, undid his tie and settled into a miserable, contemplative silence. His thoughts were interrupted a few minutes later by an icy, mocking tone from the doorway.

'I'm trying to decide if you achieve this pathetic aesthetic on purpose.'

He turned and saw Meredith leaning against the doorway, her eyes glistening as she watched him. She took a few steps into the room and the eerie light from outside caught her jewels, making them shimmer as she moved. 'What . . .'

'What I mean is, I'm just not sure if these great emotional scenes of yours aren't choreographed in some way for maximum emotional impact should anyone find you. I mean, really, look at this, for example – retreating up to a semi-floodlit room in the abandoned palace on the night of the big ball, sitting in all your finery, regretting your lost love and deploring your tragic fate. It's all very theatrical.'

'Meredith, I'm not a fake.'

'Oh, Blake, I really don't care one way or the other what you are. All I'm really concerned about is what you've done.'

'If it makes you feel any better, Meredith, you couldn't hate me any more than I hate myself.'

'I wouldn't bet on that.'

'Meredith . . .'

'I think it's time that you and I really understood each other.'

'Please don't tell Catherine. I don't want . . . I didn't mean to . . .'

'Tell her?' asked Meredith, with a light laugh. 'You're so silly. She already knows!'

Blake looked at her as if he had been sucker-punched. 'What?'

'Since February, actually. I told her over lunch one day and in return she finally confessed to Imogen about something she had done at Christmas, which caused her break-up with Stewart.'

'She had something to do with that? But . . . but how are they even linked?'

'Everything's linked – if you play the game right. And as for poor, innocent, little Catherine, who you must've thought was such a safe bet in this whole messy, bitchy situation – well, you made a serious error of judgement, Blake. You'll learn in time: never trust the nice ones. They're the slipperiest ones of all. To get what she wanted, she was willing to fake a trusting, functioning relationship with *you* for four months. She used you just as much as you did her, maybe even more – all so she could finally be it.'

'Be what?'

'Popular, of course.'

'She knew . . . She knew . . . Catherine knew . . . Is everything in this world a lie?'

'You're in no position to take the moral high ground on that one, princess.'

Blake shook his head and got off the table. He began pacing around, running his hands agitatedly through his hair. 'I know that what I've done is wrong, but it's not my fault . . . I'm confused . . .'

'Of course it's your fault. Who else's fault could it possibly be? You're just not a very good person, Blake.'

There was a long pause, during which Blake struggled to find anything to correct her with. He couldn't. 'What are you going to do?'

'I'm going to ruin you.' For a long time after that, they stood facing each other, as the music from downstairs floated up into the room. 'Do you know what it's like to have your heart ripped out backwards, Blake?'

'. . . No . . .'

'Cameron does. Thanks to you. You humiliated him, Blake. You knew how he felt about you and yet you went out of your way to drape yourself over Catherine in front of him time and time again. You sit up here so sad, so confused, so miserable, so alone and you hope that, in the end, people will feel sorry for you, because you're Blake Hartman and you're a *nice* guy. But you're not a good guy, are you, Blake? You're a leech. You go after people like Cameron and you get them to confide in you. And that's one of the most sickening things about the whole situation, Blake. *You* pursued *him*. Oh, I'm sure that in the months since you two kissed you've told yourself that that's not how it was, because he's so obviously gay, and you're not, right? Well, any time you do tell yourself something as stupid as that again, I want you to stop for a moment and consider how completely unrealistic it is to imagine that someone like Cameron Matthews would even notice someone like you, let alone fall for you, if you hadn't actively pursued him. And then, when the situation you had created all became just a little bit too real for you, you threw my best friend under a bus. You, the Nice Guy, didn't even have the courage, or the decency, to tell him yourself that you had started dating one of his closest *female* friends – a girl he sees every day. You let her do it – because you knew that if he heard the news from Catherine he couldn't cause a fuss.'

She paused, staring at him coldly. At no point had she raised her voice and she continued now with the same relentless, devastating calm.

'You see, I don't think you actually *wanted* to hurt Cameron, but you were *prepared* to, if you had to – just as long as nobody thought you were gay.' She tossed her hair lightly behind her back and prepared to leave. 'So, next year, no matter how bad things get for you – and I'll be sure to make them more or less horrendous one way or the other – the moment I begin to feel even the tiniest twinge of sympathy for you, I am going to remember what you were prepared to do to my best friend. Enjoy your summer.'

Out on the terrace, the lights of Belfast twinkled in the distance and the party-goers had gone out to savour the balmy summer night. Anastasia, Imogen, Kerry, Meredith and Catherine were standing in a group near one of the lights, when Cameron cleared his throat. 'Ladies, may I have your attention, please?' The little group turned to look at him. 'OK. Right. OK. Yes. Everyone, I'm . . . I'm gay. I'm not ready to announce it to the whole school or my parents quite yet, but I wanted you to know because, well, I'm not ashamed of it and I'm trying to take this one step at a time. I know most of you, probably all of you, already knew, but I wanted to say it properly.'

A silence greeted his words and the girls stared back at him, as if expecting the speech to continue. 'Aren't any of you surprised?' asked Cameron.

Anastasia, Imogen, Kerry and Meredith exchanged glances. 'Sure,' lied Anastasia. 'Why not?'

'You couldn't let me have one surprised reaction, could you?'

'Your favourite musical is *Evita*, your favourite book is *Wicked* and you practically faint every time James Purefoy comes on the screen in *Rome*. How surprised do you want us to be?' asked Imogen.

'I suppose having *Evita* as my favourite musical was a bit of a giveaway.'

'No, Cameron. Having a favourite musical in the first place was the giveaway.'

'Congratulations, Cameron,' said Catherine quietly. 'I'm going to go get another drink, guys. I'll be right back.'

Meredith stared after Catherine's retreating back pitilessly and waited until she was out of walking distance before deciding to go inside herself. 'If you'll excuse me too, I need another drink.'

'I'll come with,' said Kerry, linking arms with her. 'So, Meredith, isn't this the point where we say we've learned something this year?'

'Pardon?'

'Well, you know, like, isn't this when we realize how we've grown and changed etc.?'

'Don't be stupid,' said Meredith.

'They did in *Mean Girls*!' Kerry protested.

'They were weak.'

'Well, I *have* learned stuff,' said Kerry as they reached the drinks table. 'Let me see . . . Oh, OK! I've learned that gays are good. And that . . . um . . . lying is bad, sort of . . . That we should help each other, and never to match my eyeshadow to my dress.'

'You only realized that this year?' said Meredith incredulously. 'I knew that for my first Holy Communion.'

'I didn't have first Communion! I'm Presbyterian, Meredith; you really should stop discriminating against me. It's *very* politically incorrect . . . Oh my God! They have Bellinis. Fun!'

The following evening, just as an early summer twilight settled over Belfast, Meredith emerged from the main entrance to Mount Olivet Grammar School adjusting her Chanel gloves and carrying a small bag that contained a few of the things she had forgotten to clear out of her locker on the last day of school. Apart from a few caretakers, the school was empty and Meredith's heels made a soft click-clack sound as she walked across the front courtyard – the only other noise was the occasional traffic passing by on the way up the Malone Road. For a few moments, Meredith was so involved in looking for her sunglasses in her handbag that she didn't see him. By the time she did, they were standing about three metres apart from each other. She stopped, temporarily surprised.

'Hi.'

'Hello, Blake. Suitcases?'

'I'm leaving.'

'For good?'

'I don't know.'

Meredith nodded, casting her eyes contemptuously over the two suitcases and backpack that sat at Blake's feet. He was staring up at the school behind her with a slightly lost look in his eyes.

'I came to say goodbye. To this place,' he said, looking at her forlornly, as if half expecting sympathy. She continued to regard him with cold, impassive eyes. 'Can I ask you a favour?'

One of Meredith's eyebrows raised itself into a perfect arc of disbelief. 'Pardon?'

Blake's hand fumbled in his back pocket and he handed over a slightly battered-looking white envelope, on the front of which was written the word CAMERON. For a brief moment, he thought he saw Meredith swallow harder than usual. It was the only physical sign of the unexpected panic which was now blaring inside her brain. This was definitely not supposed to have happened.

'I wasn't sure whether or not I should give it to him,' Blake said, smiling nervously, sadly, 'but seeing you here . . . it kind of seems like a sign.'

'What is it?'

'It's a letter to Cameron. Explaining . . . everything. And apologizing. I owe him that, you know?'

'Maybe.'

Blake shifted uneasily where he stood. The thing about conversations with Meredith when she was angry was that they were rather like diving into a cold swimming pool – no matter how many times you had done it before, you were still always slightly taken aback at the feeling of icy shock it produced on impact. 'I don't blame you for hating me,' he said, after a moment.

The left-hand side of Meredith's mouth curved upwards and

she exhaled slightly, as if she found the idea of being blamed by Blake both amusing and absurd. She glanced down, cleared her throat and then looked back at Blake, as if asking him to make his point and end the conversation as quickly as possible. She was very busy, naturally. For a moment or so, nothing happened and eventually Meredith simply extracted the sunglasses from her bag and began to walk past him.

'Wait! I don't know if I'm coming back . . . I don't know . . . But, either way, can you give this to Cameron, please? I'm going to stay with my mom in New England, in case you were wondering.'

Meredith plucked the letter from his hand. 'I wasn't.'

The sunglasses were placed upon her face and with the letter in one hand and her bag in the other she walked away from him – her hair blowing slightly in the breeze and her Louboutins clicking on the pavement.

Belfast's dawn chorus of birds began in earnest but even that was not enough to make Meredith look up from where she was sitting at the dressing table in her closet, idly tapping a slice of lemon in her tea with a silver spoon. In front of her lay Blake's letter to Cameron, and two envelopes, both of them with CAMERON written across the front in near-identical handwriting. One, ripped open by a letter-opener, was the original envelope penned by Blake, the other was a replacement written by Meredith, who had used tracing paper to make sure she authentically forged Blake's handwriting. She would reseal the letter in the replacement envelope and if she ever decided to give it to Cameron she could claim that she had never read it.

Meredith sighed with irritation at Blake's clumsy script, but couldn't shift the slight sense of foreboding that plagued her. Personally, she felt slightly nauseous at the outpouring of clumsy sentiment, but given Cameron's worrying penchant for emotionally incontinent B-listers, there was a very real chance he might fly to Connecticut to speak to Blake. At the very least, he would write back. Like Imogen, Cameron always got carried away with his feelings.

Tapping her fingers lightly on the table, Meredith weighed up what was the best policy to take. Judging from Blake's frankly repellent letter, she felt fairly certain that if Cameron made any attempt to heal the rift between them, Blake would be so ecstatic that he would definitely return to Mount Olivet come September – because what Blake's letter really boiled down to was an enormous 'Please forgive me and give me a second chance'. On the other hand, if Cameron never received the letter, there would be no reason for him to know until the end of summer that Blake had even left Belfast and, by that time, Blake would be so crushed by Cameron's lack of a response that the chances of him never coming at all would be much higher.

There was a knock on the closet door and the family's house-keeper entered. 'The car's ready when you are.'

'Thank you.'

Meredith rose from her seat and sealed the letter in the new forged envelope. She walked down the closet to a drawer that contained various leather-bound day planners and notepads and slipped the letter in with them. She then turned the lock and placed the key in her handbag. She smiled to herself and walked out of the closet, turning off the lights as she went.

*

Five minutes later, Meredith, Cameron and Imogen piled into her car to be driven to the airport for their holiday to Mexico. From behind her enormous Cavalli glasses, Imogen looked as if she was in a foul temper at being roused from her bed so early. 'I am in *enormous* pain,' she seethed, as she clambered into the car.

'Oh God,' said Meredith. 'Holiday wax didn't go too well, then?'

'I swear, Meredith, if she'd pulled it off any harder, I'd have lost my clitoris.'

When the car arrived at Belfast International Airport forty-five minutes later, Meredith, Imogen and Cameron stepped out and waited as the chauffeur unloaded their luggage. Seeing their absurd amount of bags, Cameron stepped forward to help, earning him a grateful smile from the driver.

'Now,' said Meredith, removing their travel itinerary from her perfectly organized folder, 'we have the seven-thirty Aer Lingus flight to Heathrow and then Club Class seats on the British Airways flight to Mexico City, and there'll be another connection on to San José del Cabo from there. We have a good few hours to do a little duty-free shopping, have some brunch, pray and pop some Valium into Imogen before boarding. I've got everyone's tickets and check-in details. It's six fifteen now, so we really should be checking in as soon as possible.'

'God, I'm going to be so drunk by the time we land,' said Imogen. 'I'm going to drink that airfare right back. They won't be turning a profit on me!'

Meredith placed the folder back in her handbag and looked around for Kerry or Catherine, with increasing irritation.

'I love the dress, Mer,' said Cameron. 'Aren't you worried

about spilling something on it during the flight? It's completely white.'

'I never spill,' she replied.

Just then, their thoughts were interrupted by the sound of stilettos clacking along the concrete – all three turned in the direction of the noise, from where they saw Kerry bearing down on them with a demented scandal-produced glow across her face. She lifted her pink Dior shades as she arrived and took a moment to catch her breath. Imogen, Cameron and Meredith removed their own sunglasses, as was traditional when receiving major gossip.

'Oh my God!' Kerry wheezed. 'Biggest. Scandal. Ever . . . Blake's vanished.'

'Vanished? Where?'

'I don't know, Cameron! Catherine just found out and called me! She's on her way. She's very upset.'

Meredith replaced her sunglasses and nodded slowly, as if mildly confused by this news. Then she turned, a slight gust of wind catching her hair, and patted a shell shocked Cameron's arm. 'Oh dear,' she said. 'That is strange.'

'How upset?' asked Imogen wearily. 'I'm not sitting next to her if she's going to cry the whole way to Mexico.'

'*Very* upset,' said Kerry. 'She's acting like it was a real break-up, which is weird because it wasn't a real relationship. She was his wig, after all.'

'Beard, Kerry,' corrected Meredith. 'She was his *beard*.'
'Oh.'

As Kerry sat for a moment mulling over how she could have made such a mistake, Imogen and Meredith glanced at a still-quiet Cameron.

'Cameron, sweetie, are you all right?' asked Imogen.

'Of course I am. He can do what he likes,' said Cameron, putting his sunglasses on and linking arms with the girls. 'Now, come on, ladies, we've got a plane to catch.'

AUTHOR'S NOTE

Halfway through the writing of *Popular*, I realized that my mother and I were never going to see eye to eye about it when she casually suggested over lunch how lovely she thought it would be if everyone in it was nice to one another. That idea went in the 'Maybe' pile. Goodness only knows what she thinks of Meredith. But, despite these differences of opinion, *Popular* could not have been written without the support of both my parents, Ian and Heather, and for that I am very, very grateful. Sorry the girls weren't as nice as you'd hoped, Mum. Maybe next time.

I was extremely lucky to have an absolutely fantastic editor at Puffin, the fabulous Lindsey Heaven, and a terrific agent, Stan, without whom none of this could have been possible – and that would be the definition of anti-beau. Equally, I must thank Dan Franklin for his much-appreciated encouragement and the amazing team at Puffin, London, for everything.

So many people have helped with *Popular* and thanking them all would sound too much like the worst kind of Oscar acceptance speech, but I would like to personally express my gratitude to: the ever-supportive Laura Bradley; Lydia Forte, for her help with the Italian translations (any remaining errors are my own);

Mary Franklin and Matthew Osman; Theodore Harvey; my grandparents Richard and Iris Mahaffy; the delightful Kerry Rogan and Sarah Houghton, for the years of inspiration and hilarity; my sisters, Lynsey, Jenny and Ashleigh; Noah Smith, who was the first person to suggest I write this book; Beth Steer; Alexander Stewart; and also my very dear friend, Emerald Fennell, who has been *Popular*'s most consistent and delightful cheerleader from Day One.

Apart from that, I would just like to say thank you to all my wonderful friends from Belfast, Chicago, London, Oxford, Los Angeles and New York who went above and beyond the call of duty in offering support, laughter and Bourbon throughout this entire process. One supplied the unlikely, but fabulous, combination of fried chicken and champagne under the cover of darkness, but if I ever revealed her name she would almost certainly break off three of my fingers and beat me with them. Let's just say that if you saw two people in enormous sunglasses dashing through an Oxford quad at two a.m. with a bucket wrapped under their coats and three bottles wedged under each arm, hissing, 'If anyone sees us, just shoot them! Don't ask any questions!' it was no night phantasm. It was friendship, in its rawest form.

Finally, I must also thank one lady in particular who did not wish to be named, but whose help has been both constant and invaluable.